# THE IMPOSSIBLE HUSBAND

It was impossible that Major David Lancaster had refused to die, but instead kept on being incredibly alive.

It was impossible that he should have left the hospital, where he was safely situated, and taken up residence in Lady Jocelyn's elegant London mansion.

It was impossible that Jocelyn remain married to this impecunious officer who was so far beneath her in title and station.

But nothing was quite so infinitely impossible as that this man might not be satisfied with her aristocratic hand in wedlock but might want still more, beginning with her heart. . . .

---

MARY JO PUTNEY was graduated from Syracuse University with degrees in eighteenth-century British literature and industrial design. She lived in California and England before settling in Baltimore, Maryland, where she is a freelance graphic designer.

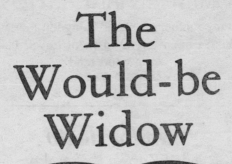

# The Would-be Widow

*by*
*Mary Jo Putney*

A SIGNET BOOK

To my mother, Eleanor Congdon Putney,
from whom I inherited my love of travel, language,
and a good read

SIGNET
Published by the Penguin Group
Penguin Books USA Inc., 375 Hudson Street,
New York, New York 10014, U.S.A.
Penguin Books Ltd, 27 Wrights Lane,
London W8 5TZ, England
Penguin Books Australia Ltd, Ringwood,
Victoria, Australia
Penguin Books Canada Ltd, 10 Alcorn Avenue,
Toronto, Ontario, Canada M4V 3B2
Penguin Books (N.Z.) Ltd, 182–190 Wairau Road,
Auckland 10, New Zealand

Penguin Books Ltd, Registered Offices:
Harmondsworth, Middlesex, England

Published by Signet, an imprint of New American Library,
a division of Penguin Books USA Inc.

First Printing, July, 1988
11  10  9  8  7  6  5  4  3

REGISTERED TRADEMARK—MARCA REGISTRADA

Printed in the United States of America

BOOKS ARE AVAILABLE AT QUANTITY DISCOUNTS WHEN USED TO PROMOTE PRODUCTS OR SERVICES.
FOR INFORMATION PLEASE WRITE TO PREMIUM MARKETING DIVISION, PENGUIN BOOKS USA INC.,
375 HUDSON STREET, NEW YORK, NEW YORK 10014.

# 1

"He turned me down, Aunt Laura. *He turned me down!*"

Lady Laura Kirkpatrick paused on the threshold of the drawing room with a startled expression, then stepped inside, pulling the door firmly shut behind her. Her beautiful niece was obviously in a fury, and better none of the servants hear what was preying on her mind.

Lady Jocelyn Kendal was known throughout the *ton* for her quality of being exactly in balance. No one could ever say she was too tall or too short, too fat or too thin. Her glossy hair was a lovely shade of chestnut brown, though not so bright-colored as to be vulgar, her hazel eyes were held to be very fine, and she had more than her share of charm and social address. It had been said that her chin was a trifle too stubborn for true femininity, but the majority of the *beau monde* thought it entirely correct that the only daughter of the late Earl of Cromarty knew her own worth.

Dressed in a pale-green gown that seemed chosen to match the richly furnished salon, she looked every inch the lady of fashion. At the moment, however, there was nothing the least balanced about Lady Jocelyn; in fact, she looked as if she were about to burst from a mixture of stunned disbelief and outraged pride. Her favorite aunt hadn't seen her so furious since the age of six years, when Jocelyn's father had insisted that she ride sidesaddle.

"Who turned you down? And for what?" Lady Laura asked as she settled into a chair, her sprigged-muslin gown flowing gracefully around her. As the younger sister of the late earl, Laura shared a strong family resemblance with Jocelyn, but the older woman had threads of silver in her hair and a warmer, softer expression on her face.

Her niece scowled. "The Duke of Candover. You know his attentions have been most distinguishing. Surely you've seen that, haven't you?" A note of pleading crept into the girl's voice.

Laura considered a moment before answering. "He has paid you more attention than he has any other unmarried girl. But surely it amounts to no more than occasional dances and a handful of rides in the park?"

"But it *is* more than he has done with any other eligible girl! The man needs an heir; after all, he's in his mid-thirties and it's high time he set up a nursery. It would be a very suitable match for both of us."

Her aunt sighed. "For heaven's sake, sit down and stop pacing. It's time for some plain speaking, Jocelyn. If I had known you were building such feather castles, I would have spoken sooner."

Jocelyn sat, her lower lip sticking out in an expression that would have been called a pout in a less-well-bred lady.

Having secured her niece's attention, Laura said, "I doubt Candover will ever marry. He's been on the town an age and has never shown more than the mildest of attentions to an eligible female."

"But he does make the effort to seek me out," Jocelyn argued. "And he always seems to enjoy my company."

"Jocelyn, it's not like you to avoid the truth." Her aunt's voice softened as she saw the real unhappiness that lay beneath her niece's fury. "Any number of men have courted you these last six years. Think of Mr. Alvery, and Lord Hanston, for example. They both offered for you." As Jocelyn nodded, Laura continued, "Has Candover ever showed the kind of ardor that they did? As much as any of the other men who have seriously courted you?"

Jocelyn shifted uneasily. "Well . . ." she temporized a moment before her innate honesty led her to admit, "no, he hasn't."

"I will say it again," Laura said bluntly. "Candover is not the marrying kind. He has perfectly acceptable cousins, so he is not lacking in heirs. The only women he has ever really pursued are demimondaines and other men's wives. If you want him as a lover, marry someone else and he'll probably oblige you, at least for a while. But he will never marry you.''

"Blunt talk indeed,'' Jocelyn said, her jaw set.

Her aunt sighed. "I'm sorry, my dear. But you are no schoolroom miss, to turn away from the way of the world.''

Jocelyn averted her face by leaning over to scoop her cat, Isis, onto her lap. The cat had been the gift of a naval suitor who claimed to have brought her from Egypt, and Isis' velvety, lion-colored fur and fine-boned elegance did resemble the felines seen in Egyptian temple art. While a very friendly pet to those she liked, Isis' triangular face had an expression of aristocratic superiority that a duchess might have envied.

Her head still down, Jocelyn scratched Isis' chin as she said in a low voice, "If I had more time, I could *make* him fall in love with me—I'm sure of it!''

Laura studied the girl thoughtfully. Jocelyn was very lovely and had a quick wit and a bright, careless charm, but even a doting aunt had to admit that being the only child of an indulgent father had made her a little spoiled. It really was beyond the girl's comprehension that in this one thing she could not have what she wanted. "Perhaps you could win him over, though I doubt it. But you don't have much more time. You'll be twenty-five in a month.''

A silence fell on the room as they both contemplated what that meant. Before either could comment further, Mossley, the butler, entered and announced, "The Countess of Cromarty.''

Jocelyn made an irritated gesture that caused the cat to leave her lap for a safer spot. "Tell Elvira I am not receiving callers. Tell her I have been transported, or died.''

Lady Laura said with amusement, "Surely you would not wish to gratify the countess with such welcome news.''

Jocelyn started chuckling as her sense of humor returned, so she wore a more pleasant expression than Elvira Kendal usually produced when her other aunt swept past the butler.

Elvira, Countess of Cromarty, had not been born to a high estate, and she had accepted her elevation to the nobility as proof that God was just. It had been widely thought that Jocelyn's father would remarry and get himself a male heir, but his experience of matrimony appeared to have soured him on that state. He had been content with his only daughter, and his younger brother, Willoughby, had succeeded to the title after the fourth earl's untimely death four years earlier.

Elvira was confident that she deserved all the dignities that came to her, but it was a source of continuing irritation that most of the fourth earl's vast personal fortune had been left to his daughter, along with the magnificent town house Jocelyn lived in. However, the bequest had been conditional, and it was beginning to appear that Jocelyn would fail to fulfill the requirement.

The countess nodded graciously at Lady Laura and said, ''I was in town shopping, so I just thought I would stop by for a few moments. I can't stay long since it is a good two-hour drive back to Charlton.'' She chose a seat without waiting for an invitation, settling her plump self down with a sigh of satisfaction as she looked around the gracious drawing room.

''I am quite aware how long a drive it is to Charlton,'' Jocelyn said shortly. She would have said more if it hadn't been for the warning glint in Lady Laura's eyes. Jocelyn hated thinking of Charlton, the principal seat of the Earls of Cromarty; she had grown up there and loved it with a passion that mere money could never have inspired. She would gladly give her entire fortune to be mistress of Charlton, but the iron laws of primogeniture made that forever impossible; the estate was entailed to Willoughby and his oldest son after him.

Prompted by Lady Laura's expression, she asked, ''Would you care to join us for some tea, Aunt Elvira?''

The countess frowned a little; she much preferred being called Lady Cromarty, but hadn't the courage to demand that of Jocelyn. Relaxing her expression, she said in dulcet tones, "How kind. I would be delighted. Do you think your cook might have made some of those delicious macaroons?"

"Very likely." Jocelyn sighed as she rang for a footman.

Lady Laura and Lady Cromarty exchanged common-places through two cups of tea and a large number of cakes, most of them consumed by the plump countess. Noticing how Elvira's gaze kept moving around the room in a proprietary fashion, Jocelyn finally said bluntly, "Stop evaluating the furnishings, Aunt Elvira. You aren't getting this house."

A lesser woman might have been embarrassed at such candor, but Lady Cromarty merely smiled blandly. "Are you getting uncomfortable with your birthday coming so soon, and you still unwed?"

"Not at all," Jocelyn said, with equal blandness. "I admit that I am having trouble deciding which offer to accept, but never fear. I will certainly be married in time to fulfill the conditions of my father's will."

Elvira's small pale eyes almost disappeared into her doughy cheeks as the subject they had all been avoiding was tossed into the middle of the drawing room like a cat among the pigeons. Jocelyn's father had been indulgent but more than a little eccentric, and he had been determined to have his own way after his death. The bulk of his enormous fortune had been left to his daughter—on the condition that she marry by her twenty-fifth birthday. The earl had firmly believed women were incapable of handling business matters, and on Jocelyn's marriage control of her property would automatically pass to her husband. If she failed to marry, most of the money and all of the unentailed property, including the town house where they were enjoying their tea, would become Willoughby's. Since he was a mild man who never dreamed of opposing his formidable wife, Elvira would be the principal beneficiary of Jocelyn's failure to marry.

"I am sure you have had your offers, dear," Elvira said in a tone that implied that she believed nothing of the kind. "But when a woman reaches your age unwed, one has to wonder. . . ."

While Jocelyn struggled to control her temper, Elvira continued, "Of course, if you *wish* to remain single, it isn't as if you will be destitute. Willoughby says you will have quite a nice competence, enough to live in some genteel place like Bath."

Jocelyn said in a silky voice, "Since I dislike Bath, it is very fortunate that the issue will not arise."

Elvira's polite mask slipped a little and she scowled at her niece. "Really, it isn't as if you need the money, while *we* have seven children to establish. It was quite infamous of your father to leave Willoughby no more than was required to maintain the estates."

Elvira's scowl turned into a shriek when a tawny body streaked over the back of the sofa to plop on her broad lap, eyeing the countess with golden eyes and a sadistic feline smirk. Jocelyn could barely contain her laughter. Isis had the usual cat genius for pouncing on those people who least wanted to be pounced on, and her intervention gave Jocelyn time to recover her temper. Making a mental note to order oysters for the cat's dinner, Jocelyn pulled the bellcord before crossing to scoop Isis from her aunt's lap. "I agree that my father's will was infamous, but I can't agree with you about the reasons."

As the butler entered, she said, "Mossley, my aunt was just leaving. Please have her carriage brought around."

Even Elvira Kendal could take a hint that broad, but she glanced complacently around the room again as she rose. No doubt Lady Jocelyn could have found a fortune-hunter who would have her, bad temper and all, but the fact that her birthday was a mere month away led the countess to believe that the chit had left it too late. Rumor said the girl had been after the Duke of

Candover, and everyone knew he'd never marry. No, the high and mighty Lady Jocelyn was about to get her comeuppance, and the fortune would come to those who most deserved it.

"Good day, Lady Laura. And do invite us to your nuptials, Lady Jocelyn. If there are any."

Accurately interpreting the look on her niece's face, Laura hastily escorted the countess from the room before the girl could throw something. When Lady Laura returned, she found her niece pacing the floor angrily while Isis sat on the sofa and washed herself, oblivious to the human storms around her.

Jocelyn looked up at her aunt's entrance, her hazel eyes flashing with fury. "Honestly, Laura, I'd marry a beggar from Seven Dials before I'd let the money go to Willoughby and that, that archwife!"

Her aunt settled into a chair with a sigh. "One could wish that Willoughby had chosen a woman of more refinement. Thank heaven none of her children take after her; young Randolph will make a worthy earl when his time comes.

"But Elvira is right, you know. Time *is* running out. I haven't pressed you about the issue because you're no green girl and you know your own business best. Losing most of your fortune is preferable to an unhappy marriage, and it isn't as if you will be left penniless. If Bath is too dire a prospect, you can always live with Andrew and me after he leaves the army."

"As if I would play permanent gooseberry when you've waited so long to have a normal life with him." Jocelyn crossed to her aunt to give an impulsive hug. "Favorite aunt! I am so glad you haven't nagged me. Every other person in the family has opinions on what I should do and whom I should marry."

"Far better you wait for the right man, as I did." Her aunt smiled and patted the girl's hand. "I had quite a battle convincing my father that Andrew Kirkpatrick was good enough for the daughter of an earl, but I've never regretted it for a moment."

"I expect that is why I am so determined to marry for

love; you and Uncle Andrew have been such a happy example." She paused, then asked curiously, "Do you really think he will leave the army? It has been his whole life, after all."

Lady Laura laughed. "It would be more accurate to say that his whole life has been devoted to fighting Bonaparte. But after the battle at Waterloo last month, I don't think Boney will be back, and Andrew has no desire for garrison duty."

Her eyes grew distant as she said thoughtfully, "The whole rhythm of my married life has been determined by fighting the French. The years we spent in India, and on the Peninsula, the times we've been separated for months, like now. Twenty-two endless years, except for that one brief spell in 1802. It has shaped my husband, my sons. . . ."

Laura's voice trailed off, then she said briskly, "I am still counting my blessings that all three of my men are safe when so many died. The boys will stay in the army, but Andrew swears he is ready to retire to the country and terrorize the neighbors as befits an old general."

She chuckled, then added, "Personally I think he will be bored in a twelfthmonth, then go into Parliament to make his opinions known. In any case, there will always be room for you at Kennington if you don't find anyone you wish to marry."

Jocelyn said emphatically, "But there *is* someone I want to marry: Candover. Ever since I first met him, three years ago." Her voice became dreamy. "Isn't he handsome? And such a horseman."

And such a challenge, her aunt mentally added. She suspected that part of Candover's charm was his unavailability, which affected her willful niece like catmint affected a tabby. Lady Laura studied her niece ruefully; not for the first time, she worried about Jocelyn's lack of interest in any of the men who had courted her. There had been the usual number of fribbles and fortune-hunters, but some had been fine men who would have made good husbands.

Unfortunately, the only men the girl had ever wanted were those who didn't reciprocate her interest.

Laura suddenly remembered the tantrum that Jocelyn had been throwing just before Lady Cromarty had called. Fearfully she asked, "What did Candover turn you down about? Surely you didn't ask him to marry you."

"Well, not quite. But I came as close as I dared."

Lady Laura moaned and stared at her niece with an expression that mingled horror and a certain grudging respect. Horror predominated. "You asked one of the most fearsome Corinthians in England to marry you?" She covered her face with her hands. "Please, tell me that I'm raving, or sickening with a fever, or something else relatively harmless."

Jocelyn pulled a long strand of chestnut hair over her shoulder and twisted it with an unusual show of nerves. "I didn't actually offer for him. I had asked him to choose me two carriage horses at Tattersall's, since women can't go there. I think that is most unreasonable, don't you?"

Lady Laura removed her hands from her face and said firmly, "You'll not sidetrack me with any of your bluestocking ideas. What happened with Candover?"

"Well, he found me a lovely pair of sorrels, perfectly matched, and such sweet goers!" As her aunt glared at her, she said hopefully, "Candover said they matched my hair. Don't you think that shows that he is aware of me?"

"It is a very long way from an offer of marriage," Lady Laura said in an awful voice. "*Then* what happened?"

"Well, when we came back from driving them, I thanked him for his help and said that I hoped to marry a man like him, someone with his style and address and knowledge of horses."

Her aunt regarded her with fascination. "How did he reply?"

Jocelyn scowled and started plaiting the curl into a

tight little braid. "He looked at me. You know that expression he has, as if a dog just slobbered on his boots?" When her aunt nodded, she went on, "Then he said that the man could not be too much like him, or he wouldn't make any kind of husband at all."

"That seems to have closed the subject rather thoroughly," her aunt said faintly. "You didn't say anything else, did you?"

"No. Although I think that underneath that sardonic expression he was amused, not offended."

"Of course he was amused. It will make a hilarious story in every club in St. James's," her aunt said hollowly as she fell back and began fanning herself with a convenient periodical.

Jocelyn shook her head firmly. "No, he won't go around telling tales, no matter what he thought of my presumption. Besides, even if he mislikes my manners, at least he must acquit me of being a fortune-hunter. I'm told he has a particular abhorrence for those."

"If you don't marry in the next month, you *will* need to marry a fortune if you want to maintain the elegancies of life," Laura said dryly. "But you are correct, Candover is a gentleman, and no matter what he thinks of your presumption, he won't hold you up to public ridicule. It is even remotely possible that you might bring him up to scratch in another five years or so; sometimes men become more concerned with posterity when they near forty. But I would wager any sum you please that you won't persuade him in the next four weeks."

She shook her head with a reluctant amusement. Life was never dull around her niece! "If you are determined that you will marry no one but him, you had best start packing. The countess will want to move in here the day after your birthday. The only reason she lives at Charlton is because Willoughby can't afford a town house that suits her standards."

Jocelyn looked mutinous. "I will not give Elvira the satisfaction!" She glanced sideways at her aunt, then said slowly, "It is a desperate idea, but I have been thinking of accepting Sir Harold Winterson. He's always fancied me, and the man must be seventy if he's a day. Surely he's too old to be interested in his marital rights."

"Jocelyn!" her aunt said with real shock. "That is the most improper thing I have ever heard you say. To marry a man while speculating on his life expectancy . . . Why, every feeling revolts!"

Since her niece appeared unmoved by the appeal to propriety, Laura continued, "Moreover, it is the utmost foolishness. I knew a girl who married a man about Sir Harold's age, hoping to be a rich widow soon. That was twenty years ago, and her husband is still very much with her, while she has lost her youth. It is unlikely that he will live another twenty years, but who knows?"

As Jocelyn's face fell, Laura moved in with the clincher. "More than that, there is no age at which one can assume a man will not be interested in exercising his marital rights. In fact, when December marries May, he often has at least a temporary return to his own spring-time."

Jocelyn shuddered. "You've convinced me. Sir Harold is a sweet old gentleman, but I have no desire to be a wife to him." She sighed regretfully. "You're right, it was a mad thought. Although the idea of marrying a man on his deathbed has merit, Sir Harold is quite vigorous for his age. One would have to be sure the man was really dying."

Lady Laura watched her with foreboding. When Jocelyn had that expression on her face, her aunt knew from experience that there was trouble ahead. She gave a resigned smile and said, "I would like to believe I have dissuaded you from that plan through moral logic, but I have the dismal feeling that it is only the practical problems that discourage you. If you have any more outrageous schemes in mind, don't tell me. I'm afraid my poor old nerves couldn't stand it."

She added with mock mournfulness, "And to think they say boys are hard to raise. My two never gave me half the trouble you gave your father."

Jocelyn smiled merrily. "Yes, Papa was always so proud of me when I was outrageous. He used to say he was glad the blood hadn't run thin." She sighed and smoothed her green muslin dress over her knee before adding softly, "I do miss him."

"I know you do, dear. I miss him, too. There was no one like him. Just don't let that ridiculous will of his drive you to something you'll regret." She eyed her niece thoughtfully and offered a distraction. "Today I got a letter from Andrew."

Jocelyn looked at her with trepidation. "Does he mention any of the officers I met in Spain? It has been over a month since Waterloo." She stopped, unwilling to continue. She and her aunt had pored over the casualty lists after the battle; in the weeks that had passed, many of the wounded would have died.

"The news isn't too bad," Laura said briskly as she removed the letter from her sewing basket. She scanned it briefly, reading aloud what the general said about men that Jocelyn would know. At one point she said sadly, "Here is a tragedy. Remember Colonel Kingsley? He was blinded in the battle. He had been engaged but his fiancée has jilted him. Apparently she was there in Brussels."

"How horrible!" Jocelyn cried. "That any woman who claimed to love a man could do such a thing when he needed her most. He was the most handsome man, and so charming."

"We shouldn't condemn her out of hand. Perhaps she knew her own weaknesses and was wise enough to end things quickly. Not all people are capable of being noble."

Jocelyn shook her head. "Sometimes I think you are entirely too fair-minded, Aunt Laura. *I* have no problem at all condemning her. Did Uncle Andrew mention anyone else I know?"

Turning to the last page of the missive, Laura said, "Where is that about Richard Dalton? I know you liked him."

"Oh, no, Laura, please don't say he has died of his

wounds." Jocelyn's face paled. "He was the best company—quiet, but so even-tempered, and such a dry wit. Remember how he was always whistling when he was thinking? He was my favorite officer."

"No, he hasn't died. Andrew says he has a very serious leg injury and was sent to London for treatment. Based on the date of this letter, he must have arrived in town a fortnight ago."

"How splendid! Perhaps I can visit him tomorrow. Remember how he was the one that rescued me when I got lost trying to find Uncle Andrew's winter quarters?"

"Remember!" Laura rolled her eyes in mock horror. "I could show you the exact gray hairs I acquired when you rode into Fuente Guinaldo with all those soldiers and not so much as an abigail to bear you company."

"Well, the maid I had then was such a hen-hearted creature," Jocelyn said with a grin. "How was I to know that she would flatly refuse to leave Lisbon?"

"The girl had a good deal better sense than you did," her aunt said dryly. "It is a miracle that you weren't robbed, murdered, and worse by French troops, bandits, guerrillas, or heaven knows who else. Such a madcap you were to come bolting to Spain like that."

"Well, things had been sadly flat in London," Jocelyn said with a twinkle. "I had the most delightful time in Spain. I'll admit I was a bit worried when my guide ran off and I had no idea of where to find the regiment, but once Captain Dalton and his patrol found me, I was perfectly safe."

"All I can say is that you have the hardest-working guardian angels of any girl in England." Laura consulted the letter again. "Anyhow, the captain has been taken to the York Hospital. Major Lancaster is there too, but I don't believe you met him; he was on detached duty with the Spanish army the winter you were in Spain."

Just as well Jocelyn didn't know him, her aunt thought; the major was dying, and the two women had shed enough tears over the casualties of Waterloo.

Having spent her life as a military wife, Laura had seen her friends decimated.

"I wish I had fallen in love with one of the officers in Spain," Jocelyn said thoughtfully. "Half of them offered for me, and they were real men, not like the perfumed gallants of London." Returning to her obsession, she went on, "I think that is what attracts me so much about Candover. No one could deny that he is manly. It might be difficult to win his love, but I think that once he gave his heart, he would love forever."

"Perhaps, my dear. But that may be your imagination." Lady Laura's voice was very gentle. She understood her niece's passionate idealism, the desire to find the one true love that would last forever. Laura suspected that it was a reaction to the disgrace her mother had brought on the Kendal family, but she didn't dare ask; Jocelyn never referred to her childhood. Yet who was Laura to say that love everlasting was an impossible dream, when she herself had found such a love?

And now her niece was caught between the desire to wait for the perfect love and the cold certainty of losing a fortune by waiting too long. Laura shook her head and stood. Only Jocelyn could decide whether to marry one of her eager suitors, or to wait and hope that the Duke of Candover might someday return her feelings. It would be easy to imagine oneself in love with someone as handsome and charming as the duke, but it was foolish for Jocelyn to gamble her inheritance on the slim chance of winning a man widely assumed to have no heart.

"I'll see you at dinner," she said. As she left the room, Laura thought about her late brother with a mixture of regret and irritation. He had loved his daughter sincerely, but his combination of indulgence and arrogance hadn't always benefited the girl's character; while Jocelyn had a warm heart and great loyalty, she was also entirely too used to having her own way, and often trod on the feelings of others without thinking. After all, she had been raised to think that a

Kendal of Charlton was just a little closer to God than the rest of the human race, certainly much closer than the Hanoverian upstarts that sat on the throne of England. Laura could only hope that her niece's determination to thwart her Aunt Elvira would not lead her into anything too regrettable.

As she sat alone in the drawing room, Jocelyn frowned and started drumming her fingertips on the satinwood table next to her. In spite of Lady Laura's horrified reaction, Jocelyn was convinced that becoming a widow would be ideal, for it would give her freedom and time to win Candover without relinquishing her inheritance. But how could she reach that enviable state, and do it soon enough to save her fortune and independence? She thought of Sir Harold and sighed; her aunt was right, it would be quite insupportable to be in the position of longing for the old gentleman's death so she could have her freedom.

Jocelyn knew that she could marry one of her fashionable suitors and have a marriage *à la mode*, with each going their own way after an heir or two had been produced. Unfortunately, under her highly polished exterior beat the heart of a romantic. She wanted a real marriage, like Laura and Andrew Kirkpatrick had. She loathed the idea of having a husband who was scarcely more than an acquaintance, with both of them taking lovers for amusement. Whenever she thought of that possibility, she remembered her mother and shuddered.

Softly she said to Isis, who had returned to her lap, "I'm *not* like her, not at all. I always knew that when I met the right man I would know it, and I did. I'm sure Candover was badly hurt when he was younger and that is why he is so afraid of love now. But even the most damaged spirit can learn to love again, and someday . . ." Her words trailed off in a flood of desolation; though her heart believed that someday he might return her love, Jocelyn's worldly mind said that she was prey to delusions. Isis purred sympathetically, sensing the distress, and Jocelyn automatically scratched the cat's neck.

She would not feel sorry for herself! Jocelyn tilted her head to gaze at the drawing-room ceiling, gorgeously painted and gilded forty years earlier by Athenian Stuart. As a child she would lie on her back on the Persian carpet and make up stories about the paintings inset in elaborate medallions, with Aunt Laura sometimes lying beside her and admiring the fantasies her niece contrived.

Lady Jocelyn Kendal clenched her fists and muttered an oath that one of her warrior ancestors would have approved of. She might never win the duke's love and Charlton might be lost, but Cromarty House was *hers*. No matter what it took, she would find a way to keep it out of Elvira's grasping little hands.

## 2

The soft footfalls of her maid awakened Jocelyn from a restless slumber where she had rolled onto her stomach and burrowed under the pillows. She turned over with a yawn, then sat up so Marie could arrange the tray of hot chocolate and bread. "Thank you, Marie. Any more developments in your campaign for Morgan?"

The round, dimpled maid gave a fetching smile as she carefully spread a linen napkin for her mistress. Her parents were French émigrés, and she herself had a variable accent which was quite English normally but which became very French when she talked to a man who caught her fancy. And she fancied the new footman, Hugh Morgan, a great deal.

"He wishes me to meet his brother Rhys, a soldier just back from Belgium. The brother was wounded at Waterloo and is recovering at the York Hospital. I think it is a very good sign that Hugh wants me to meet a member of his family, no?"

"Definitely," Jocelyn agreed as she sipped her chocolate. She thought for a moment, then added, "I am going to visit a friend at the York Hospital myself today, and I will take Morgan along. I'm sure he will want to visit his brother. I'll wear the blue eau-de-Nile silk muslin." She just hoped that Captain Dalton would be in the mood for visitors; if he was in great pain, he might not wish to put on a stoic facade.

She shrugged and slid out of the bed, slipping into the silk wrapper Marie held out for her. As she recalled, the captain had little or no family and would probably welcome distraction in the form of a visitor. There had been nothing the least bit romantic between them, but they had always enjoyed each other's company, and

Jocelyn knew without vanity that men enjoyed looking at her.

The Duke of York Military Hospital was not far from the Chelsea Royal Hospital but was much grimmer than the masterpiece Christopher Wren had designed for army pensioners. The York was a drab monolith dedicated to the treatment of seriously wounded soldiers, and many who entered never left alive.

Jocelyn repressed a shudder as she stood outside. She hated to leave the July sunshine to enter the gloomy hospital, but sternly reminded herself that it was far worse for the patients and marched up the wide steps, her footman close behind. Hugh Morgan had been excited when she informed him where they were going, as he had not yet been able to visit his brother. Hugh was a tall, handsome young man, and his dark curls and melodious Welsh voice had created quite a stir belowstairs. Still, Jocelyn was confident that Marie could overcome the competition of the other maids; the minx was a born flirt.

As Morgan held the door, Jocelyn stepped into a large, high-ceilinged marble foyer where bustling people crisscrossed back and forth, their footsteps echoing from the hard surfaces. No one took the least notice of them, so after looking around uncertainly, she walked up to a man who looked like a porter.

"Excuse me, we are looking for the Waterloo soldiers."

The man looked her up and down, then said brusquely, "Most of 'em are in the west wing," and jerked his thumb to his left. She almost gave him the setdown he deserved, but decided that it wasn't worth the effort, and headed in the direction indicated.

The building was crowded with casualties and it took a long time to find Rhys Morgan's ward. By the time they reached their destination, Jocelyn had experienced sights and smells that knotted her stomach and made her regret the breakfast she had eaten, and there was a greenish-white tinge to Hugh's country complexion.

Rhys Morgan was in the corner cot of perhaps forty that were jammed into a room too small for its population. Some patients sat on their beds or talked in small groups, but many lay still. The bare walls reflected an unrestful clamor, and a miasma of illness and death hung over the room. When Jocelyn entered, she became the target of dozens of curious eyes, most admiring, some insolent, a few openly hostile toward her obvious wealth.

Jocelyn knew they had found their man when Hugh croaked, "Rhys, lad!" He started to push past her, then looked down apologetically. With a nod, she released him to his brother and became a witness to their reunion. The wounded man had been lying back and staring at the ceiling, but he looked up as his name was called. The face was startlingly like his brother's, but wore a look of blank despair that was only partly lifted as Hugh rushed up and grabbed his hand, Welsh words pouring forth.

The raw feeling in Hugh's face made Jocelyn uncomfortable; she had heard the Welsh were an emotional race compared to the English, but she had never before seen it so vividly demonstrated. As she shifted her gaze away, her eyes were caught and held at the bottom of Rhys' bed. Where there should have been two feet under the covers, there was only one; at a guess, his leg had been amputated just below the knee.

She swallowed, then went up and touched Hugh's arm. He turned with a guilty start. "I'm sorry, my lady," he said as he flushed. "I forgot myself."

She gave a smile that included both of them. "Nonsense, no apologies are necessary. Corporal Morgan, may I introduce myself? I am Lady Jocelyn Kendal, and I have the honor of being your brother's employer."

Rhys pushed himself upright in the bed as he took in the vision of elegance before him. With a bob of his head, he stammered, "My pleasure, ma'am."

Hugh hissed, "Call her 'my lady,' you looby."

A wave of color rose under the fair Celtic skin as the soldier attempted to apologize.

Jocelyn smiled and said, "It is of no importance, Corporal. But tell me, are you two twins?"

Rhys replied, "Nay, I'm a year the elder, but we were often taken for twins."

"You are very like."

"Not any more," Rhys said bitterly as he glanced at the bed where his leg should have been.

Jocelyn felt her throat start to tighten; she felt in no way qualified to deal with this kind of distress. In her best social manner, she said, "I'll go find my friend now and leave you to visit. When I am finished, I'll come back here."

Hugh looked uncertain. "I should go with you, my lady."

"Nonsense, what could happen to me? It may take me a while to find the man I am seeking, so don't be alarmed if I am not back right away. Corporal Morgan, do you know where the officers are quartered?"

He seemed to straighten a bit as she asked for help and called him by his rank. Had he been lying there, feeling as if his useful life was over? "The floor above, ma'am . . . my lady."

"Thank you. I will see you both later."

Jocelyn smiled and left the room, conscious of the stares that followed her. She had found the encounter unnerving; while she had been living in comfort in London, these men had been getting blown to pieces for their country.

Climbing a staircase to the next level, she found a long, empty corridor with individual doors instead of open wards. As she tried to decide what to do next, a thickset man of middle years emerged from a nearby room and brushed past her. He looked like a physician, so she flagged him down.

With an impatient glance he asked, "Who are you looking for?"

"Captain Richard Dalton of the 95th Rifles."

"Down the hall." The doctor waved his hand vaguely behind him, then marched off before she could get more specific directions. The first door Jocelyn opened released a nauseating stench and she hurriedly closed it. Aunt Laura had done nursing in Spain and had once described gangrene, but the reality was far worse than Jocelyn had imagined. She had seen enough of the man's face to believe it was not whom she sought; she was unable to force herself to open the door and confirm that fact.

She peeked in several more rooms to find empty beds or unconscious men before opening the last door on the corridor. Jocelyn had just time enough to see several figures grouped around a table before a blood-freezing scream of agony shattered the air. She slammed the door shut, dizzily hoping she had not disturbed the occupants of the room; then she turned to run blindly away into a larger open space at the end of the hall. It had seemed such a simple task to find someone here; instead, she was coming face to face with a degree of suffering she had never been exposed to in her life.

Her eyes clouded with tears, she didn't even see the man until she slammed into him. There was a hard clatter of something falling, and a strong hand grabbed her arm. When the firm grip didn't release her, Jocelyn gasped, on the verge of a hysterical scream. Before she made a sound, a deep, soothing voice said, "Sorry to have gotten in your way. Do you think you could hand me my other crutch?"

Blinking back her tears, she hastily bent to pick up the crutch that had skidded across the floor. Turning to give it to the man, she heard the deep voice say with surprise, "Lady Jocelyn! What on earth brings you to this wretched place?"

Her eyes came into focus and she realized that she had found the man she was looking for. Captain Richard Dalton was a brown-haired young man of medium height, with hazel eyes much like her own. His face was drawn with fatigue and pain, but his expression showed pleased surprise at the sight of her.

"Captain Dalton! Oh, I'm so glad to see that you are up and about. I came here to see you, actually. My Aunt Laura had heard from General Kirkpatrick that you had been returned to London. I certainly had no intention of putting you back into a hospital bed.'' She tried to keep her tone light, but she still felt unsteady from the sights she had seen and the unexpected accident.

The captain laughed. "Never fear. It takes a good deal more than a collision with a beautiful woman to do me an injury. I think I can say without reservation that running into you is the most enjoyment I have had in weeks." More quietly he added, "I don't blame you for running away from the cutting ward; any sane person would.''

Jocelyn started to relax. Richard's teasing flirtation was pleasant and unthreatening and it helped restore her normal balance. She said, "Aunt Laura sent her apologies that she could not accompany me today, but she intends to call on you later in the week."

"I trust she is well?" He smiled reminiscently. "We used to call her 'the angel of the regiment.' I think she knew every man who served under General Kirkpatrick. From the youngest soldier to the most grizzled old sergeant, everyone adored her." He hesitated, then said, "Would you mind terribly if I sit down? I think I've been upright for about as long as I can manage at the moment.''

Jocelyn's face flamed. "Of course you can sit down! I appear to be causing all kinds of problems for you."

The captain swung over to one of several upholstered chairs by a window, saying, "Welcome to Casa York. The accommodations lack elegance, but the chairs are not uncomfortable." With a courtly wave of his hand he gestured her to the chair opposite him as he lowered himself with a wince. The two were the only occupants of what appeared to be some kind of salon, with card tables and chairs scattered around. The drab walls and furnishings hardly seemed designed to aid convalescence, and the windows faced another depressing wing of the hospital.

"Will you be leaving here soon?" Jocelyn asked.

Richard sighed. "It may be a while. The surgeons keep poking around, looking for bits of shell and bone they might have missed, and they have doubts about how well the leg is healing. We had one long argument about amputation, which I won, but now they are trying to convince me that I'll never walk without crutches again. Needless to say, I have no intention of believing them."

Jocelyn leaned forward impulsively to give his hand a quick squeeze. "In any such disagreement, I'll lay my blunt on you."

"Thank you," he said quietly. There was a long moment of silence, then he said with determined cheer, "I'm in far better case than most of my fellow patients. David Lancaster, for example. But, then, you never met him. He was stationed elsewhere when you came to enliven our winter."

"Aunt Laura mentioned him. Is there news of him that I can take to her?" Jocelyn asked.

"Nothing good. He is dying," the captain said bleakly. "He has grave spinal injuries, and is paralyzed from the waist down." Richard leaned his head against the back of his chair as if suddenly exhausted. Jocelyn knew he was only about twenty-seven, but his drawn face appeared years older. "He can eat almost nothing, and it is an open question whether he will die of starvation, pain, or of the opium they've been giving him to make living bearable. None of the doctors can imagine why he is not dead already, but they agree that it is just a matter of time."

"I'm sorry. I know the words are inadequate, but any words would be," Jocelyn said sadly. After a moment she asked, "He is a particular friend of yours?"

"Yes, and the best of good fellows," Richard confirmed. "Death itself is not so bad, though most of us would prefer a quick end on a battlefield to the kind of slow nightmare David is living. What makes it worse for him is concern for his younger sister. When he is gone, she will be alone in the world, with no protection or prospects." He stopped, then said, "I am sorry to be depressing you with the story of someone you don't even know. His sister, Sally, is an independent creature with a good situation, and will manage quite well on her own.''

Jocelyn hardly heard his later words as an idea blazed into her consciousness. She had thought just the day before that widowhood would be the ideal state, but it was hardly something that could be arranged without assassination. Yet here was a perfect meeting of needs: she could offer the unknown major a settlement that would ensure his sister's security; in return, he could marry her. She would have the legal status needed to retain her fortune while he would be able to die in peace. It was outrageous . . . yet who would be harmed by it?

Speaking quickly before she could lose her courage, she said, "Richard, I have just had a most bizarre inspiration that might solve a problem of mine while helping your friend." Quickly she sketched in the requirements of her father's will, then with some trepidation she explained the solution that had just occurred to her.

To her relief, the captain listened to Jocelyn's proposal with no signs of revulsion or shock. "You are on the horns of a dilemma, but I have trouble believing you can't find a husband in the usual fashion. Are the men of London mad, blind, or both?"

With a wry smile, Jocelyn replied, "It is very lowering to admit, but the man I want has shown an unflattering lack of interest in me. I am reluctant to marry only for the sake of an inheritance, then regret it the rest of my life. You do understand, don't you?" Her last words were a plea: it was important that someone accept her actions as reasonable, and she was relieved when he nodded.

"I quite see your point. It would be utter folly to marry the wrong man because of a ridiculous will." He turned her proposal over in his mind, then said slowly, "If you and David can reach an agreement, it would be a great comfort for him. His sister is a governess here in London and comes to sit with him every afternoon and evening. I know they are very close, and if she were provided for, he would rest easier."

With a surge of excitement, Jocelyn asked, "Would you be able to introduce me to him?"

Resolutely the captain reached for his crutches, then pulled himself upright. "Of course. No time like the present."

He made surprisingly good speed on his crutches, leading her to one of the rooms she had glanced in earlier, where the patient had appeared unconscious. Dalton politely held the door open for Jocelyn, then swung across to the bed and lowered himself into a wooden chair.

As she stared down at the emaciated figure on the bed, it was hard to believe that a man so thin and motionless could still be living. Major Lancaster appeared to be in his late thirties, with dark hair and pale skin stretched across high cheekbones to form a face of stark planes and angles.

Dalton said softly, "David?" and touched his arm.

The major opened his eyes at the sound of his friend's voice. "Richard . . ." The voice was no more than a low whisper of acknowledgment.

Dalton said, "There is a lady here with a proposition that might interest you, if you are able to talk with her."

With a thread of humor, the major said, "I have nothing more pressing on my schedule."

Dalton said, "Lady Jocelyn Kendal," and stood, motioning her into the chair.

She slipped into the seat and looked down, then drew her breath in surprise. The major's eyes were the only thing about him that were alive, and they were vividly green, reflecting not only pain but also intelligent awareness and, amazingly, humor. He looked her over appreciatively and said, "So this is the legendary Lady Jocelyn. Have you brought her here for me to look at, Richard, as a dying man's last request? Unfortunately, looking is all I can do."

Jocelyn said with surprise, "You have heard of me, Major Lancaster?"

"But of course," he said. "Every man in the regiment was at pains to tell me what I had missed by spending the winter with the Spanish." With a ghost of laughter he added, "But they scarcely did you justice."

As she studied the major's spare face, Jocelyn realized his eyes were striking not just for the unusual shade of transparent green but because the pupils were tiny pinpoints, making the irises even more startling. It must be the opium; society ladies who were overfond of laudanum had eyes like these.

As she sat by the wreck of what had been a warrior, her throat closed up and left her silent; to look into Major Lancaster's green eyes and say that she was here in anticipation of his death was, quite simply, impossible.

Richard Dalton correctly interpreted her agonized look and moved forward to help with brief, impersonal phrases that summarized her situation and purpose in visiting.

Major Lancaster seemed unperturbed by the bald implication of his imminent death, merely turning his gaze back to Jocelyn and saying in his shadow of a voice, "How much of a settlement were you proposing?"

Jocelyn hadn't thought that far; her own background left her quite unable to judge such things. Hesitantly she asked, "Would five hundred pounds a year be acceptable?"

The major raised a brow in surprise. "It's positively munificent. That would take a great weight from my mind." He smiled at Jocelyn. "Shall I formally offer you my heart and hand?"

His ability to joke under these circumstances almost undid Jocelyn's heavily stressed self-control. She laid her hand briefly on his and said, "That won't be necessary. I will have my lawyer draw up the settlement papers. Your sister is named Sally Lancaster?"

"Sarah Lancaster, actually. And have your lawyer also draw up a quitclaim for me to sign, relinquishing all other claims against your property."

"Is that necessary?"

"Yes. Legally your property would become mine on

marriage and on my death half would go to my heir, Sally. Since the purpose of this exercise is for you to retain your fortune, we don't want that to happen." He looked amused at her aghast face. "Yes, it is ridiculous, but it is the law."

"That never occurred to me," Jocelyn said. Good God, suppose she had made this strange proposal to a man less scrupulous than Major Lancaster! It could have meant disaster.

The major's eyes closed and his voice was almost inaudible as he said, "If your lawyer is worth his hire, he would have thought of it."

Realizing with sharp compunction that the interview must be tiring him, Jocelyn rose and said, "I should be able to arrange for a special license and the legal papers by tomorrow morning. Will this same time be agreeable to you?" Looking at the spare figure under the blanket, she wondered if he would still be alive in another twenty-four hours.

Uncannily, the major read her mind. Opening his eyes, he said, "Don't worry, I will still be here." He glanced at the silent Captain Dalton. "Will you stand witness for me?"

"Of course."

Jocelyn nodded at the captain. "Thank you for your good offices, Richard; perhaps providence took a hand as well. I will meet you both here tomorrow morning at eleven, with everything necessary for the ceremony." She turned and whipped out of the room before her self-control deserted her entirely.

As the door closed, David Lancaster said, "My thanks also, Richard. There are other men here whose families could use the money more than Sally, but I am selfish enough to be glad she will be provided for."

"It is a very generous settlement," his friend said. "Your sister will have considerable freedom and comfort."

"And most important, security. I know that she is very self-reliant, but someone with no family to fall back on lives perilously close to disaster. An accident or illness could push her into abject poverty. Now that won't happen.'' David exhaled in a long, shuddering sigh. Turning his head, he said, ''It is time for more laudanum. Over there, on the table . . .''

The captain carefully poured a dose of Sydenham's Laudanum into a spoon, then lifted his friend enough to swallow the solution. Conversationally, he said, ''Of course, your sister is not entirely without family.''

''She would starve to death before she would ask help of one of our brothers. Can't say that I blame her; I would do the same.'' He closed his eyes as the opium started to take effect, making him drowsy. ''Now she will have no need to ever ask anything of them.''

As Richard Dalton hoisted himself onto his crutches to leave, David opened his eyes and said in a stronger voice, ''Actually, I would have helped Lady Jocelyn even without the settlement. I rather like the idea of being married to her, even if it's only for a few days. She's lovely . . . and she has a heart, for all she's a lady.'' His eyes closed again, his voice drifting off in the barest of whispers. ''She's a dream girl. . . .''

The captain left the room with satisfaction, grateful that Lady Jocelyn was bringing a little pleasure into David's last days. He only hoped Sally Lancaster wouldn't cut up rough about the marriage; around her brother she was like an angry mother cat guarding her only kitten. At least the income would give her something to think about after he died.

Jocelyn plopped down on a step between floors and buried her head in her hands for a few moments while she collected herself, her mind a jumble of thoughts and feelings. *What have I done?* Dimly she was grateful that her problem was solved—always assuming Major Lancaster didn't die in the night—but at the moment she half-wished she had never set foot in the York Hospital. Though neither of the men had shown disgust at her impulsive suggestion, she felt like a carrion crow; she was unhappily aware that were it not for her ignoble desire to spite Aunt Elvira, she would never have thought of marrying the major. But she had made the offer and been accepted; she could not possibly withdraw now, when the major was depending on her. Jocelyn felt a little better when she reminded herself that he had been pleased to accept her proposition.

She remembered Major Lancaster's courage, his amused green eyes, and could have wept for the waste. How many other men and boys, equally fine, had died as a result of Napoleon's ambition, or been maimed like Captain Dalton and Corporal Morgan? It didn't bear thinking of, so Jocelyn stood and carefully donned her gracious-lady facade. By the time she reached Rhys Morgan's ward, she appeared composed again, though a knot of misery still twisted in her midriff.

Hearing an anguished Welsh voice, she paused in the door of the ward, just out of sight of the Morgans. Rhys was saying, "And who would ever want a cripple like me? I can't fight, can't go down in the mines, can't work on a farm. I wish the damned cannon had blown my head off rather than my leg!"

Hugh's softer voice started making soothing noises, too low for Jocelyn to hear. She squared her shoulders before entering the ward; here at least was something worthwhile she could do for a man who would be around long enough to benefit.

Smiling brightly, she approached the bed, the two brothers turning to face her. Both were silent, Hugh's unhappy face showing the guilt and misery of a whole man in the presence of a disabled one.

While Hugh stood, Jocelyn addressed Rhys. "Corporal Morgan, I have a favor to ask."

He swallowed in embarrassment and said, "Of course, my lady," his face clearly reflecting disbelief that he could in any way assist her.

"I know it would be very dull after all you've done and seen, but would you consider coming to work for me? My aunt is setting up a separate household and we'll need more servants. Tall, handsome footmen are all the rage, and with you and your brother looking so much alike, I would be the envy of Mayfair."

The corporal's face reflected shock and dawning hope. With a glance at his amputated leg, he faltered, "I think I would be more qualified to work in the stables than in the house."

She smiled. "You may suit yourself. There are several positions to fill. Besides," she added teasingly, "if you won't come for my sake, do it for your brother's. The poor man is positively endangered by all the maids in the household. With you there, it will take some of the pressure off him."

Both Morgans stared at her, then Hugh blurted out, "My lady!" while his face turned red, and Rhys leaned back on the pillows and laughed with the air of a man rediscovering humor.

"I'll be pleased and honored, my lady," the corporal said after he stopped chuckling.

"That is settled, then. As soon as the doctors are ready to release you, why not come to my house? I'm sure it is a much nicer place to recuperate than this, and no doubt Hugh will be happy to have you closer."

She smiled and left the room, Morgan catching up a moment later after taking leave of his brother.

When they reached the outside, Jocelyn took a deep, deep breath of the warm July day. Even with the smells of the city in summertime, the air was blessedly clean after the hospital.

Behind her, Morgan said hesitantly, "My lady?"

She turned to face him. "Yes, Morgan?"

Hugh's blue eyes were deeply earnest. "My lady, I will never forget what you have just done. If there is ever anything I can do for you, anything at all . . ."

Jocelyn waved her hand dismissively. "Do not give me too much credit. It was easily done, and I'm sure your brother will be a worthy addition to the house." She thought a moment, then said, "There is something you could do for me tomorrow."

"Yes, my lady?" he asked eagerly.

"I expect that everyone in the household knows about my father's will and the necessity that I marry soon?" She was unsurprised when he nodded; servants always knew exactly what was going on. She continued, "Tomorrow morning, I am coming back to the hospital to marry Major David Lancaster. His condition is grave, and the ceremony will be very quiet. Will you come with me, and be a witness, and tell no one until after it is done?"

The footman's face reflected surprise, but he quickly suppressed it and said, "Of course, my lady."

"Good. Now, where do you think my carriage has gotten to?"

Morgan went to summon the carriage, but was undeterred by her refusal to take credit for creating a situation for Rhys. Many employers could have done the same, but how many would? Lady Jocelyn was just like they said in the servants' hall: a heart of gold, and always refusing to accept thanks for her kindness.

As he helped his mistress into the barouche, Hugh silently prayed that someday he would have the opportunity to repay her for what she had done for his brother.

## 3

**B**efore returning to Upper Brook Street, Jocelyn paid a visit to her lawyer and man of business, Stephen Hamilton. In the four years since the fourth Earl of Cromarty had died, the lawyer had become inured to the surprise visits of the impulsive Lady Jocelyn, but today her requests raised even his experienced eyebrows. However, he knew better than to try to change her mind about something she was determined on, and by the time her ladyship left, he had promised to procure the special license, arrange for a clergyman, and have the settlement and quitclaim documents ready in the morning.

As Hamilton gloomily watched her drive away from his chambers, he reflected that the late earl had been right: the girl needed a man to keep her in line, but a dying officer wouldn't be able to do the job. Lady Jocelyn had said that the attachment was "of some duration," whatever that meant, but he had his suspicions. With a sigh, he turned and rang for his clerk to begin drawing up the documents her ladyship required.

Jocelyn was grateful that Lady Laura was out when she returned from her mission. It would take several hours to compose herself to a point where her sharp-eyed aunt would not see that something was amiss. Far better to explain tomorrow, when the deed was done.

The next morning she awoke with a bizarre sense of unreality and lay staring at the blue satin canopy above her. *Today is my wedding day.* It was not as if it was a real marriage; she would likely marry again later, even if it wasn't to the Duke of Candover. After all, she wanted children and family as much as any woman even if she refused to be rushed by her father's foolish will. Yet, in spite of her rationalizations, today she was taking the step that was for most girls the most momentous of a lifetime, and she was doing it almost at random.

As she stared blankly up, she decided to add something special to the tragic little ceremony that would take place later that morning. When Marie brought her chocolate and bread, she sent the girl down to the kitchen with orders to pack a basket with champagne and glasses, and to gather a bouquet of flowers.

Jocelyn chose her dress with care, selecting a cream-colored percale morning gown with pleats and subtle, cream-on-cream embroidery around the neckline and hem. Marie dressed her chestnut hair rather severely, with most of it pulled back into a twist and only the most delicate of curls left near her face. Seeing that her mistress looked pale, Marie deftly added a bit of color with the hare's foot. Even so, Jocelyn thought, she looked like she was going to a funeral.

At fifteen minutes before eleven o'clock, she arrived at the entrance of the York Hospital to find her lawyer waiting with the license, legal papers, and a vague, elderly cleric named Burns. Hamilton had a scowl on his face; he did not at all approve of such havey-cavey proceedings, even though he was glad that his largest client was keeping her inheritance and her need for his services. With Morgan carrying the basket of champagne and flowers, they entered the hospital and headed toward the west wing in a silent procession. No one challenged them or asked their business; Jocelyn had the eerie feeling that she could have ridden a horse into the building and no one would have given her a second glance.

Major Lancaster and Captain Dalton were engaged in a game of chess when Jocelyn arrived with her entourage, and she was absurdly pleased to see that her intended husband was not only alive, but propped up against pillows so he looked less frail and vulnerable. She smiled at the major and said, "Good morning, David." It was a liberty to use his first name, but she wanted to reduce the impersonality of this strange marriage.

The major caught her unspoken cue and smiled back. "Good morning, Jocelyn. You are looking very lovely today."

When Hamilton saw the expression in Lancaster's eyes, he began to relax, his sense of propriety appeased, since it was obvious that the attachment really was of some duration. The girl must have met the man in Spain the time she had rushed off to spend the winter. He chuckled to himself for even having considered such an absurd possibility that she had chosen someone randomly; after all, the girl *was* a lady.

"Major Lancaster, if you will sign these, please." The lawyer handed him a sheaf of papers and a pen. After scanning everything quickly with an alert eye, the major signed the documents, keeping those copies intended for him and handing back the others.

Ignoring the business aspects of the wedding, Jocelyn arranged the flowers on the bedside table in the vase she had brought. Unfortunately, the brilliant summer blossoms made the rest of the room look even more drab. When that task was done, Jocelyn moved to the side of the bed and gave the major her hand. His grasp was warm and strong on her cold fingers, and he gave a small squeeze of encouragement. She looked down into the green eyes, and was caught by the warmth and peace she saw there. Whatever else he was, David Lancaster was not a man who either wanted or needed pity. She smiled back rather tremulously and said, "Shall we begin?"

The details of the ceremony were never clear to her after. She remembered fragments: "Do you, David Edward, take this woman . . ." "I do." "Do you, Jocelyn Eleanor . . ." "I do." *"Till death do us part."*

The sense of unreality ended when she found herself holding Major Lancaster's hand with a death grip. She should think of him as David now; after all, was he not her husband in the eyes of God and man?

David gently pulled her hand and she leaned over to kiss him. It had been no part of her plan, but it seemed right, and she was surprised how warm his lips felt under hers. When she drew back a little, he said softly, "Thank you, my dear girl." She was fighting back tears when the moment was shattered by a low, intense voice from the doorway.

*"What is the meaning of this?"*

Jocelyn jerked up as if she had been caught in the act of theft, and spun to face the door. A scowling young woman stood there, her fists clenched by her sides as she regarded the tableau before her. While everyone in the room watched in stunned silence, the newcomer marched to the bed with tight, controlled steps, looking as if she would be snarling were she not in a sickroom. When she halted, her gaze moved from David to Jocelyn, the angry eyes brightly green.

With dry amusement, Jocelyn realized that her new sister-in-law had arrived and was not best pleased by what she found. She examined the other woman critically, thinking that she would have been taken as a governess anywhere. Sally Lancaster was a short wiry creature, almost relentlessly plain, her dark hair pulled into a tight knot. Her drab dress was unfashionably high at the neck and she wore a highly practiced look of disapproval on her face. The fine green eyes were her only claim to beauty, and at the moment they sparked with fury.

With a cool inclination of her head, Jocelyn said, "You must be Miss Lancaster. I am Lady Jocelyn Kendal. Or rather, Lady Jocelyn Lancaster. As you have no doubt guessed, your brother and I have just married."

The girl said incredulously, "David?"

He reached out his other hand to her and said quietly, "Sally, it's all right. I'll explain later."

As Sally took her brother's hand and glanced down at him, her face softened and she no longer looked like an avenging angel, just a tired young woman little older than Jocelyn herself, with a look of despairing anxiety on her face.

Jocelyn turned to her footman and said, "Morgan, the champagne, please." Opening the basket, he produced a bottle and glasses, and the bustle of pouring and handing around champagne dissipated the tension in the room. Even Sally accepted one, though she still looked like a rocket ready to explode. Jocelyn insisted Morgan take a glass also, and only then did she wonder if once again she had made a ghastly mistake: it was obviously grotesque for anyone to wish the couple health and happiness.

In his capacity as best man, Captain Dalton saved the moment. "To David and Jocelyn. As soon as I saw you together, I knew you were intended for each other." He managed to look quite at ease even balanced on his crutches, and his toast was close enough to what one would hear at a normal wedding to be unremarkable. Probably only Jocelyn understood the irony of the remark, and she smiled at the captain with gratitude as the guests drank to the couple.

Then David raised his glass in another toast, glancing around the room before saying in a faint, clear voice, "To friends, both present and absent." Everyone could drink to that, and the atmosphere took on a tinge of conviviality as people began chatting. Jocelyn kept a wary eye on Sally Lancaster and was not surprised when the governess said with false sweetness, "Lady Jocelyn, may I speak with you outside for a moment?"

Jocelyn followed her out of the room with resignation; she would have to deal with her prickly sister-in-law sooner or later, and it seemed better that she make the explanations than David. He was obviously tiring rapidly and had hardly touched his champagne.

In the hallway, Sally carefully closed the door, then whirled on Jocelyn. "Would you kindly explain what that was all about? Is it a new fashion for wealthy society ladies to marry dying Waterloo soldiers, as one would chose a new hat? Will you be telling your friends what an amusing game you have found?"

Jocelyn gasped at the accusation; did her sister-in-law really believe the marriage was the result of some bored, selfish whim? It explained the woman's hostility. Jocelyn thought of the major's warmth and understanding touch, and felt angry that Sally dared think that she would marry for such a callous reason. *Was your reason that much better?*

With irritation tinged with guilt, Jocelyn shrugged and said in the icy voice of an earl's daughter, "That is a ridiculous statement and does not dignify an answer. Your brother is an adult—he doesn't need your permission to marry."

Sally's green eyes narrowed down like a cat's and she said tightly, "I think you forced him to do it in some way. David has never even mentioned your name, and I can't believe he would marry without telling me unless he had no choice."

Jocelyn realized the other woman was jealous of her brother's attention, but was still irritable enough to say acidly, "Perhaps he knew that you would throw a tantrum, and preferred a peaceful ceremony."

Sally's face whitened, and Jocelyn felt ashamed of the thrust. More gently she said, "We decided very suddenly, just yesterday. Perhaps there was no time for him to notify you."

Sally shook her head miserably. "I was here yesterday—I am every afternoon. My employers have been very generous in letting me arrange lessons so I would have time with David. But why didn't he want me here?"

Before Jocelyn could think of an appropriate reply, Captain Dalton joined them, having apparently guessed that the two ladies would need a referee. Closing the door with the tip of one crutch, he said without preamble, "Sally, David did it for you." He glanced over and said, "Lady Jocelyn, with your permission, I will explain the situation." She nodded and he proceeded to sketch out Jocelyn's need to marry and why David had agreed.

Sally still looked mutinous. "He had no need to get married for such a reason. I can take care of myself perfectly well."

Dalton unobtrusively leaned against the wall, the fatigue on his face showing why he needed the extra support. "Sally, it will make David much happier to know that you are provided for. Can't you let him have that?"

Sally's face crumbled suddenly and she started weeping softly. "I'm sorry, Richard. You're right, of course. It just seems so strange, coming on top of everything else. What right does she have to come in and take over his last days like this?"

Jocelyn's nerves had had quite enough. With a scowl she said, "The right your brother gave me. Now, if you will excuse me, I will rejoin my husband."

As she reentered the sickroom, she saw that Sally was now sobbing against the long-suffering captain's shoulder. He put an arm around her and smiled wryly at Jocelyn over the bent head; the man had real talent for dealing with distressed females.

Inside, Morgan was packing away empty bottles, leaving two full ones and several glasses on the major's bedside table. David himself was lying down again with a look of exhaustion, and Jocelyn felt a stab of compunction. She crossed to the bed and said gently, "It is time I left you to rest." She leaned over to kiss him lightly for the last time, then said huskily one of the Spanish phrases she had learned, *"Vaya con Dios."*

Their eyes met for a moment, and she again felt desolation at the waste of it all. Then she collected her entourage and left. In the hall, Sally had regained her composure, but her glance was hostile. Jocelyn dug into her reticule, removed one of her cards, and handed it to the other woman. "Here is my direction. Let me know when . . . anything changes, or if there is something I can do that will make your brother more comfortable."

Sally's lips tightened, but she accepted the card without comment. With a nod at Captain Dalton, Jocelyn turned on her heel and left without looking back.

Glaring as the vision of elegance disappeared, followed by her faithful retainers, Sally muttered between clenched teeth, "Slut."

Captain Dalton didn't bother to express surprise at her shocking language. He merely gave a tired smile and said, "She isn't, you know. She is merely a woman trying to find a solution in a world made by men. In the same circumstances, I expect you would behave much the same."

Sally looked at him, then drew her breath in contritely. "Perhaps you're right, though I beg to differ. In any case, it's past time you went and lay down. I'm sure you have been up much longer than your doctor would approve of."

With a low chuckle, Richard said, "I haven't listened to him yet, why should I start now? But you are right, I am ready to lie down for a while." He looked at her seriously. "Sally, think carefully about what you say to David. He is pleased about what happened. Don't spoil it for him."

She flushed a little that he felt it necessary to warn her, but said, "I suppose I deserve that. Don't worry, I won't distress him. I'll go in now and let him know that I haven't murdered his lady wife."

"Good girl." He pushed himself forward from the wall and gave her a wan smile. "Will you be here tomorrow?" She nodded and he headed down the hall toward his own room.

Sally looked after him, seeing the strength in the broad shoulders that swung the crutches. He and David had known each other for years during the Peninsular campaigns, and he had been a good friend these last awful days in London. She didn't know if she could have borne the strain if it wasn't for his quiet, pragmatic support, even though he was almost as grieved about David's condition as she was herself.

When she entered her brother's room, he appeared to be asleep but his eyes opened when she sat down. "Forgive me, little hedgehog?" he asked in a tired thread of whisper.

Her heart came near melting of anguish as he used the old nickname. "Of course I do. It was just such a shock to come here and find a wedding. Is it time for some more laudanum?" Without waiting for the answer, she reached for the bottle and poured a dose.

After swallowing it, David said, "You're here early today."

"Yes, the children's godmother came this morning and whisked them off on some expedition, so I was free unexpectedly." She gnawed at her lip a moment, then said in a voice carefully purged of accusation, "Why didn't you tell me about this wedding?"

David smiled with a hint of his old mischief. "Did Richard explain what was behind it?" When she nodded, he continued, "If I had told you in advance, you would have given me a lecture on how capable you are of taking care of yourself, and said it was quite unnecessary for me to provide for you. Am I right?"

"You know me too well," Sally said with a rueful smile.

His voice was fainter as he drifted toward sleep. "Mind you, you *are* very capable, but you're still my little sister, and I'll be much happier knowing you have five hundred a year."

Five hundred a year! Sally stared at her dozing brother. Captain Dalton hadn't mentioned how large the settlement was; whatever else the arrogant Lady Jocelyn might be, it wasn't stingy. Five hundred pounds was four times Sally's annual salary, and she was reckoned a very well-paid female. She would be able to live in considerable comfort, and even some style.

Would she still want to teach? Sally enjoyed her job and the Launcestons were the best employers she had ever had, but she had no idea whether she would stay with them. She shook her head and dug in her shapeless brocade bag for her knitting; there would be time enough to decide later. Sally had made four pairs of gloves and two scarves during the hours she sat with David. She wasn't really fond of knitting, but had found it impossible to concentrate on reading when David was laboring for breath next to her. Knitting at least kept her hands busy.

She looked glumly at the current sock; three stitches had been dropped, and it would take her half an hour just to repair the damage. Well, she had the rest of the day, and David would sleep most of it. She glanced at the bone-thin figure, then turned away with a shudder. Had it only been two weeks since he had been brought back to London? It seemed that she had been coming to this grim hospital forever, and every day he seemed more frail, until it was hard to understand how he still lived.

Sometimes, God help her, she wished it was over, and she could give in to pure, primitive grief. Other times she wondered how she would find out when he died. Would she be with him? Or would Captain Dalton send a message to her? Or would she arrive and find his room empty, and know the worst?

Sally found she had pulled the yarn so tightly that it had broken and with shaking hands she knotted it together again. *You must be calm. David doesn't need to deal with your grief on top of his pain.* She looked around at the dark, ugly room, hearing the distant sounds of suffering men, smelling the countless wretched smells of a hospital. It was a poor spot to die, but she supposed any place was.

That afternoon Jocelyn joined her aunt for tea in the sunny parlor that was Laura Kirkpatrick's special retreat. After they had been served and were private, she smiled brightly and said, "You will be pleased to hear that my marriage problem has been solved and Aunt Elvira can resign herself to struggling along on Willoughby's present income."

Laura put her cup down in surprise. "You have accepted one of your suitors? Which one? There is just enough time for the reading of the banns, but it will have to be a very small ceremony."

"Better than that." Jocelyn handed her aunt a sheet of paper. "The deed is done. Behold, my marriage lines!"

"What on earth?" Laura glanced at the paper, then went very still. When she glanced up, there was the beginning of anger. "What is the meaning of this?"

"Why, it should be obvious. I found a dying man,

and in return for a substantial consideration, he did me the honor of making me his wife.'' Jocelyn's laugh was brittle.

"But you have never even met David Lancaster!''

"I got the idea when I was visiting Richard Dalton and he told me of his friend's condition,'' Jocelyn said defensively. "It seemed perfectly reasonable—Major Lancaster's sister will be provided for and I will fulfill the conditions of Father's will. Richard wasn't shocked when I suggested it, and neither was . . . my husband.''

The reference to David Lancaster exploded Laura's control into fiery fragments. "They are men who have lived on the edge of death for years. Of course they will see things differently than society will! Why, Richard Dalton wasn't even born in England, and neither of them are from our class. They can't begin to understand how our peers will react to such an action.''

Jocelyn felt the beginnings of anger herself. "Is that why you are concerned, because of what others will say? I had thought you were above such things. Besides, half the *ton* would be amused if the story became known; they would just laugh and credit me with being ingenious.''

Spots of bright color stood out on Laura's cheeks, but her voice was level again as she said, "I can't deny that what people say is of concern to me. The Kendal family has already had more than its share of scandal.''

As Jocelyn's face paled at the thrust, her aunt continued implacably, "What truly bothers me is that you should use such a fine man in a contemptible way, and that you have involved friends of ours in something that could bring censure on them. Why didn't you talk it over with me first?''

Jocelyn tried to maintain calm, but the pain in her chest was overwhelming. Her voice breaking, she cried, "You didn't *want* to know what I was going to do. Please, Aunt Laura, don't be angry with me! I never would have married him if I had known how it would upset you. It was an idea of impulse. Major Lancaster welcomed it, and then it was too late to withdraw. Please . . . please try to understand!''

Lady Laura felt some of her anger fade in the face of her niece's distress. She knew how vulnerable Jocelyn was to the disapproval of those she loved, but Laura felt too revolted by the marriage to give instant forgiveness. While her niece had meant no harm, the girl's impulsive thoughtlessness had led her badly astray. It would not have been so unacceptable if the man was a stranger instead of someone Laura knew and liked; that fact might not be logical, but it made perfect emotional sense. She said slowly, "I don't know, perhaps your actions weren't so very dreadful, but it is going to take time for me to accept them.''

She stood, adding, "I think I will go down to Kennington in the morning. I have been intending to open the house, and I might as well get started." With a trace of acid in her normally soft voice, she said, "Now that you are a married woman, I can leave you alone without occasioning comment.''

Jocelyn looked so starkly unhappy that her aunt said gently, "I will be back in a week or two, and no doubt I'll be over my anger by then. I think I will not go to the Parkingtons' tonight. You may go alone if you wish.''

Then she left the room. With shaking knees, Jocelyn sank back into her chair. As if the last two days had not been difficult enough, now she had alienated her dearest friend, the woman who was the closest thing she had to a mother. As she stared ahead unseeing, she saw her deed through her aunt's eyes and felt bitterly ashamed.

She automatically sipped some of her rapidly cooling tea, hoping it would brace her a bit. Well, there was no help for it: she must lie in the bed she had made, even if it wasn't a conventional marriage bed.

Jocelyn decided to go to the Parkingtons'. She could certainly use the distraction.

# 4

The Parkingtons' informal ball was a small one, since most of the *ton* had already left London. Jocelyn was restless, bored by the chatter that seemed so meaningless compared to the stark realities of the military hospital. Then she drew in her breath sharply at the sight of a latecomer, her heart beginning to pound with uncontrollable excitement when she saw that it was indeed Rafael Whitbourne, the Duke of Candover.

Candover had obviously delayed his departure to the country, and just looking at him made Jocelyn feel better. It wasn't only that he was handsome, although he was; his height and his darkly sardonic expression made him stand out in any company. What Jocelyn found irresistibly attractive was the suggestion of power and forcefulness that showed through the languid manners of a fashionable gentleman.

As Jocelyn saw him work his way around the room, it took all her willpower not to put herself in his path with a besotted expression on her face. The magnetism he radiated reminded her of why she had refused to accept other suitors, and justified the painful ceremony earlier in the day. Why settle for less when there was a man like this in her world?

She monitored his progress from the corner of her eye as she chatted easily to other guests, and she was rewarded when Candover sought her out after the small orchestra started playing dance music. The first dance was a waltz, and whirling around the floor in his masterful arms was so intoxicating that it drove all her worries from her head.

As they exchanged the normal pleasantries, she studied him carefully, admiring the firmness of his features, the clarity of those cool gray eyes. He was known as Rafe by the handful of people who were his intimates, but she would never venture to call him that without an invitation. She thought she was laughing and chatting in quite her normal manner, and it was a surprise when the duke said thoughtfully, "Forgive me, Lady Jocelyn, but you appear a bit out of sorts today."

She was surprised at his perception, but answered gaily, "It was an odd sort of day, your grace. I got married this morning and have not yet accustomed myself to the fact."

The pale eyes showed surprise. "Indeed? I had not heard that you were contemplating the fatal step. And surely the Parkingtons' house is an odd place for a honeymoon."

She studied him through her long lashes. She was looking her best tonight, in a celestial-blue silk dress that made her changeable eyes look blue, and the duke's gaze was openly admiring. On impulse, she decided to inform him of her circumstances, and her availability. With a shrug, she said, "It is not generally known, but my father made the most ridiculous will, with the condition that I marry by the age of twenty-five or be essentially disinherited."

"Absurd!"

"Quite, especially when you consider that we were on the best of terms," Jocelyn agreed. "But there was nothing to be done about it, so this morning I contracted a marriage of convenience." She was unable to prevent a note of bitterness as she continued, "I had hoped to have a real marriage."

"If by that you mean a love match, you know how rare that is in our order, and how seldom it is successful."

"Rare, my lord, but not impossible."

"You are very young, my dear. Life has a way of stripping away optimism."

There was a note of sadness in Candover's voice, and she glanced up in surprise. The remark was quite unlike anything she had ever heard him say, and she wondered if he was letting down his formidable barriers just a little.

"I do not know if I am an optimist, but I know that I will not stop looking for love."

"Your husband of convenience will not object?"

"He will not," Jocelyn said firmly. In the arms of the man who had fascinated her for the last three years, she had no desire to think of the soldier who had touched her life and feelings so briefly.

The waltz came to an end and the duke returned her to her chair as he studied her with great deliberation, his gaze lingering on her low neckline and the curves visible through the gauzy summer gown. It was a bold appraisal, far more speculative than any he had ever done before. With a slow, devastating smile, he said, "I am leaving London in the morning, but I look forward to calling on you when I return to town in September."

Jocelyn almost melted at the promise in his gray eyes, but she rallied to return a devastating smile of her own. "I shall await that with great pleasure."

She did her best to seem cool, but as Candover left her, she was possessed of an excitement too intense for words. Finally, the only man she wanted was looking at her as a woman, and all because she was now married. That look in his eye was worth even the price she had paid these last two days. Surely if he drew close, her love must ignite a matching love in him? The thought was almost frightening in its implications.

The two months until September stretched endless and empty before her.

Sally had tossed restlessly all night after she left David, angry at the memory of the cool society beauty who so casually used and discarded her brother. While she was able to get through her usual lessons with the three Launceston children the next morning, her mind would not cease its churning, and as she left for the hospital, Sally realized she had been jolted out of her fatalism. For the last weeks she had accepted passively the doctors' verdict on David's fate. Now her anger had broken loose into a refusal to give in so tamely. David was in no condition to fight for his life, but she most certainly was. And if there was anything or anyone at all who might hold out promise for recovery, she would pursue it.

Before she even went to David's room, Sally sought out her brother's physician, Dr. Ramsey, determined to question every possibility. Dr. Ramsey was a solid man with an air of permanent fatigue, and unlike many of his colleagues, he was willing to admit the limits of his knowledge. He blinked warily behind his spectacles when Sally caught him between patients, knowing from experience how tenacious she could be with her questions.

"Yes, Miss Lancaster?" he said with a rising inflection that implied he had very little time to talk with her.

"Dr. Ramsey, isn't there anything more that can be done for my brother? He's just fading away in front of my eyes. Surely there must be something you can do."

The physician removed his spectacles and polished them. "I admit Major Lancaster's case puzzles me. He is holding on to life with remarkable tenacity, but there is so little that can be done in cases of paralysis. . . ."

His voice trailed off in depression, then he continued, "What kills so many battle casualties is infection or the shock of surgery. Your brother has survived both, but his condition continues to deteriorate." Returning the spectacles to his face, he said more firmly, "George Guthrie himself did the operation, and there isn't a finer surgeon in the whole army. He and I have discussed your brother's case repeatedly, but I fear that all we can do is make his last days as comfortable as possible."

Sally caught his wandering eye and said carefully, "I don't wish to criticize your care. I know you have been doing everything you can, and I am grateful. But do you know of any physicians or surgeons in London that have a different approach, perhaps something that seems radical by normal standards? After all, there is little to lose."

Dr. Ramsey stroked his chin thoughtfully. "Well, there's a mad Scot called Ian Kinlock. You could locate him through St. Bartholomew's Hospital, I believe.

He's said to be quite impossible, but he has done some remarkable things. Worked in India and China, I understand, and perhaps he has learned a useful trick or two."

He looked at Sally's modest dress and said warningly, "He's a private practitioner and his fees are very high. Apparently he charges people with money a great deal, then gives free care to gutter scum. Quite, quite mad. You'll never persuade him to call on a patient at the York Hospital."

Sally said with a determined gleam, "I have just come into some money unexpectedly. We shall see."

She turned and strode down the hall, while Dr. Ramsey watched with a rare smile. *God help Ian Kinlock.* Then he entered the next room to see how much longer the double amputee would survive.

Sally's mind was calculating as she went to David's room. She knew that looking for a new physician was grasping at the thinnest of straws, but as long as there was any hope at all, it was worth trying. More than that, she liked the idea of spending Lady Jocelyn's money in a way that might possibly benefit David. St. Bartholomew's Hospital was one of the oldest and busiest in London, and she recalled vaguely that it was a center for surgery. It was over near St. Paul's cathedral, and she would need to hire a hackney coach. . . .

Distracted, she almost walked into a hefty young man hovering outside David's door. He was wearing a powdered wig and blue livery, and after a moment she recognized him as the footman who had been present at the mockery of a wedding the day before.

"Come to see if your mistress's husband is dead yet?" she asked caustically. She felt ashamed of herself when the young man flushed scarlet; he was too easy a target, and it wasn't fair to blame him for Lady Jocelyn's want of conduct.

"I came to take my brother home, Miss Lancaster," he said stiffly. "Lady Jocelyn sent the coach with me and told me to ask after the major while I was here."

"Your brother is also a patient here?" Sally asked in a more conciliatory tone.

"Yes, he was in the Guards. Lady Jocelyn has offered him a position and the chance to convalesce in her town house."

The footman's words were intended to demonstrate his mistress's kindness to someone who clearly did not value her ladyship. Instead, they sowed the seeds of an idea that burst instantly into full, radiant flower in Sally's mind. This ghastly hospital was enough to make a well person ill, and she would have moved David out sooner if she had a better alternative. But she couldn't take him to her employers or have afforded to hire good lodgings and servants to care for him.

Now, however, an alternative had presented itself. Under English law, David *owned* the no-doubt luxurious house in Upper Brook Street that the Lady Jocelyn called home, and the witch had no right to refuse him admittance. If she tried, Sally would bring the place down around her ladyship's shell-pink ears.

"How convenient that you have brought a coach," she said. "We can use it to move Major Lancaster to Lady Jocelyn's house."

Hugh Morgan looked first startled, then alarmed. "I don't know, miss. She asked me to inquire after him, but she said nothing about bringing him home."

Fixing the hapless footman with the quelling stare she used on her charges, Sally said firmly, "No doubt she was worried about moving him. However, I was just talking with the doctor, and he sees no harm in it."

Since Morgan still looked unconvinced, Sally moved in with the killing stroke. "After all, they are married. What was hers is now his. And surely dear Lady Jocelyn cannot wish her husband to stay in this, this"—she waved her hand around eloquently—"unwholesome place now that the doctor says he can be moved."

Morgan could not help but agree when he remembered how passionately grateful Rhys was to be leaving. And her ladyship seemed very fond of the major; surely she would be pleased to have him home. With a decisive nod, he said, "I'll help my brother move, then be back for Major Lancaster with a litter and someone to help me carry it. Will you pack his things, miss?"

"Of course." As she watched him leave, Sally marveled at the ease with which he had been convinced. She would have thought he would be more wary of his mistress's wrath. Dismissing the thought, she sought out Dr. Ramsey again. That gentleman agreed that if the trip from Belgium hadn't killed the major, a journey across London probably wouldn't, and if it did, it would just be hastening the inevitable.

Ignoring the doctor's last sentences, Sally returned to her brother's room to inform him of what she had arranged. "Good news, David. Lady Jocelyn's carriage is here and the doctor says you can be moved. I'm sure that you'll be happy to get out of the hospital."

"She wants me to come to her house?" he said with surprise and the beginning of a smile. "That was no part of our bargain. It is most kind of her."

The idea that his "wife" cared enough to send for him made David look so pleased that Sally didn't attempt to correct his misapprehension. Instead, she vowed that Lady Jocelyn would make him feel welcome if Sally had to hold a pistol to her head.

"I shan't miss this place," David said as his gaze flickered over the drab walls. "Except for Richard."

"Richard can come and visit you. He's getting around very well now and will welcome an excuse to get out. I'll go give him your new direction before I leave." She paused, then said, "Perhaps it would be best if you took a heavy dose of the laudanum. The trip is bound to be a rough one."

David grimaced in agreement. "Too right. I think I would prefer not to be aware of what is going on." It was one of the few references he had made to what Sally knew was constant pain, and she hoped the journey would not injure him further. If he died of the carriage ride, she would never forgive herself.

* * *

It was crowded in the closed carriage with Hugh Morgan, his crutch-wielding brother, Sally, and Major Lancaster jammed in together. Hugh had obtained planks and blankets from somewhere and rigged a pallet across one side of the vehicle to hold the semiconscious major, but Sally still winced as they jolted on every cobblestone between Belgravia and Mayfair.

When they reached Upper Brook Street, Sally said, "If you don't mind staying with the major for a few moments, I'll go and inform Lady Jocelyn that he has arrived."

She marched up the marble steps and used the massive dolphin-shaped knocker. When a butler opened the door, she said, "I am Miss Lancaster, Lady Jocelyn's sister-in-law. If you direct me to her ladyship, I will ask her where she wishes her husband to be carried."

Husband? The butler's eyes visibly bulged; it was a tribute to Hugh Morgan's discretion that none of the servants had heard of the marriage. Pulling himself together, he said, "I believe Lady Jocelyn is in the morning room. If you will follow me . . ."

The house was every bit as luxurious as Sally had expected, a perfect background for its flawless mistress. She refused to be daunted by the towering, three-story-high foyer, even when an upward glance revealed that the majestic columned galleries were each decorated by a different order of pillars. The ground-floor columns were Ionic, the first-floor Tuscan; after squinting a bit, she decided that the top floor showed Corinthian. She had hoped to find evidence of vulgarity, but to her regret, the house was furnished with impeccable taste.

Sally stuck her jaw out pugnaciously as the butler ushered her into the morning room, where Lady Jocelyn sat at a writing table, her graceful, daffodil-colored dress a perfect complement to her warm chestnut coloring. Sitting on the desk was a bouquet of flowers and a furry feline statue, not a plump cozy tabby, but an elegant, thin-boned cat of obviously aristocratic origins.

In Sally's jaundiced view, the cat looked as expensive and unlovable as its mistress.

The butler said, "Lady Jocelyn, your 'sister-in-law' wishes to speak with you." His inflection masterfully implied both that Sally was an impostor and that if she was indeed genuine, Lady Jocelyn owed her faithful retainer an explanation.

Jocelyn looked up with surprise, then paused, her eyes narrowing. "Thank you, Mossley. That will be all."

When her ladyship used that tone, she got instant obedience, and the butler beat a hasty retreat. He considered pressing his ear to the keyhole, but decided with regret that it would be inconsistent with his dignity, particularly if he were caught.

Jocelyn had been dreamily remembering her meeting with Candover the night before, and it was a rude shock to have this angry young woman intruding on her, a hostile reminder of yesterday's unhappy events. She speculated briefly on what might have brought Sally to Upper Brook Street. If her brother had succumbed to his wounds, surely the governess would be too busy and distraught to come in person? Perhaps she had come to harangue her unwanted sister-in-law again. Her stomach knotting in anticipation of more unpleasantness, Jocelyn made no attempt to rise or invite Sally to sit. With cold politeness she asked, "What brings you here today, Miss Lancaster?"

The surly creature scowled at her, then said abruptly, "David is outside in your carriage. It will take two footmen to carry him inside, and you will need to direct them to a room."

"What on earth are you talking about?" Jocelyn asked in astonishment.

If Miss Lancaster stuck her jaw out any farther, she was in danger of dislocating it. "I have brought your *husband* to stay here." The emphasis was heavy and unmistakable.

"How dare you!" Jocelyn leaped to her feet as her temper ripped loose of its moorings. "Your brother and

I made a bargain, and it had nothing to do with taking a dying man into my home. Why, it would disrupt my whole household.''

"It isn't 'your' house. It's his."

As Jocelyn stared at her visitor with dawning fury, Sally said fiercely, "Under English law, the wife's property becomes her husband's on marriage. If you don't let him stay, I'll . . . I'll get him to sign all of your property over to the Army Widows' and Orphans' Fund. He'll do it if I ask him to."

Jocelyn could feel her hands curling into fists; she hadn't felt such a desire to visit physical violence on someone since her nursery days. Through clenched teeth, she said, "What a touching example of sibling devotion. However, the major himself suggested that my lawyer draw up a quitclaim that waived all future claims against my estate."

Her eyes raked Sally as she added contemptuously, "Obviously your brother inherited all of the Lancaster family honor, as well as any claim to looks. If you do not leave in the next thirty seconds, I will have my servants remove you."

She was reaching for the bellcord when Sally's face crumpled into raw emotion. "Lady Jocelyn, I know that you don't like me any better than I like you. But haven't you ever had anyone in your life that you loved?"

"How is that to the point?"

"If you had any choice at all, would you leave them to die in that stinking hospital?"

As Jocelyn hesitated, Sally pleaded, "Don't send him back there, *please!* If you want to bar me from visiting here, I will not dispute it. If you want me to return the entire settlement, I will. But I beg of you, don't send David back to the hospital. Even if he has no legal right, surely you have a moral obligation to your husband."

Jocelyn felt as if a cold hand had grasped her liver and twisted. In her anger at Sally and her desire to put the whole unpleasant business behind her, she had forgotten that the issue wasn't this drab termagant, but

David Lancaster himself. She felt again his warm hand supporting her when they had married, and her opposition dissolved. No matter how disruptive and upsetting it would be to have him in the house, in common humanity she could not turn him away.

She rang the bell. As Sally watched silently, Jocelyn told the butler, "My husband is in the carriage outside. He is very ill and will need to be carried in. Put him in the Blue Room."

When Mossley had left, his face carefully impassive, Sally said brokenly, "Thank you."

Jocelyn said coldly, "I'm not doing this for your sake, but for his." Turning to her writing desk, she lifted a leather bag that jingled, then tossed it to Sally. "I was going to have it sent, but since you are here, I will give it to you in person. Your first quarter's allowance."

Sally gasped at the weight as she caught the pouch, then automatically pulled at the drawstring to look inside.

"You needn't count it," Jocelyn said acidly. "It is all there, one hundred twenty-five pounds in gold."

Sally's head snapped up. "Not thirty pieces of silver?"

Jocelyn said softly, each word carved from ice, "Of course not. Silver is for selling people. Since I was buying, I paid in gold."

As Sally teetered on the verge of explosion, Jocelyn continued, "You may come and go as you please. If you like, I will have the room next to your brother's made up for you, for . . . as long as you need it. Does he have a personal servant?" When Sally shook her head, Jocelyn said, "Then I shall get one for him. He will require a good deal of care. Let me know if he needs anything."

Sally turned to go, then turned back to say hesitantly, "There is one other thing. He thought that it was your idea to bring him here, and . . . it pleased him very much. I hope you will not disabuse him of the notion."

Jocelyn stared at her frostily, the picture of aristocratic disdain. "Should you find yourself unable to survive on five hundred pounds a year, I'm sure you can have a lucrative career in blackmail. You needn't worry that I will distress your brother unnecessarily. Now will you remove yourself from my presence?"

As Sally beat a hasty retreat, she could feel her body shaking in reaction. If she had had any doubts that Lady Jocelyn was a brass-hearted virago, they were laid to rest now. She could only hope that her beastly ladyship wouldn't be unkind to David. He seemed to cherish the illusion that she was a good person, and discovering her real character would distress him.

It took only a quarter-hour to get the major and his few belongings settled in a sumptuous room with a diagonal view to Hyde Park. It appeared to be the best guest chamber, and Sally again conceded—with enormous reluctance—that Lady Jocelyn did not do things by half-measures. David was white-faced with pain from the move, and Sally was grateful that she had carried the bottle of laudanum over in her knitting bag. When the footman had left, she gave her brother a large dose of opium.

Burying her own feelings about Lady Jocelyn, Sally said, "Your wife was good enough to offer me a room here, but I think it best that I sleep at the Launcestons'. The littlest girl has nightmares sometimes and likes me to be there. But I will be here in the afternoons and evenings, as I was at the hospital, and Richard Dalton said he would call tomorrow. You had better get some rest now. The trip must have been tiring."

David smiled faintly. "I'll be fine, little hedgehog. You are the one who needs some rest."

"Actually, David, I was going to go to St. Bart's now. Dr. Ramsey said there was a very fine doctor there, someone who will be able to help you."

"Perhaps," David said, unimpressed.

Sally noticed that his eyes kept drifting to the door. Was he expecting his so-called wife to visit him? It was one more heartache, and Sally had had enough of those. She stood and said, "I will see you later. Lady Jocelyn

said she will hire a servant for you. She has been everything generous.'' Sally bent to kiss his forehead, then
quietly left.

Outside, she met Hugh Morgan, who said ingenuous-
ly, "I'm to take care of the major. He's a real gentleman.''

"Yes, he is. I'm sure you will suit him very well.'' As
Sally left, she felt a certain unwilling amusement at the
perfect poetic justice Lady Jocelyn had visited on
Morgan, the accidental instrument for bringing the
major to these hallowed precincts. Sally thought he
seemed a nice young man; David would be in good
hands. Now to find the mad Scot at St. Bartholomew's.

It took Jocelyn a good ten minutes to calm down after
her repellent sister-in-law left. She had been sitting at
her escritoire, admiring the flowers that Candover had
sent that morning. The note simply said "Until
September,'' and was signed with a boldly scrawled
"C.'' Holding the note and remembering the warm way
he had looked at her, she had been lost in dreams;
finally she would have a chance to show him her love.
He had revealed something of himself the night before,
and in time she might know the mysteries that lay
behind those cool gray eyes.

Then that unspeakable female had blundered in with
her threats and her emotional blackmail. Had it not
been for Sally Lancaster's green eyes, it would have
been impossible to imagine that she was related to a
civilized man like David Lancaster. Jocelyn's mouth
curved involuntarily as she remembered her own remark
about buying the major with gold. Aunt Laura would
have gone into a spasm if she had heard her niece say
something so unforgivably vulgar, but it had been worth
it just to see the expression on Miss Lancaster's face.
"Sally.'' A name for a housemaid . . . quite appropriate.

Jocelyn sighed, her temporary amusement gone, and
absently reached to scratch between Isis' ears. How
could she have thought getting involved with someone's

life and death would be simple? She would rather not think of the major's imminent death, and she certainly had not intended to be a witness to it, but it could not be avoided now. Whenever she thought of David Lancaster, she wanted to cry. It was like a candle going out, reducing the amount of light in the world.

She pulled her mind back to practical considerations. Fortunately Morgan had welcomed the opportunity to serve the major; the footman had a kind heart and a steady hand, and Jocelyn had heard from Marie that he aspired to be a valet someday. Now he could get some real experience.

Jocelyn made a mental note to have Mossley arrange for straw to be spread on the street in front of the house to reduce traffic noise. She would also notify the cook that invalid fare would be required, if the major could be induced to eat.

Most of all, she reminded herself forcefully to be patient with Sally Lancaster. It would be impossible to avoid her sister-in-law entirely and Jocelyn did not expect the woman to improve in civility. It was understandable that Sally was irritable and upset; after all, she was devoted to her brother and had no one else to care about. And with her looks and disposition, she probably never would again.

Jocelyn did not even bother feeling guilty for the uncharitable thought.

## 5

Sally thought the York had inured her to hospitals, but St. Bart's seemed ten times as crowded and twenty times as noisy. It had been founded in the Middle Ages by monks and appeared not to have been cleaned since. St. Bartholomew's and St. Thomas' hospitals treated the bulk of London's indigent poor, and a clamorous, odorous lot they were. Still, the hospital trained some of the country's best surgeons. As she passed through endless crowded wards, she supposed it must be because the surgeons had so many patients to practice on.

It took half an hour of walking and asking questions to locate anyone who knew anything about Ian Kinlock, and at first she was told that he never came in on Tuesdays because "that was 'is day for the swells." Another listener chimed in that he'd seen the doctor 'imself that very day. Another hour of searching brought her to the dingy cubicle where Kinlock was alleged to be found after he'd done his day's work in the cutting ward.

It was already late in the afternoon when Sally found the room, but she had two hours more of waiting while she studied the rough wooden desk and chairs. The desk had two locking drawers, perhaps for him to keep his instruments. A jumble of books, papers, and anatomical sketches covered every available surface; brilliant Kinlock might be, but neat he definitely wasn't.

With nothing better to do, Sally finally began straightening papers without actually moving things to new places. As she tidied up a pile on top of a low bookshelf, her fingers brushed what felt like a china mug and she pulled it out, only to find herself holding a hollow-eyed, grinning human skull.

She was proud that she didn't drop it from shock,

although her fingers shook a bit as she carefully put the ghastly relic back on the bookshelf. As she did so, an impatient voice with a definite Scots burr said from the doorway, "The skull belongs to someone who had the foolishness to meddle with my office. Are you trying to become a mate to it?"

Sally was sure she jumped a foot into the air. When she spun around to face the owner of the voice, she saw a man of middle height with massive shoulders, rumpled white hair, a blood-splashed smock, and an impressive scowl.

Sally knew without conceit that she could scowl with the best of them, so she did. "Dr. Ian Kinlock?"

"Correct. Also Mr. Ian Kinlock, when I am acting the surgeon. Get the hell out of my office."

He turned his back on her with an assumption that she would obey, then threw himself into the desk chair and unlocked one of his drawers, pulling out not instruments but a bottle of raw scotch whiskey. Ignoring his visitor, he uncorked the bottle, took a long, long draft, and slumped against the chair back with his eyes closed.

When Sally approached, she realized that he was younger than she had first thought, certainly under the age of forty. The thick hair might be prematurely white, but the lines in his face were from exhaustion, not age, and the compact body had the lean fitness of a man in his prime. "Dr. Kinlock?"

His lids barely lifted to reveal tired blue eyes. "You still here? Out. Now." He took another pull of whiskey.

"Dr. Kinlock, I want you to see my brother."

"Miss Whatever-the-hell-your-name is, I have seen over fifty patients today, performed six operations, and just lost two patients in a row under the knife. If your brother was Prinny himself, I would not see him. Especially if he were Prinny. For the third and last time, get out, or I will throw you out."

He ran a tired hand through his white hair, adding a smudge of blood to its disarray. For all his profanity, there was a forceful intelligence about him, and Sally was determined to get him to David as soon as possible.

"David was wounded at Waterloo. He's paralyzed from the waist down, in constant pain, and wasting away like a wraith."

Kinlock's eyes showed the barest flicker of acknowledgment. He said brusquely, "With that kind of spinal injury, he is a dead man. For miracles, try St. Bartholomew's church across the street."

"Didn't you take an oath, Doctor? To help those in need?"

For a moment she thought that she had gone too far and that the doctor would murder her on the spot. Then the anger dissolved and he said with great gentleness, "I will make allowances for the fact that you are concerned about your brother. I should even be complimented by your touching faith that I might be able to help him. Unfortunately, the amount we know about the human body is so minuscule when compared to the amount we *don't* know that it is a wonder that I can ever help anyone."

He paused to take another swig of whiskey, then continued in the same reasonable tone. "Waterloo was fought when? The eighteenth of June? So it has been almost five weeks. With a spinal injury severe enough to cause paralysis, the surprise is that your brother is still alive. Half the bodily functions are knocked out, there are infections, ulceration from lying still too long—a man just can't survive long like that, and from what I've seen in like cases, it's a mercy when they die. So take my advice: say good-bye to your brother and leave me alone."

He started to turn away to his desk, but Sally reached out to touch his sleeve. "Dr. Kinlock, none of those things have happened to my brother. It is just that he is in such pain and is wasting away. Couldn't you just look at him? Please?"

At her words, Kinlock's dark, bushy brows drew together in thought. "A great deal of pain? That's odd, one would expect numbness. . . ."

He pondered a moment longer, then turned back, his eyes sharply analytical as he rattled off a series of medical questions. Sally could answer most of them; not for nothing had she badgered the doctors at the York Hospital for information.

Finally he asked, "How much laudanum has he been taking?"

"About a bottle a day," Sally said.

"What! Bloody hell, no wonder the man can't move!" As Sally stared, he continued, "Opium is a wonderful medication, but not without drawbacks." He put an elbow on his desk and rested his chin on his hand as he thought about what she had said. Finally he turned back to Sally and said, "Give me the direction and I'll come and see him tomorrow afternoon."

"Couldn't you make it tonight? He's so weak. . . ."

"No, I could not. And if you'd want me to after I've just put away this much whiskey, you're a fool."

"Tomorrow morning, first thing then? I'll give you one hundred twenty-five pounds." Reaching through the side slit in her dress to the pocket she wore slung around her waist, Sally pulled out the pouch of gold and handed it to him.

Kinlock whistled softly at the weight, then tossed it in the air while he eyed her with grudging respect. "You're a determined little thing, aren't you? Nonetheless, I have patients to see tomorrow morning; the afternoon is the best I can do, and I won't make any promises about the precise hour. Take it or leave it." He handed the bag back to her.

Stung by the dismissive phrase "little thing," Sally said, "I've always heard surgeons are a crude, profane lot. So good to know that rumor spoke true in this case."

Instead of being insulted, Kinlock laughed, his face lightening for the first time. "You forgot to mention abrasive, insensitive, and uncultured. Accuracy, lass, accuracy. By the way, what is your name?"

"Sally Lancaster."

He nodded. "Aye, ye look like a Sally. Write down the address, I'll see your brother tomorrow afternoon." His Scots accent was becoming more pronounced as the whiskey took effect.

While Sally wrote the direction, Kinlock crossed his arms on the desk, laid his head on them, and promptly fell asleep. She carefully tilted the slip of paper against his whiskey bottle, assuming that it would be easily found and remembered in that position, then turned to leave.

When she reached the door, she glanced back to regard the slumbering figure with bemusement. What on earth did a Sally look like? A mad Scot indeed, abrasive, insensitive, and all the rest. But for the first time in the last month, she felt a faint flutter of hope that David might have a future.

Lady Jocelyn finally threw her quill across the desk in exasperation, leaving a scattering of ink blots on her account book while Isis raised a contemptuous nose at her lack of self-control. All afternoon she had tried to attend to correspondence and monthly accounts, but she was unable to concentrate for thinking of the man lying upstairs in the Blue Room.

She rested her chin on her palm and thought how ridiculous it was to be so shy about visiting him. After all, she was his hostess. Lord, his wife! His prickly sister had gone out and not returned, and had reportedly turned down the offer of a bedchamber, for which be thanked. At least the chit wasn't entirely lacking in sense; if they had to meet daily over the breakfast table, there would be murder done.

"You're quite right, Isis. Since I'm not getting any work done anyhow, I might as well check that the major is comfortable." Or alive, for that matter. Jocelyn pushed herself away from the desk decisively. "Do you think he'd like some flowers? He seemed to like the ones in the hospital." The cat yawned luxuriously. "So pleased you agree with me. There should be some nice roses in the back garden."

A few minutes later, Jocelyn knocked lightly at the door to the Blue Room, entering when there was no response. The major appeared to be asleep, so she set the vase of cream and yellow roses on a table by the bed and went to look at him more closely. So thin, and so pale . . . A dark shadow of beard was beginning to show, and moved by some impulse of tenderness, she reached out gently to touch his cheek, feeling the rasp of bristles beneath her fingers.

Disconcertingly, his eyes opened and he looked at her with a faint smile. "Good day, Lady Jocelyn. It was good of you to bring me here."

With that look of gratitude on his face, she could not have disabused him of the idea even if Sally Lancaster hadn't warned her. Still, innate honesty compelled her to say as she withdrew her hand, "Much of the credit belongs to your sister. It was she who thought of asking the doctor if it was safe to move you."

With a faint chuckle, he said, "Doubtless the doctor said that it really didn't matter one way or the other." His eyes circled the room with its high, molded ceiling and silk-clad walls. "And your house is an infinitely pleasanter place to die than the hospital."

"How can you be so calm, to talk of your death as if it were a change in the weather?" Curiosity compelled Jocelyn to ask the question past the lump in her throat.

He gave the impression of shrugging, though he scarcely moved. "When you've spent enough time soldiering, death *is* like a change in the weather. I've been on borrowed time for years. I suppose I never really expected to make old bones."

She looked so lovely, standing there in her daffodil dress with the afternoon sun sculpting the perfect features. Her brows were knit as if she were concerned about him, and David found he was a little less resigned to dying than he had been. It would have been a great pleasure to meet and court this lady when he was well and whole. But even then, his circumstances would never have made him a suitable partner for a woman of her station. So he smiled and said, "You must not trouble yourself about me."

There was a glimmer of tears on her cheeks, and he found that by concentrating all his strength, he could lift his hand and brush them away, his fingertips lingering on the rose-petal softness of her skin. "Don't weep for me, my lady. If you remember me at all, I would rather you did with a smile."

The tears didn't entirely disappear, but she did smile, raising her hand to cover his. "I'll do my best, Major." The great hazel eyes looked at him solemnly, then she said hesitantly, "This is all so strange."

"Yes. But for me at least, not unwelcome. I am only sorry to be disturbing your peace."

"Perhaps it is time it was disturbed. Too much tranquillity can't be good for the soul." She released his hand and he let it fall back to the bed, exhausted even by that small effort. He wished he had had the strength to touch the chestnut hair, to see if it felt as silky as it looked.

Her sweet musical voice took on a businesslike note as she asked, "Is Hugh Morgan acceptable to you as a servant? If not, I'll find another."

"Perfectly acceptable. I don't mean to be a demanding guest, or to overstay my welcome."

She bit her lip, then said with a slight quiver, "If there is anything you wish, you have only to ask. Do you object to my visiting you?"

"Why should I possibly object?"

"The impropriety . . ." She was startled when he started to laugh, then had to join in. "Quite ridiculous, isn't it? There can be no impropriety when we are properly leg-shackled."

The interview had tired him, and he could feel himself drifting off again, but he could not resist saying, "My only regret is that I am in no condition to compromise you."

Jocelyn looked uncertain, then smiled and leaned forward to brush a gossamer kiss on his lips before she turned to leave the room. He admired the grace of her walk and the way the sun burnished her hair to auburn warmth. A dream girl.

Jocelyn closed the door behind her, then leaned against it, feeling as drained as the major looked. Damn the man, why did she have to like him? Every time she saw him, it got worse. Strange, the feeling of intimacy between them, perhaps because there was no time for polite preliminaries, no time at all. . . .

The visit reinforced her resolution to be more tolerant toward Sally Lancaster, whose loss would be far greater when the major died. Jocelyn went downstairs vowing not to let David's sister irritate her so easily in the future.

The afternoon was far advanced the next day when Ian Kinlock finally showed himself in Upper Brook Street. In the elegant town house, he looked as out of place as a dancing bear, and as powerful. Sally was so glad to see him that she bit back her first impulse to comment caustically on the lateness of the hour. Judged by his stained and rumpled appearance, he had been busy about his business all day, and he looked tired and cranky enough to leave if she antagonized him.

Nonetheless, his voice was gentle and reassuring as he questioned David about his injury and subsequent treatment. He firmly insisted that Sally leave before he would do a physical examination; she was unsure whether he was more concerned with sparing her blushes or David's.

For an endless half-hour she paced along the gallery, looking over the railing into the foyer two floors below, then stalking back to a bust of some marble gentleman with a wreath who guarded the head of the stairs. Captain Dalton had visited earlier in the day, and she wished now she had asked him to stay and bear her company. Instead, she hadn't even mentioned the new doctor, as if speaking would take the magic of hope away.

When Kinlock opened the door, she was on him in a flash, asking eagerly, "Well?"

"Come in, Miss Lancaster. I want to discuss this with you and your brother." He looked more pleased then forbidding, and she felt a stirring of anticipation. David was white-lipped from the pain of the examination, but he was propped up against the pillows, his eyes alert.

Sally went to sit next to him, seizing his hand and holding it tightly.

Kinlock delivered his verdict while pacing and punctuating his speech with sweeping gestures and a stabbing forefinger. Sally thought briefly that the man never seemed to relax before concentrating her attention on his words.

"First, Major Lancaster, there is still a shrapnel fragment in your back, positioned lower than the ones that were removed after the battle. That is the source of most of the pain."

He glared at them from under his bushy brows to be sure they were attending, then went on, "Based on your responses, I think you are not actually paralyzed. Swelling around the shrapnel would have produced that effect in the days after the injury, but the swelling has abated now."

David looked startled, then said, "If I'm not really paralyzed, then what is the problem?"

"I think you are suffering from a combination of things, most a result of too much laudanum." He shook his head dourly. "I have worked in both China and India and seen a good many opium-eaters. While it's a very useful drug, opium can cause unpredictable side effects, including extreme muscular weakness.

"They started giving you massive doses because the pain of that shrapnel fragment must be excruciating." The major's lack of comment confirmed the doctor's statement, and Kinlock continued, "I'll not disagree with that, since it did keep you from thrashing around and damaging yourself further. However, large doses of opium can make it impossible to keep any food down; you've said broth is the only thing you've been able to eat since you were injured. By the time the swelling around the fragment had subsided to a point where you might have been able to move, you were so weak from hunger, and so affected by pain and the laudanum, that you might as well have been paralyzed. Certainly the effect was similar."

The major's face showed amazement and a kind of

anger. "So the medicine is the cause of most of my problems."

"Aye, I'm afraid so. Dissolve opium in sherry, add a few spices, and people treat it like a sweet. Ridiculous!" He shook his white head in irritation. "As Paracelsus said, 'Dose alone makes a poison.' And as *I* say, anything that is potent enough to heal can also harm."

There was no doubt the Scot had his audience enthralled; both pairs of green eyes were watching him like cats measuring the life expectancy of a mouse. Ian Kinlock drew a breath, then got to the core of the discussion. "If you stopped taking laudanum and could eat again, you would start gaining weight and health immediately, though you would have the pain to contend with. You might even be able to move your legs and walk, though the attempt could cause the shrapnel to shift and cause permanent nerve damage. Still, you could manage in a Bath chair and your life would be in no immediate danger. That is the conservative course of treatment."

His last words fell into absolute stillness. He knew he shouldn't give them too much hope, but when so many cases ended tragically, it was irresistible to talk about one that looked so promising. "The alternative is an operation. Surgery is always dangerous, and removing the shrapnel might cause the very spine damage you are assumed to have already. Plus there is always the chance of inflammation. But . . . if the operation went well, it is possible you could be walking in a week."

Miss Lancaster's eyes were round and awestruck, but the major's mind had already moved on to the next question. "How soon can you operate?"

Kinlock considered the contents of his medical bag. "If you're sure that is what you want, I could do it right now. I have everything I need, and the actual operation won't take long. Certainly the longer you delay, the weaker you will be."

"Then do it now. I don't care what the risks are. If there is any chance of success, it is preferable to living like this." David thought a moment, then asked, "I assume I should stop taking the laudanum immediately?''

"Well, you'll need it for the operation, and it might be best to cut back on it gradually. If you try to quit all at once, you'll have a couple of very miserable days of craving, itching, hallucinations, and God knows what else.''

"A pleasing prospect," David said dryly. "Nonetheless, ever since I started on the laudanum I've felt that a stranger has taken over my mind. I thought it was because I was dying. Now that I know that isn't the case, the sooner I stop taking the damnable stuff, the better.''

Kinlock studied his face, then nodded slowly. This was a strong man, in spite of his physical state, and if he could face the prospect of quitting the drug quickly, more power to him. "Take laudanum for twenty-four hours more. It would be too much strain on your body to withdraw the drug at the same time as surgery. If you're doing well, you can try stopping then, but don't force yourself if it is too difficult.''

Based on the look in the major's eye, Kinlock's later words were wasted: the man had obviously decided to quit the drug as soon as possible. The doctor shrugged; at the moment, getting him through surgery was the main concern. "I suggest you take a very large dose now because you are in for a difficult few minutes. If you'll come outside with me, Miss Lancaster, I will discuss what I need with you.''

After helping her brother with the laudanum, Sally followed Kinlock into the hall. The doctor looked around curiously. "Is this your brother's house?" he asked as he eyed Sally's governess clothes dubiously. The girl didn't look like she belonged in this setting, though the major did.

"It belongs to David's wife.''

"Wife! Why wasn't she here?''

Kinlock looked outraged, so Sally said with reluctant fair-mindedness, "The marriage took place only a couple of days ago and was essentially one of convenience. They scarcely know each other. Lady Jocelyn doesn't even know you are here."

For the first time, she realized how her high-and-mightiness would react if David made a miraculous recovery, and she had a surge of unholy glee. Sally luxuriated in the vision for a moment, ignoring all the incredible complications, including the horrid possibility that Lady Jocelyn might be permanently connected to the Lancasters.

She was drawn back to the present when Kinlock said, "I'll need at least two men to hold him, plus someone to hand me the instruments. And I need towels, sheets, and plenty of hot water and soap to clean up beforehand."

When Sally seemed surprised, he said, "I don't know why, but cleanliness seems to reduce infection." He turned to reenter the bedchamber, saying, "Arrange for what is needed, and I'll prepare him for the operation."

She stared after him for a moment, then hastened to the arrangements. Lady Jocelyn had said to ask for anything she needed, and by heaven, she would.

Sally was grateful that surgical preparations included covering most of David's body with sheets, except for the small area of back where the actual incision would be made. Looking at a square of blank skin made it a little easier to forget that the person she loved most in the world was about to be sliced open . . . She stopped her thoughts, went to stand by the bed.

"Dr. Kinlock—or should I call you Mr. Kinlock, since you're wearing your surgeon's hat?—I will assist you with the instruments myself."

His blue eyes were keen as he looked at her. "Are you sure, lass? It might be better to have someone less close to the patient. It wouldn't do if you fainted or had the vapors."

She could feel her chin starting to jut out. "I won't."

"Very well." He spent several moments explaining the names of the instruments and the order they would be needed. She was impressed by their sparkling cleanliness; though she knew very little about medicine, it seemed obvious that clean was better than filthy.

The two footmen moved into position, Hugh Morgan near the foot of the bed, an older man of slighter build to the head. The operation proceeded with remarkable speed, with Sally handing Kinlock the instruments as he brusquely requested them. She was amazed at the deftness of his hands; it was only minutes before he told her to hold the shallow incision open with two hooked tools. She looked away as he probed, then he extracted a small fragment of metal that fell into the basin he requested with an audible clink. David had scarcely moved throughout, except for a convulsive shudder at the initial incision, and the footmen's services were barely needed.

After sewing up the incision, Kinlock requested an open jar from the table. It smelled wretched, and when Sally glanced inside, she saw a disgusting gray-green mass. She was horrified to see him smearing it across the wound, but clamped her jaws shut on her protest; it was too late not to trust him.

The release of tension was so great that she was barely aware of Kinlock putting on a dressing and bandage and giving low-voiced instructions to Morgan. Feeling a little faint now that her part was played, Sally went outside and slumped onto a sofa that was set against the gallery wall. She was dimly aware when the smaller footman left, then eventually Kinlock himself came out.

Her attention caught, Sally turned to him fearfully. "Do . . . do you think that it went well?"

He sat down on the opposite end of the sofa, as weary as the first time she had seen him. She was frightened when he buried his head in his hands, but then he looked up with a reassuring smile. "Aye, it went very well. The fragment was easily removed, and from the tests I just performed, he has normal sensation in his legs. There is still a small chance of infection, but I think he's going to be all right."

Sally hadn't cried when they had told her that David would die, but now that she heard he would live, she dissolved in racking sobs that seemed like they would never end. Kinlock put his arm around her shoulder comfortingly, saying, "There, there, you're a braw lassie, it's over now," and similar remarks, as she buried her face against his chest.

She heard herself saying, "Thank God," over and over, and knew it was a genuine prayer. Sally finally pulled away from him and fished a handkerchief from her pocket. "I'm sorry, it just seems like such a miracle. I can't quite believe it."

Kinlock gave a tired smile that seemed boyish compared to his usual expression. "Nothing is certain, but I think you have your miracle. Did you stop at St. Bart's church the other day?"

"No, but I certainly will tomorrow!"

"It would be appropriate." He stood, lifting his instrument bag. "Tell me, would this grand establishment run to whiskey?"

"I should think so. Shall we go downstairs and find out?"

When they reached the front salon, Lady Jocelyn's well-trained servants speedily produced decanters of whiskey and brandy. Sally had to give them credit; not once had they indicated contempt for her lowly self by so much as the flicker of an eye, though no doubt they had plenty to say in the servants' hall. No matter; at the moment she was so giddy she scarcely needed brandy, though she accepted a generous portion.

She noticed Ian Kinlock's hands were shaking as he poured himself the whiskey, and she asked curiously, "Are you always this way after surgery?"

He looked a little shamefaced. "Aye. My hands are steady as a rock during an operation, but after, I have trouble believing I had the temerity to do it. It's uncommonly difficult to cut into a human body, knowing how hard it is on the patient, but sometimes it's the only cure. Like today." He tossed off a good third of his glass, then sat down with a sigh, kneading his forehead.

"What was the awful-smelling dressing that you used?"

"Sure you want to know?" he asked with a half smile.

"Yes, please."

"Moldy bread and water."

"No! After making such a point of clean instruments, you put that filthy stuff on David?" Sally was genuinely horrified.

Kinlock shrugged. "It seems strange, I know, but all over the world, there is a folk tradition of using moldy materials for dressings. In China, they use moldy soy curd. In eastern and southern Europe, I'm told the peasants keep a loaf in the rafters. When anyone is injured, they take it down, cut off the mold, and make a paste with water, then apply it to the wound."

He chuckled reminiscently. "In fact, this particular mold that I use was originally given to me by a Russian sailor. He called it something in his barbarous language that he said meant 'mother.' When I used it, I found I lost fewer patients to infection and mortification, so I've been feeding it bread and water for the last eight years."

Sally was fascinated. "I had no idea such a thing was possible."

"Folk medicine is a particular interest of mine. My more scientific colleagues scorn it, but sometimes it works, and part of my aim in life is to find out what is worthwhile. For example, I've seen no evidence that putting a knife under a childbed cuts the pain in half, but willow bark *is* very good for fevers. When I can, I test different traditional remedies and use the ones that seem valid."

"And your other aims in life?"

"To save as many people from the Reaper as I can, for as long as I can. In the end, death always wins. But not without a struggle, by God!" His expression was bleak and faraway for a moment, but then it lightened and they drifted into general conversation.

Sally talked of her governess job, Kinlock about his training in Edinburgh and London, then his years as a ship's surgeon, which had led him to many strange parts of the world. Sally could feel his passion for his calling in every word he said. Mad Scot indeed! She blessed Dr. Ramsey for sending her to this man. Perhaps he was the only one in England who could have saved her brother.

# 6

Jocelyn was tired when she returned from a series of social calls and almost walked past the salon when she returned home. She paused at the sound of a woman's voice. Could Aunt Laura have gotten over her anger and returned to London so quickly?

When she entered the room, she found her uncouth sister-in-law in the process of getting drunk with some rough-looking fellow Jocelyn had never seen before. She felt her face stiffen that they should take such liberties in her house, but remembering her resolution to be more patient with Sally, she merely nodded a greeting and turned to leave.

Sally's schoolteacher voice carried clearly across the intervening space. "I've bad news for you, Lady Jocelyn."

Jocelyn turned swiftly, feeling an incredible sense of sadness and loss. So David was dead, his body was growing cold upstairs, the green eyes closed forever. She had not even been at home; that brief visit yesterday had been good-bye.

No wonder Sally was drinking. Feeling almost physically ill, Jocelyn stared blindly as Sally continued, "He's going to live. Dr. Kinlock here performed a rather splendid bit of surgery, and it seems likely David will recover completely."

It took a moment for Jocelyn to hear the words. Then the wave of relief was so intense that she reached out to steady herself against a chair back as she absorbed the shocking news. But in the midst of her gladness one powerful thought resonated: *You're in the suds now, girl!*

Sally's hostile voice continued implacably while the doctor watched in puzzlement. "I know you wanted him dead. It has just occurred to me that perhaps I should stay here to guard him until he can be moved. Since he isn't going to die on his own now, you may wish to remedy the situation.''

Jocelyn's face went white and she blindly fumbled her way around the chair until she could sit down. Her lips felt numb as she said, ''That is a despicable thing to say. While my intention was to become a widow, I had no desire to see David dead. If you are capable of appreciating the distinction.'' She felt something cool in her hand and looked up to see the doctor pressing a glass of brandy on her, his eyes detached and professional.

''Drink that, Lady Jocelyn. It will help with the shock.''

She sipped the brandy automatically, coughing as it burned its way down, then feeling a spreading warmth that helped her mind start working again. As she stared off into space, she tried to sort out her feelings.

Nothing could make her sorry that David Lancaster was going to live, and his survival didn't mean that she couldn't have an affair with Candover. But now, even if the duke fell in love with her, Jocelyn could not marry him, or anyone else.

For her, divorce was quite unthinkable. She had suffered all her life from the aftermath of her parents' divorce, and she could never face one of her own. Besides, even if she was interested, divorce took an act of Parliament; perhaps one a year was granted, and she had the vague idea that only men could seek them, that a woman couldn't, under any circumstances. Would David demand one so he could regain his freedom?

She shook her head to clear it; time enough to talk to her lawyer later. Jocelyn looked up at the surgeon, seeing him clearly now. His manner might be rough, but surgeons were famous for that, and his gaze was both intelligent and kind. She smiled and said, ''My thanks, Mr. Kinlock. It is a good day's work you have done. I have not known Major Lancaster long, but he is a fine person and the world is a better place for his survival.''

Before Sally's disgusted eyes, Kinlock almost started

purring under the hundred-candlepower warmth of Lady Jocelyn's smile. Really, even the most intelligent of men seemed unable to recognize a highbred tart for what she was. At the unwarranted thought, Sally flushed a bit; it must be the brandy working on her empty stomach. Her accusation that Lady Jocelyn might harm David had come from the same source; as soon as she said the words, she wished she could have recalled them, and not just because Dr. Kinlock had glanced at her disapprovingly.

Apologies were not one of Sally's specialties, but she managed to say, "I am sorry for what I said, Lady Jocelyn. It was quite uncalled for. I'm sure David will be well cared for here until I move him. I will start looking for another place immediately so you will not be inconvenienced."

Jocelyn glanced at her vaguely. "No need to hurry. This house is large enough to house a regiment, or at least a company." She stood. "Mr. Kinlock, you will send me a bill for your services? I trust you will make it consonant with the results."

"Miss Lancaster was going to take care of it."

"Nonsense, the responsibility is mine." She gave another of her dazzling smiles, and Sally had to admit that if a smile like that had been directed at herself, even she might be willing to overlook Lady Jocelyn's numerous defects of character.

Her ladyship added carefully, as if she was having to search for words, "It is getting late. Pray let my carriage take you to your homes. Unless you wish to stay overnight, Miss Lancaster?"

Guilt at her own rudeness made Sally's voice brusque. "No need. Dr. Kinlock says David will sleep all night, and I should return to my employers. I can walk; it will be light for hours still." She would need to keep her situation now; Lady Jocelyn would demand the return of the settlement, since she hadn't gotten what she had paid for.

Kinlock looked keenly at Sally, then said, "We are

happy to accept your kind offer, Lady Jocelyn. I shall make sure Miss Lancaster reaches home safely. If you will call the carriage, we will be on our way."

"It isn't necessary," Sally hissed at Kinlock as Lady Jocelyn gave orders for a carriage.

The doctor gave a maddening chuckle. "In my professional opinion it is. How often do you drink brandy?"

"Not very often," Sally admitted. "But I am merely hungry, not foxed." Her statement was undercut by a hiccup.

Ignoring her remark, the doctor took her off to the chaise when it pulled up in front of the house a few minutes later. As Lady Jocelyn said a polite farewell, Sally sank gratefully into the soft velvet squabs, since she was unaccountably a little dizzy and inclined to giggle. She had no memory later of what, if anything, they talked about on the ride home, but when they neared the Launcestons' Wimpole Street town house, Kinlock signaled the driver to let them off.

Sally blinked and said, "Are we there?"

"Not yet. There is a tavern here with good food and I'm going to see you eat some before I take you home. Otherwise your employers will be sacking you for drunkenness."

His tone was amused, but Sally still took offense. "I am not drunk. Jus' a little trifle well-to-go. Don't need to eat."

"Well, you might not be hungry, but I am. Come along now."

Once they were ensconced in the dark, friendly environs of the tavern and two hot meat pies had been served, Sally admitted that the doctor was right. After putting away the pie, bread and cheese, apple tart, and two strong cups of coffee that he ordered her to drink, she realized she must have been a bit drunk or she wouldn't feel so much soberer now.

"I'm sorry to be such a nuisance, Dr. Kinlock. It was just the relief. I don't think I've eaten a full meal since Waterloo." She flinched when she thought of the endless spring while England waited for a battle, the agonizing wait for the casualty lists, then the terror of seeing that David was severely wounded. The waiting, all the endless waiting . . . She said hurriedly, "And now you'll have to walk home, when Lady Jocelyn's carriage could have taken you."

Kinlock was unperturbed. "No need to worry. I live above my consulting rooms just over on Harley Street. I eat here often, actually; that's how I knew about the food." He surgically sliced an apple into eighths and ate a segment as he looked at her curiously. "What is the story behind that so-called marriage of your brother's? Don't try to tell me there's nothing havey-cavey about it, because I won't believe you."

Sally sighed, then told him the story of Lady Jocelyn's desire to become a rich widow. He showed no signs of shock; she rather thought it would take a good deal to surprise him. When she had finished, he shook his head with a rueful chuckle. "Poor woman! No wonder the two of you are at daggers drawn; your interests in the major's health are entirely different."

"To say the least," Sally said stiffly. "Do you blame me for wondering if she might put a period to his unwelcome existence?"

"Whisht, lassie, you don't believe she's a threat to him any more than I do," he scoffed. "Didn't you look at her when she thought he was dead?"

"She did look unhappy," Sally conceded reluctantly. "Maybe she was afraid a death in the house would upset her servants."

"She may not want to be married to him, but your brother is a very likable man and she was genuinely happy to hear that he would be well," Kinlock stated. "The lawyers can find some kind of solution for them," he added dismissively.

"I certainly hope so! The thought of having Lady Jocelyn as a permanent sister-in-law has no appeal for me."

"Nonsense, she's a charming woman, for all she's a member of a class of useless wastrels."

Sally eyed the doctor, then wisely refrained from comment; Lady Jocelyn was not someone they were likely to agree on. Under the circumstances, politics would be a safer topic of conversation. "Are you a radical?"

He shrugged. "Perhaps, if it is radical to despise lazy people who have never done a particle of good for anyone else. Women who assassinate character and spend more money on one dress than the average family sees in a year, men whose idea of sport is slaughtering helpless animals and gambling away their fortunes." He smiled wickedly. "I've often thought hunting would be a good deal more fair if the foxes and pheasants were armed and could fight back."

Sally pictured a fox aiming a shotgun, then started laughing. "An amusing thought, though I suppose if I were a better person I would be shocked. I can certainly think of a few members of the quality who would be improved by buckshot in the breeches."

Hmm, she really ought to watch her tongue more. Kinlock was so unconventional that he made her forget her manners. She glanced across at the craggy face shadowed by the startling white hair, the expressive features that could reflect such extremes of anger and compassion. She would never be able to repay him for what he had done.

She stood suddenly. "It is time I returned to the Launcestons." She was suddenly very tired indeed, and she knew that tonight she would sleep better than she had in months.

Jocelyn sat drinking tea for a long time after the surgeon and Miss Lancaster had gone. So she really was married, to a complete stranger of unknown parentage and habits. Lady Laura would say it served her right for her improper actions, and on the whole, Jocelyn was inclined to agree.

Surely a man so fair-minded about protecting her property when they married would not hold her to the marriage, would he? She shifted uncomfortably.

Knowing he would live might make the major a very different man: he might be angry that she had taken away his own freedom to marry, or he might revel in having married one of England's greatest heiresses.

Drawn by some instinct, Isis had come to sit on her lap and purr, bumping her tawny head into her mistress's ribs in a much-appreciated display of affection. Stroking the sleek fur, Jocelyn thought how ironic it was that her own romanticism had led her to the most impersonal of marriages; she rather expected that God was mocking her pretensions.

As the room cooled, eventually Isis jumped down, hitting the carpet with an audible thump and proceeding about her own concerns. With a sigh, Jocelyn rose and went to the Blue Room, where Hugh Morgan watched over his sleeping patient. Because of the incision on his back, the major lay on his stomach, his breathing steady and his face boyishly peaceful. The footman assured her that all was well and thanked her for inquiring after his brother, Rhys, who was almost like his old self now that he was out of the hospital.

After a solitary dinner, Jocelyn took her anxieties to bed. She tried to be philosophical about her unexpected husband. After all, in a hundred years they would all be dead, and who would care then? Nonetheless, she tossed for hours before falling into a troubled sleep, only to be awakened by urgent knocking. As she struggled for wakefulness, she saw Isis sleeping in her usual spot at the foot of the bed, her sharp ears pricked toward the door, where Marie conversed with someone in a low voice.

The maid entered with a troubled face. "It's Hugh Morgan, Lady Jocelyn. He says the major is very restless, and it's that worried he is."

Suddenly alert, Jocelyn slid out of bed and into the wrapper Marie held out. "I'll come take a look. Did Dr. Kinlock leave you his direction, Morgan?" she asked, belting the robe while they hastened toward the front of the house.

"Aye, Lady Jocelyn."

"Well, we won't disturb him needlessly, but it's good we know where to find him."

Major Lancaster had rolled over onto his back and was twisting restlessly back and forth. His movements were weak, but Jocelyn felt a thrill at seeing that his legs were moving as well as the rest of him: Dr. Kinlock was right, and there was no lasting paralysis. She moved next to the bed, then laid a hand on his forehead. If he had felt feverish, she would have sent for the doctor immediately because of possible inflammation, but his face was cool to her touch.

David stirred beneath her hand and murmured, "Jeannette, *mignonne*?" with an admirable French accent.

Unaccountably irritated, Jocelyn removed her hand and said crisply, "No, it's Jocelyn. A proper English-woman, not one of your French or Belgian hussies."

His eyes opened and after a moment showed recognition. With a hint of laughter he said, "How do you know that Jeannette wasn't my horse?"

"*Mignonne*?"

"A soldier and his horse become very dear to each other," he said gravely, but with a twinkle in his eyes.

"I can't believe we are having this conversation under these circumstances," Jocelyn said as she surrendered to laughter. "Do you remember what happened? Dr. Kinlock? The operation?"

From the look in his eyes, she saw that he remembered, and with a flash of insight she realized that he was afraid to ask about the outcome. Quickly she said, "You're going to be all right. You may not be very aware of your body now, but you have the use of your legs again."

He closed his eyes suddenly, too weak to suppress the tears of relief, and it seemed the most natural thing in the world to take his hand. While he struggled for control, Jocelyn calmly repeated what the doctor had told her earlier in the day, ending with a question. "How do you feel now?"

"Compared to the way I've felt since Waterloo, fairly

good. By any normal standard, rather rotten.''

"Will you please be serious?'' Jocelyn begged. "Are you in pain?''

"Of course I am! What kind of a fool do you take me for?'' he asked indignantly. Remarkable how outrageous he could be with no more than a cocked eyebrow.

"Major Lancaster, I have a feeling you are going to be very difficult now that you are convalescing,'' Jocelyn said with resignation. She studied the thin face for a moment, realizing there was something different in the expression, something beyond the irrepressible humor.

The eyes. For the first time, the green eyes looked normal, without the opium-induced pinpoint pupils. The last dose of laudanum must have worn off, so she reached for the bottle on the bedside table. "Dr. Kinlock said to give you some laudanum if you woke up in the night. You need rest to recover.''

"No!'' His arm flailed out with more strength than she would have dreamed he possessed, knocking the bottle from her hand to shatter in a dark stain across the rich Oriental carpet. As she stared at David in shock, the spicy scent of cloves and cinnamon spread subtle tendrils through the room. His usual humor was replaced with a kind of desperation as he said weakly, "I'm sorry, I hope I didn't hurt you. But I won't take any more opium, ever.''

When Jocelyn just looked at him expressionlessly, David marshaled his whirling thoughts, knowing that he must convince her or she would have some of the damned drug down him for his own good. "I didn't realize it at the time, but taking so much opium was like having my soul stolen. I would rather die than have that happen again.''

The grave hazel eyes studied him thoughtfully, then she nodded. "Very well, Major, I won't force it down you, though I make no promises about what Dr. Kinlock will do. If you won't sleep, will you eat? We need to build your strength somehow.''

He concentrated on how he felt. "Do you know, I believe that I am hungry, for the first time since the battle."

"Does the idea of a roast joint with Yorkshire pudding appeal to you?" she asked. Watching his face, she continued sweetly, "Well, you won't be getting that. Perhaps some soup? And an omelette and some raspberries with custard."

He couldn't help laughing, even though it hurt. "You've had your revenge, Lady Jocelyn. Though I doubt I could handle a joint even if one were available at this hour."

She turned to Morgan, who had been hovering in the background during the exchange. David found himself admiring the pure line of her profile as she said, "Morgan, please wake the cook and have some food brought up."

The footman hesitated, doubt on his face, before saying, "He won't like getting up this late."

She raised a brow and said with no diminution of sweetness, "If Monsieur Cherbonnier objects to the conditions of employment in my house, tell him that he is under no compulsion to continue accepting the exorbitant wage I pay him. I expect to be served within fifteen minutes. Is that clear?"

Morgan gulped as he bobbed his head, then set off on his errand.

David shook his head in wonder. "Lady Jocelyn, should you wish employment, you might get a position as a sergeant-major. You would do well at that."

She grinned, unabashed. "My servants lead a fairly easy life, I think. Certainly it is impossible to get them to leave, so I think there is no great harm in their being challenged occasionally." Returning to seriousness, she asked, "Is there someone you would wish notified of your return to health? I'll send a note to Captain Dalton in the morning, but have you no relatives?"

He shook his head slightly. "Some cousins on my mother's side, but Sally will write them, and the bond is not that close. My brothers would hardly be interested in my continued existence."

"You have brothers?" she said in surprise.

David sighed; he wouldn't have mentioned them under normal conditions. "Of a sort. Three older half-brothers. My mother was a second wife, much younger than my father. The surviving sons of the first wife resented her, said her birth was inferior, which by their standards was true, and they took it out on Sally and me." He shrugged. "We both learned to fight at an early age, a very useful skill. After my father died, the oldest son threw us out of the house with no more than my mother's jointure."

"Why, that's outrageous!"

"Many things in life are, but there's no help for it. My father assumed—wrongly—that his heir would make reasonable provisions for us. After my mother died, her income stopped, but by then I was in the army and Sally was almost through school. We managed well enough."

The hazel eyes were thoughtful as she said, "No wonder the two of you are so close."

"Yes. Sally's worth more than all three of our brothers put together."

Jocelyn said wistfully, "It would be nice to have a brother or sister. At least," she added, "one that I got on with."

"I would offer you one of my half-brothers, but I doubt you'd get on with them. They don't even get on with one another."

"They sound like a pack of pit dogs."

"That's it exactly," David said in a pleased tone.

"I have my share of dirty dishes among my relatives," Jocelyn said. "My Aunt Elvira, for example. She is the one whose greed drove me to my imprudent marriage."

David closed his eyes. He had known the topic must come up, but he felt unequal to it at the moment. "Don't worry, Lady Jocelyn, I think this tangle can be solved without damage to either of us."

She gave him a keen glance, wondering what he had in mind. "Time enough to talk of that later. Now, unless my ears betray me, I hear the feather footfalls of Morgan."

Sure enough, solid steps could be heard in the hall and in a moment Morgan entered with a tray containing several covered dishes. To his shame, David was still too weak to feed himself, even after Morgan propped him up in the bed, and he protested at first when Jocelyn started to feed him.

"Lady Jocelyn, you really shouldn't."

She had cast him a reproachful look. "Don't you think I will do it well?"

"You know that's not what I mean!" He had to stop to swallow a spoonful of richly flavored onion soup. "You shouldn't be doing this kind of menial task for me."

She shook her head mournfully. "Just because I have a title, no one thinks I am good for anything. Perhaps you should drop my style and call me simply Jocelyn." As he opened his mouth to answer, she popped another spoonful of soup in it.

He rolled his eyes at her and got a chuckle in response. All in all, he couldn't remember a meal he had enjoyed more, in spite of his feeling of helplessness. Both soup and omelette were excellent, though he could eat only a small portion of each, and the company was outstanding. Finally he said, "I think that is enough. I'm sorry I can't manage any of the berries."

"Quite all right," Jocelyn said blithely. "I really ordered them for me, anyhow. I'm always quite peckish when I'm up at this hour." A downstairs clock struck three times as she ate the berries, and David found that it was a pleasure to watch her enthusiasm. In her directness she was like a child, but even in his lowest moments he had been aware that the body was very much that of a woman.

When she had finished, she asked, "Since you won't take laudanum, would some brandy help you sleep? You really do need some rest."

"Perhaps a little. I'm feeling fairly good, actually."
It was true; while David felt weak, tired, and in pain,
there was none of the mind-numbing dullness he had
known with the opium.

With a few crisp orders, Jocelyn procured some
brandy, then sent Morgan off to wake another footman
so the Welshman could get some sleep. A few mouthfuls
of brandy spread their warmth through David's body
and he could feel himself slipping into the first natural
sleep he had known in weeks. Before he lost awareness,
he thought Jocelyn's hand brushed his hair, but perhaps
that was only wishful thinking.

When Hampton, the other footman, arrived to keep
watch, Jocelyn poured herself some of the brandy
before she trailed off to bed. She had a suspicion that
within a week the major would be quite impossible to
keep in bed.

# 7

Jocelyn was wrong when she guessed that within a week it would be difficult to keep Major Lancaster immobilized; when she stopped by his room the very next morning, she found him sitting on the edge of the bed, his head braced on his hands. Arms akimbo, she surveyed him dispassionately. "Dr. Kinlock will have your head for a haggis if you don't lie down."

Morgan said plaintively, "He wouldn't take 'no' for an answer, my lady."

"I'm sure. Have you had breakfast yet, Major Lancaster?"

He glanced up with a slightly twisted smile. "Enough of one. If your Monsieur Cherbonnier hasn't packed his bags and left already, you can tell him that his excellent cooking is making a new man of me. And if you want me to call you Jocelyn, you'll have to call me David."

There was a strained note in his voice, and as she moved closer, Jocelyn saw the beads of perspiration on his face. "David, are you all right?" she asked with concern.

He closed his eyes and drew a deep breath. "The doctor warned me that there would be a couple of days of reaction when I stopped the opium. It's beginning."

She put a hand firmly on his shoulder. "Dr. Kinlock said that if one cuts down on the drug gradually, there is little problem. Surely, it would be better—"

"No!" He opened his eyes, the spare face damp and haggard, the green eyes too bright. More calmly, he said, "No, I meant what I said last night. I shall manage. But irritability is one of the effects, and I can feel that coming. I would rather you didn't see me this way."

She bit her lip but refrained from argument. Glancing

at Morgan, she said, "You will let me know how he goes, Morgan?"

The Welshman nodded, and she turned and left without looking back. David murmured, "A rare woman, who knows when not to argue."

"Aye, she's that, Major."

"Help me into the chair, please."

"Wouldn't you be better off lying down, sir?"

"Later, perhaps. But as long as I can, I prefer to face this sitting up."

"Craving, itching, hallucinations, and God knows what . . ." As Morgan half-carried him to the chair, David reflected that Kinlock had known what he was talking about. He hoped the good doctor was also right about this lasting only two days.

Jocelyn had sent a note to Captain Dalton about the major's health, but the messenger crossed him and he showed up in midmorning without having heard of his friend's miraculous improvement. Knowing the major wasn't well, the butler brought Dalton to Jocelyn in the morning room, and when he was announced, she looked up to see his face expressionless, his knuckles white on the crutches. Expecting the worst as she herself had done yesterday, he asked tightly, "Is David . . . ?"

She stood quickly, "Richard, he's going to be all right. He was operated on yesterday, and they expect him to make a complete recovery."

His face froze for an instant before he asked, "He is really going to live?"

"Live, and walk. As good as new, or near enough."

The captain swung across to the window and looked down into the mews, pushing the lace drapery away with a hand that trembled. Jocelyn saw in his reaction a reflection of her own feelings the day before, and she made a pretense of sharpening a quill and searching in the escritoire for her stationery box.

When Dalton finally spoke, it was in a voice so soft she barely heard it. "When the butler brought me here, I thought you were going to say he had died last night."

His fingers tightened on the drapery, and he said more to himself than to her, "You can't imagine what this means. When so many have died, to know that at least one friend will survive against all the odds."

"I think I can guess, a little."

Having assimilated the news, his mind moved a step further. Turning to face Jocelyn, he asked, "What will this mean to you?"

She spread her hands. "Richard, I just don't know. But I hope that, unlike Sally Lancaster, you will acquit me of a desire to slip poison in his soup."

"Sally never said that!"

"Indeed she did, though she did not specify the method."

The captain laughed, and she remembered that he was a very handsome man. He should laugh more often. He said, "If you were going to murder someone, I assume it would be pistols in Bond Street rather than something sly like poison."

Jocelyn beamed. "You understand me very well."

"I doubt it," he said with a smile. More seriously, he asked, "Is David well enough to receive visitors?"

"Well, he threw me out of his room this morning, but I expect he will be happy to see you," Jocelyn said acerbically. She briefly explained the operation and David's refusal to take more opium. "Do you think you might persuade him to take at least a small dose of laudanum? It can't be good for him to withdraw so suddenly."

"If that's what David wants, I won't attempt to influence him," the captain said bluntly. "I know precisely how he feels. Don't worry, he can be stubborn, but he's not a fool. He wouldn't insist on something that would destroy him just as he is on the verge of recovering."

"I suppose you're right," Jocelyn said with a sigh. "I'm told you were here yesterday, so you can find your own way up." She assumed Richard wouldn't want her to watch his struggle up two long flights of stairs. After a moment's consideration she added, "While David is here, please make yourself free of my house. I'm sure your presence will speed his recovery."

Understanding, he smiled warmly. "And your home is a good deal pleasanter than the hospital. Lady Jocelyn, it is a great pleasure knowing you."

After the door closed behind him, she was uncertain whether to smile at the compliment or scowl at the muddle she was in. Then a happy thought struck her: there was one task she could do that would give her great pleasure. A few minutes later, she was penning a note about her recent marriage to Elvira. Jocelyn only wished she could be there to see the reaction when the countess discovered that her niece's fortune had been removed from her clutches.

Jocelyn was just affixing the wafer to the letter when Mossley appeared. "The Misses Halliwell are here, my lady."

She looked up in surprise, then muttered a curse below her breath. In the midst of so much high drama, she had forgotten that this was one of her regular at-home days. While it would be a quieter day than during the Season, she could expect a steady stream of visitors for the next few hours. Charm, Lady Jocelyn, remember you've a reputation to maintain.

With slightly gritted teeth, she went off to receive the Misses Halliwell, three harmless but addlepated spinsters much given to incomplete sentences and pointless stories. The next few hours seemed to drag endlessly; on one level she offered tea, cakes, and *on-dits* with practiced ease, but part of her mind was fixed upstairs in the Blue Room. How was David managing? Had he collapsed from pushing himself too hard, or was he going through some ghastly torments from the drug withdrawal?

It was some comfort to know that she would be notified of any dire emergencies. Nonetheless, when the trickle of visitors had temporarily lulled, she told Mossley to deny her to any latecomers and marched up the stairs to see what was happening.

Her knock was greeted with a cheerful "Come in,"

though she couldn't identify the voice. When she swung the door open, her bemused gaze was met by the unexpected sight of a gentlemen's card party in full swing. Hugh and Rhys Morgan had joined Captain Dalton and David around the table and a lively game was in progress. Hugh jumped up, Rhys appeared shy, and David looked as if he ought to be lying flat in his bed.

"After I have been imagining all manner of disasters! Here you gentlemen have been amusing yourselves while I have been playing hostess to half the bores in London."

Hugh stammered apologetically, "I'm sorry, my lady, but the captain insisted."

She cast a quick glance at Richard Dalton, whose eyes held a message. Though David appeared on the verge of collapse, he had a feverish air that suggested it would be impossible for him to rest. Jocelyn assumed the card game was intended as a distraction, and she mentally applauded the captain's ingenuity.

As she looked at the culprits, her lips began to twitch in mirth. "Major, are you corrupting my servants?"

In spite of his physical condition, David answered easily enough. "On the contrary, I'm participating in a salutary lesson on the evils of gambling. Never play with Richard, Lady Jocelyn. We are using buildings for stakes, and by now he is now in possession of the Horse Guards, Carlton House, St. Paul's, and Westminster Abbey."

"Indeed? Who holds the York Hospital?"

"None of us wanted it," Rhys blurted out, then blushed so hard his ears turned red.

She was hard-pressed to suppress a smile. Hugh was right, his brother already looked happier and healthier than he had in the hospital. Perhaps she could turn Cromarty House into a convalescent home, since wounded soldiers seemed to flourish here. Two pairs of crutches leaned in a tangle against the wall, and she realized that Hugh was the only undamaged man present.

"Well, this is obviously no place for a mere female. Shall I order some refreshments for you?"

The men all seemed to relax a trifle. Had they expected her to kick up a dust? "That would be very good of you, Lady Jocelyn," David said. "I seem to be continually ravenous."

"Well, you are some weeks in arrears of food. Enjoy yourselves, gentlemen."

She withdrew in good order. Interesting; she was beginning to understand just a little the comradeship of arms, of how men who fought together also took care of one another. She could sense the bond between the three military men, even though two were officers and old friends and the third a stranger and a common soldier. Some fusty fellow, perhaps Samuel Johnson, had once said that every man was sorry if he hadn't been a soldier. She hadn't understood the remark before, but now she had some inkling of what it meant.

What a pity men couldn't find such satisfactions without killing so many of their fellows.

David realized that he could no longer keep up even a semblance of playing cards. Instead of hearts and spades, he was seeing shifting patterns that wouldn't hold still long enough to define. Time had slowed down until it ceased to have meaning; a month or two before Lady Jocelyn had paid an amused visit, and some food had appeared and disappeared, so it was probably early afternoon now. Just how long could two days last?

His voice sounded metallic in his ears when he said, "Sorry, gentlemen, it's time I withdrew from the game." There was a film of sweat on his hand as he laid the cards down on the tooled leather table, and it was a struggle to add lightly, "Richard, you'll have to win Kensington Palace another time."

"Just as well, I could never afford to maintain it." Richard's voice was wonderfully soothing, and it must have been his hand warm on David's shoulder. But surely it was Hugh that got him onto the bed; neither Richard nor Rhys would have been able to offer much help from their crutches. He wished he could sleep and let the time pass that way, but his mind seemed stuck in a peculiar waking dream, where his present surroundings mingled with his past and with nightmares he had experienced.

Sally was there for a while, her face concerned even after he assured her he was all right and that she needn't stay. Kinlock was there too, frowning over his pulse rate and saying he was a thrice-damned fool. David had meekly agreed, but insisted that since he had already gotten halfway through the withdrawal period, why waste the suffering if he would just have to do it again later?

His logic must have worked because Kinlock didn't force any more laudanum on him—a reasonable man for a quack. Once or twice David wondered dazedly if he should ask for opium, to retreat once more into the velvet numbness of the drug, anything to stop the way his body ached in every bone and muscle. He even opened his mouth to ask, but his voice wouldn't come, as if his better judgment refused to cooperate in such cowardice.

Someone was sponging his face with blessedly cool water, and he knew from the jasmine scent that it must be Lady Jocelyn. He tried to turn away, to tell her that she shouldn't, but her clear voice told him firmly not to be a lackwit. A strong-minded woman, his wife. Wife? Impossible. Sadly, impossible.

Then the black depression seized him and drew him down into endless dark. Perhaps it was night, or perhaps the sun had died. He fixed his gaze on a candle, sure that if he blinked there would never be light again. *How long could two days be?*

Dawn. It was half over; of course he could hold out another day. He had eaten whenever food was offered, knowing that his body needed it desperately, and he was stronger today. The feverish, hallucinatory quality of his vision hadn't gone, but now he could move a step or two on his own, where a day earlier it had been only just possible to stand.

Endless time, aching time. The burning interior plains of Spain, glittering cruelly brown, then breaking into hard yellow shards under the impact of monster raindrops. The shards washed away in a flash flood of jangling pieces, leaving the green, beloved hills of Hereford, the hills he hadn't seen in twenty years. He had been twelve, still bearing the marks of a beating from one of his brothers, when the carrier's wagon had come for him and Mother and Sally and their belongings. He loved Westholme as much as he had hated his brothers, but he refused to look back in case anyone watching would think it weakness.

He stood and started to lurch toward the window, knowing that outside he would see Westholme, but Hugh Morgan caught hold of him. He had struggled a bit, sure that salvation was near at hand if only he could reach it, but he was no match for the young Welshman's gentle strength, and then he was lying down again.

If only he could sleep . . .


It was after two in the morning when Jocelyn let herself in the front door. She had known the wretched dinner party would run very late and had told her servants not to wait up for her. As expected, she had had an argument on her hands; from butler to abigail, the staff appeared to think her incapable of turning a key in a lock or undressing herself. It never occurred to them that sometimes she preferred to be alone.

She would far rather have stayed home, but a month earlier she had promised Lady Westley faithfully that she would attend. ("My dear Lady Jocelyn, it will be all of my husband's dire relations. I simply must have someone to lend some charm!") She wondered ruefully if Lady Westley had gotten as much charm as she hoped for; Jocelyn's shimmering green taffeta dress had probably been livelier than the woman inside it. She rested one kidskin slipper on the bottom step while she mustered the energy to climb the stairs, but her unfocused gaze fell on the door of the salon and she remembered with a shudder the nasty little scene that had taken place there earlier in the day.

It had been another cat fight between her and Sally Lancaster as Sally had urged that her brother be given laudanum, to keep his mind from snapping or his heart from giving out under the strain. Dr. Kinlock had clearly been troubled by his patient's condition, and he had asked Jocelyn her opinion, since as the wife, she should have a say in Major Lancaster's treatment.

Jocelyn could understand Sally's concern; indeed, she shared it. But the other woman hadn't been present when David had smashed the bottle of laudanum to keep it away; she hadn't heard his voice. Jocelyn had pointed out that David was an adult and his decisions should be respected. Sally had again accused her of hoping David would die, her words spitting out like hornets. Only when Richard Dalton had sided with Jocelyn had Sally retreated, her eyes wide with the fear behind her fury.

Jocelyn found she was gripping the newel post so hard that her fingers were imprinted with carved acanthus leaves. With an effort, she released it and started up the two long flights of stairs. Was it only a week ago that she and Aunt Laura had discussed marrying to preserve her fortune, so she wouldn't have to survive on a mere competence? How trivial.

Strange how quiet the house was at this hour, the dark three-story-high foyer lit only by the few lamps that had been left for her. Jocelyn could almost believe she lived here alone, rather than sharing her roof with fifteen other people. Sixteen, counting her newly acquired husband.

She had reached her floor and was halfway down the gallery to her room when her tired eyes suddenly realized that the shadowed shape in front of her was the man who had been at the center of her thoughts for these last endless days. Major Lancaster was slowly making his way down the hall ahead of her, his steps weaving as one hand slid along the wall to support his unsteady progress.

Jocelyn stopped dead in her tracks. She wouldn't have believed David could make his way so far alone. He must have escaped his keeper; perhaps an exhausted Hugh Morgan had fallen asleep during his long vigil. She muttered a minor curse that the footman hadn't called someone to relieve him if he was that tired; devotion was all very well, but good judgment counted for something, too.

She must have made some sound because David turned to face her. In a galvanizing rush of panic, she saw that he was lurching sideways, that if he moved a step farther to his right he would collide with the railing and pitch over to the deadly marble floor two stories below. With a sharp gasp of alarm, Jocelyn flew across the dozen feet that separated them, and hurled herself against him, using her weight to push him away from the treacherous railing.

Her impetus pushed them both into the wall and knocked her breathless as her arms went around him to prevent him from falling. He was so thin his ribs could be counted through the blue dressing gown, but his body felt surprisingly solid against her. More than that, when he was lying down, she hadn't realized how tall he was: easily six feet, and with an impressive breadth of shoulder. She could feel his heart beating against her, but the warmth of his body felt normal rather than feverish. As she caught her breath, his arms circled her strongly, and with pleased surprise he murmured "Jeannette!" into her ear.

She was looking up, her mouth opening to correct his misapprehension, when his lips descended on hers. Her initial impulse of shock was rapidly replaced by more interesting thoughts. Jocelyn had been kissed a good many more times than a high stickler would approve of, and she knew quality when she experienced it. *If this is how he kisses when he is ill, what on earth would he be like when he is recovered?* She spared a moment of envy for the absent Jeannette before the intoxicating sensations stopped rational thought altogether.

Only when she started to get a little weak in the knees

did her rational mind return to duty. Good God, one of them needed to be able to support them, and she doubted it would be David. Turning her face away from his regretfully, she said in her best earl's-daughter voice, "Major Lancaster!"

Unfortunately, she penetrated his mental mists immediately. His arms loosened around her and he might have fallen had he not been braced against the wall. "Good Lord! Lady Jocelyn, I'm sorry." Then the green eyes came more into focus than she had seen them for the last two days and he said with a little choke of laughter, "Or perhaps I'm sorry that I didn't appreciate my misdeed when I was misdoing it."

It is hard to be severe with someone when your arms are around him. If she had released him, it would have improved the dignity of her position, but he might have fallen on the floor, rendering conversation difficult. So Jocelyn consigned dignity to the devil and said with as much severity as she could muster, "Major, what are you doing wandering around at this hour? And in a house full of overpaid servants, why is this little drama taking place in complete solitude?"

He gave her questions serious thought as his right hand absently stroked her bare arm. "Perhaps everyone is in bed? It must be very late."

"A profound statement, Major. So pleased you are back in the land of the living." Her words were wry but heartfelt; he was clearheaded now as he hadn't been in two days, and she was sure that he had survived the drug reactions. From now on, recovery was a foregone conclusion.

Trying to ignore the delicious ripples spreading along her left arm, Jocelyn considered what to do next. She could yell until someone woke up and came to help her get the major back to his room, but she wasn't sure how much longer she could support his substantial weight. "Major, if I help you, do you think you can get as far as my chamber? It's just behind you."

With some awkwardness, they rearranged themselves, and with his left arm draped across her shoulder, they made it to Jocelyn's room. Gravity contributed to getting him onto what was luckily a rather low bed, and as Jocelyn lifted his legs up onto the covers, he said, "I appear to be in your debt once more."

"Think nothing of it, Major. You have no idea how boring my life was until our paths crossed." Jocelyn gazed down at him with an amusement that turned to dismay when she realized that he had already fallen asleep. She supposed it was not surprising after three days and nights without any real rest, but had to bite her lip in consternation as she considered her options. If he was moved now, he would probably wake, which would be a great pity when he needed rest so desperately. Furthermore, there would be all kinds of alarums and diversions to deal with—apologetic servants, discussion, noise—when all she really wanted to do was go to sleep herself. She couldn't go to a guest room because none was made up, the major's own Blue Room being the only one kept always at the ready.

She glared at the major's peacefully slumbering form for a moment, then defiantly pulled the pins from her hair. So what if he was in her bed? After all, they were married, more or less. She undressed, putting on her most opaque nightdress and tying her wrapper over it, then pulled a quilt from her wardrobe and spread it over her guest, crawling under half of it herself.

Fortunately, it was a very large bed.


When Jocelyn woke the next morning, it was with a familiar sensation of weight on her chest. "Isis, move!" she ordered, raising her arm to push the cat away. When her fingers encountered fabric, not fur, memory flooded back and she turned her head to find herself looking at David Lancaster at extremely close range. His face was only inches from her own, and as his green eyes opened, she was in an excellent position to see their expression change from sleepy relaxation to shocked surprise and finally to unmistakable amusement.

*Drat the man. He probably doesn't know what*

*embarrassment means*. "Major, do you remember what happened last night?"

"I'm not sure. What did happen?"

Jocelyn unaccountably felt like giggling. "Not much."

He sighed regretfully and rolled away, releasing her from the arm that had been holding her close. "Then I guess I remember. Wasn't I wandering along the gallery and you caught me and brought me in here? Then I must have fallen asleep instantly." He chuckled suddenly, then added, "Surely it would be most unflattering to you if more had happened and I didn't remember, wouldn't it?"

It certain would be unflattering if he didn't remember that kiss! Better not to mention it. Jocelyn sat up in bed and said severely, "I always seem to be having the most extraordinary conversations with you." She paused a moment, then asked curiously, "Just where were you heading last night with such determination?"

He crossed his arms under his head, his forehead wrinkled with thought. "Hereford, I think."

"Hereford?" Jocelyn asked incredulously.

"Why not? It's a very lovely place," David said as he glanced at her. Before he could stop himself, he added, "Almost as lovely as you are."

She colored and started to edge away from him. "Major, I am beginning to think you are a practiced flirt."

He shook his head and said absently, "No, not in the least." He had thought she was beautiful from the moment he had first seen her leaning apprehensively over him in the hospital, but in morning *déshabillé* she was breathtaking, long waves of chestnut hair spilling over her shoulders and her flawless complexion glowing in the rosy dawn light.

She edged a little farther away. "Then why are you looking at me as if I am a particularly tasty morsel at a midnight supper?"

He burst out laughing. "A singularly appropriate metaphor."

Her blush deepened, but she recovered quickly. "Perhaps I had best order some breakfast for you if you are that hungry."

Their conversation was interrupted when Jocelyn's maid hurried into the room. "My lady, the major is missing . . . Oh!" Her eyes rounded in shock as she took in the picture before her.

In her best grand-lady manner, Jocelyn said, "As you can see, the major is *not* missing. He was wandering last night and it was easier to guide him here than rouse the whole house. If your slumbering swain is awake, inform him that he can assist Major Lancaster back to his own room."

Marie bobbed her head and backed out of the room, still staring, but with a disgraceful hint of a smile playing around her lips.

David pushed himself up, then cautiously swung his legs over the bed and stood, one hand braced against the bedpost. "Everything appears to be in working order." He glanced across at Jocelyn. "I thought I had persuaded you to call me David the other night."

She said dispassionately, "I think it might be easier to keep you at a distance if I call you Major."

Using the bedpost as a pivot, he swung his whole body around to face her. For once, his voice was serious as he told her, "I'm not going to do anything that you don't want."

For some reason, her eyes dropped. "I didn't really think you would." Glancing up with a smile, she said ruefully, "But we are in the very devil of a bind."

He looked at her for a long moment, then said in a neutral tone, "I believe there is a way out."

"Do you really think so?" She was unflatteringly eager.

"I'll have to look at the will. Do you have a copy in the house?" When she nodded, he said, "Then bring it to me in about two hours. That will give time for breakfast, a bath, and a shave. One should never look at legal documents on an empty stomach."

She laughed. Then curiosity got the better of her and she asked, "Who is Jeannette?"

He grinned but was saved from answering when Hugh Morgan rushed in, his broad face still showing the fear he had felt on waking to find his patient gone. Gushing explanations and apologies, he supported the major out of the room.

After closing the door behind them, Jocelyn looked up to find Isis sitting on the windowsill where she had spent the night after her spot on the bed was usurped. "Well, cat friend, it looks like our major is definitely recovered. But what are we going to do with him?"

Isis yawned, then watched her mistress through disdainful half-closed eyes. Cats arranged their relationships much more neatly.

## 8

When Jocelyn joined Major Lancaster some two hours later, it was almost impossible to recognize the man who had been at death's door a handful of days before. Bathed, shaven, and sitting at ease by the window, only his dressing gown indicated his convalescent status. He stood as she entered and executed a commendable half-bow with no hint of the ordeal he had just undergone.

She shook her head in admiration as she seated herself, placing a tied roll of papers on the small table between them. "Major, you are a wonder. Even Dr. Kinlock thought it would be a week until you were up and about."

David was still very thin, his cheeks almost hollow, but his color was healthy. Although his thick brown hair had been combed into a semblance of military order, it was rapidly, and charmingly, reverting to an unruly natural wave rather like the fashionable Brutus cut. Jocelyn suddenly realized that he was younger than she had supposed, somewhere in his early thirties.

He also had a most attractive smile. "Healing quickly is an excellent trait to have in the military, where time is often in short supply. Care to join me for some coffee? Hugh Morgan just brought a fresh pot."

"Thank you, I believe I will." As he poured two steaming cups of the fragrant brew, she glanced around the room. "Speaking of whom, where is Morgan?"

"I thought he might wish to catch up on his other duties, or spend some time with his brother." Correctly interpreting Jocelyn's raised brow, David said reasonably, "Well, you can hardly think that I need a full-time nursemaid anymore."

"I suppose not. Perhaps I will suggest that Morgan divide his time between you and his brother for the rest of the summer. London is so thin of company now that the footmen have very little to do.'' She smiled. ''Rhys Morgan has won a number of hearts belowstairs; if Hugh were not such a good-tempered young man, his nose would be put out of joint.''

At David's inquiring look, she explained, ''All of the maids in the house were panting after Hugh until his brother arrived, but my abigail informs me that more than half of them have transferred their affections to Rhys.''

''Which does your abigail prefer?''

''Marie has been sadly torn.'' Jocelyn laughed. ''She says 'there is something about a soldier,' but after careful reflection decided that she prefers Hugh, even if he hasn't a romantic wound and tales of exotic lands. I was glad to hear that, as I think her regard is the one Hugh values most.''

''You are a liberal employer to allow such goings-on in your house. Many prefer their servants not to keep company.''

She shook her head in amusement as she stirred milk and sugar into her coffee. ''It is human nature for males and females to keep company, and employers who deny that merely force their servants into slyness. As long as no one's work suffers, I see no point in issuing commands that won't be obeyed, and this way, I am kept informed of what is happening.''

''Lady Jocelyn, I do believe that you are a romantic.''

''Alas, too true.'' And look at the trouble it had gotten her into! She handed over her bundle of papers. ''Here is the copy of my father's will you requested.''

''With your permission?'' She nodded, and David immediately started scanning the document. The last will and testament of a wealthy peer is necessarily a lengthy document, but he made short work of it, returning to study only one section at greater length. Finally he said, ''It is as I surmised. There are no conditions attached to your inheritance apart from the simple one of marriage by your twenty-fifth birthday. Even divorce or murder cannot take it from you.''

"Are those the only two options?" Jocelyn said with alarm.

"Not at all. You could live in a state of permanent separation, but that has an untidiness that will probably not appeal to you." He looked at her carefully, analyzing her reaction, then finished, "Or you can seek an annulment."

"An annulment?" she said slowly. "I have heard the term, but I really don't know what it means."

"An annulment is much simpler and faster than a divorce, and nothing like as scandalous, since no misconduct is involved."

He was speaking with the impartiality of a lawyer, and she looked at him askance, wondering if he had personal feelings about the matter. "Do you mean that any couple could get an annulment if they decided they didn't suit? If that were true, surely annulments would be very common."

"At the risk of getting too technical, there are two kinds of annulment. The first voids the marriage for nonconsummation; and it would dissolve the marriage as if it never happened. This wouldn't do for you since you need to have been married.

"The second kind is called voidable, and preserves any legal consequences of the marriage. This would fulfill the terms of your father's will and would allow you to retain your inheritance."

A little confused, Jocelyn asked hesitantly, "What would make a marriage voidable?"

His voice dry, David replied, "The ground that would work in this case would be impotence."

As she stared at him, her eyes rounded in sudden shock. "You mean that because of the paralysis, now you can't . . . ?" She was horrified and felt a wave of compassion so intense that she was left wordless. What a tragic loss for the major. More than that, what a waste!

David gave a half-smile. "You needn't look so appalled, Lady Jocelyn. In fact, I have no reason to believe that is the case, but given the nature of my recent injuries, it will be simple enough to claim that the marriage cannot be consummated and should be annulled." His smile broadened. "I admit this is legal hairsplitting, but as long as I don't know for certain, I can sign a deposition about my incapacity with a reasonably clear conscience."

Jocelyn blushed violently and applied herself to the coffee, thinking that she hadn't anticipated how uncomfortable this discussion would become. After a long sip, she asked, "So if we both sign something for the lawyers, we will soon be free?"

She was dimly aware that men took their amatory performance very seriously; surely David was unusual in his matter-of-fact offer to claim an embarrassing disability. She thought of mentioning the fact so she could thank him for his gallantry, but could not think of any words that would not discomfit her to total speechlessness. To change the subject she asked, "Where did you learn so much about the law?"

"I read law for a year and a half. It was thought to be a suitable profession for me."

"No wonder you are so knowledgeable. What happened that prevented you from completing your training?"

"I decided that I quite literally preferred death to life as a lawyer. The army was the logical choice; I was clearly unsuited to the vicarage."

"I should think so! I cannot imagine you as a man of the cloth." She chuckled at the picture of the mischief he might cause in a parish, then said, "You've confirmed me in my prejudices about the law. Since lawyers are usually prosy old bores, I can only assume that the law is boring."

"The practice of law certainly is, but the law itself is quite fascinating. The great body of Anglo-Saxon common law is part of what makes our country unique. It derives from precedent and common sense and is quite different from the French Code Napoléon, for example, which is derived from the Roman Justinian Code. Common law has the admirable ability to grow and change with the times, and I have no doubt that two thousand years from now our descendants will still be governing themselves with a recognizable form of it.''

She said admiringly, "What a wonderful thought! Major, you have just done the impossible, you have made the law sound romantic. Perhaps you should have become a lawyer, after all.''

He shook his head. "No, it wouldn't have served. The day-to-day practice is an indoor, paper-shuffling business, and I would have hated it.'' He smiled suddenly. "It can't be often that a solicitor draws up a will like your father's. What on earth was he thinking of?''

Jocelyn wrinkled her nose. "You've read the will, it should be obvious what was in his mind. I believe he described me as 'a headstrong wench with too many romantical notions, and too particular in her tastes.' ''

David made a noise that sounded suspiciously like a smothered laugh, but his face was sober when she glared at him.

"Mind you, my father had a point," she admitted with an engaging twinkle, "but since everyone agreed that I was just like him, it seems most unfair to penalize me.''

At that, the major could no longer contain his laughter. "Quite right, it was most unhandsome of him," he said finally.

Jocelyn had been unable to avoid laughing herself. Shaking her head, she said, "I know my father was most sincerely concerned for me. He really believed that for a woman not to marry was a ghastly fate. Also, while he didn't mind seeing the title go to his brother, Willoughby, and my cousin Randolph after that, he didn't want to think that his own line would die out if I chose not to marry.''

"I can understand his feelings.''

"So can I. But I would not be forced into marriage.'' Her eyes had a steely glint, but her expression softened to regret. "It is paradoxical. Because of the way he raised me, I can never be content with the ladylike life he wanted me to have.''

"What do you mean?"

Her gaze was fixed on the nearby greenery of Hyde Park, but her inner eye saw another scene. "He raised me to be his heir. Oh, not legally—the entail made that impossible. But we spent so much time together, as if I were his son. We would ride around the estate, discussing drainage and livestock and crop rotation, all the things the lord of the manor must know. The Kendal estate, Charlton, is in my blood and mind and soul."

She felt her eyes beginning to mist and her final sentence was scarcely more than a whisper. "And Charlton can never be mine."

She was glad that David's voice drew her back from the pain she always felt when she thought of her lost home. "I know it is a limited consolation, but now you are in a position to buy another estate. With time and love, you can make it your own."

Jocelyn glanced shyly at him. "You understand, don't you? I've seldom talked of this. My kind of attachment to the land is quite unsuitable in a mere female."

She sighed. "It may take years to find the right property. Very seldom does an estate like Charlton come onto the market. But I will instruct my man of business to investigate everything that becomes available. I suppose that is the main reason why I wanted so much to retain my fortune. I could afford the life of a social butterfly on the competence that would have been mine if I hadn't married, but becoming a woman of property will require a large amount of money."

David sipped his coffee thoughtfully, then smiled. "It is an ambition worth the having, Lady Jocelyn, and I think you will achieve it. But have you never wished to marry?"

She glanced down and toyed with her delicate china cup in an uncharacteristic display of nervousness. "Oh, I most certainly want to marry. There is someone . . ." She concentrated on mounding the sugar high in its bowl with the little silver spoon. It seemed important to explain herself to David Lancaster, and he was very easy to talk to.

"I have known the gentleman for the last three years, but it has been most difficult to get him to cooperate. I am not certain, but I think he must have been very badly hurt by some woman in the past and has avoided marriage ever since. Yet he has shown some preference for my company, and I have often thought that, given time, we might reach an understanding."

Just thinking of the Duke of Candover produced the familiar knot of longing in her breast, and it was with some difficulty that she added lightly, "No doubt it sounds very foolish."

"Love is very seldom wise." David's voice was gentle.

She raised her eyes to his with a smile of gratitude. "You are a very understanding man. I wish you were my brother, but I suppose Miss Lancaster would be loath to share you."

There was an odd note in his voice as he said, "You would like me for a brother?"

"I know that is impossible, but I would hope we can be friends." Her lovely face was earnest as she said, "Too much has happened in these last days for us to be strangers."

"You are certainly correct about that." He reached across the table to take her hand. "Friends, then."

His hand was firm and warm on hers, but his face looked shadowed and she said with sudden compunction, "I have been tiring you. I'm sorry, you seem so well that I keep forgetting how ill you have been. Do you wish to lie down?"

"That sounds appealing. I imagine I shall do little but eat and sleep for the next week or two."

"Do you need assistance?" Jocelyn asked uncertainly. Her memory of the night before made her shy about getting so close to the major again. He might not remember what happened, but she did. What if she had an overwhelming urge to discover how well he kissed when he was fully aware?

She blushed at her shameless thought, but luckily David said, "I can manage ten feet to the bed, Lady Jocelyn. Thank you for your concern."

"I will see you later, then."

Jocelyn's hand was almost on the knob when the door swung open and her Aunt Elvira exploded into the room. The Countess of Cromarty was in a rare taking, her beefy face a close match for the fuchsia plumes bobbing on her head.

"You shameless baggage! What is this nonsense about your having married? Just last week you hadn't brought anyone up to scratch! Or did you buy a husband, some fortune-hunter willing to take you in spite of your sly ways and wicked temper?"

Jocelyn was momentarily staggered under the wave of vitriol. Though she and the countess had never gotten on well, they usually maintained at least the appearance of civility. But then, Elvira had never been deprived of a fortune before. Her aunt was drawing her breath for another barrage when a cool voice cut across the room.

"Would you be so kind as to introduce us, Jocelyn?"

She had momentarily forgotten that David was present, but now she stepped aside so that her aunt could see that she had invaded a gentleman's bedroom. Unfortunately, the countess was beyond questions of propriety, and the sight of Major Lancaster produced a distinct growl in the back of her throat.

Jocelyn wished she could spare David this scene, but that was impossible unless she bodily removed her aunt. Reluctantly she said, "David, this is my Aunt Elvira, the Countess of Cromarty. You may recall my mentioning her. Elvira, Major David Lancaster." She deliberately introduced her aunt to David, knowing that the status-conscious countess would see it as the insult it was.

Elvira snarled, "So *you* are the one taking part in this farce. Why, I have never even heard of you. You're a nobody!"

Looking very tall and very distinguished, David bowed, then gave a winning smile. "Well, I am definitely somebody, though not in any worldly sense. Of course you are sorry that your niece has thrown herself away on someone of no great rank or wealth; with her beauty, birth, and charm she could look to the highest in the land. Indeed, I have pointed that out to my dear girl many times."

He moved forward easily and put his arm around Jocelyn's waist. "I could not agree with you more about the unsuitability of the match. Still, the attachment has stood the test of time and it became very hard for me to refuse Jocelyn's earnest pleas when to marry her was my own dearest wish."

Seeing that his dear girl had turned to stare at him with blank astonishment, he grinned and dropped a quick kiss on her chestnut hair. Continuing smoothly, he said, "So in a moment of weakness, I agreed. Your outrage cannot possibly be greater than my own misgivings. It is a tribute to your perception that you realize no man could be good enough for your niece. I can only swear I will spend my life trying to be worthy of her."

Jocelyn's astonishment almost turned to uncontrollable giggles. With heroic willpower, she cooed, "David, darling, you do say the sweetest things! As if any woman wouldn't be proud to be your wife."

She turned to her aunt and said soulfully, "Had I sought to buy such a husband, it would be impossible. Such nobility of nature, such high principles, are beyond price. And the heart of a lion—he is a hero of Waterloo, you know." She slipped her arm around his waist and laid her head against his shoulder. "I am the most fortunate of women."

Elvira stared in stupefaction. Whatever she had expected, it was not this picture of mutual adoration. And while she might not know Major Lancaster, he undeniably had the air of a gentleman. "You have been attached for some time?"

"Oh, we have known each other this age," David said blandly. "But the difference in our stations and the wars conspired to keep us apart." He gave Elvira a seraphic smile. "I do hope you will wish us happy."

Even Elvira's erratic social sense could not overlook such a disarming plea. "Well, it still seems like a deuced hole-in-corner business to me," she huffed. "No engagement, no banns, no one from the family present. At the very least, you should have invited Willoughby and me; as head of the family, he should have given you away."

Jocelyn let her mouth droop tragically. "There was no time. David was so ill. Indeed, had his life not been despaired of, I could never have persuaded him to marry me. Pray tell my uncle I meant no slight."

Routed and romped, Elvira muttered, "It still seems havey-cavey to me." Her eyes narrowing, she added, "If by some chance this wasn't a real marriage, merely one of convenience, you wouldn't inherit, you know. How did you two meet?"

Jocelyn said firmly, "Aunt Elvira, it was very thoughtful of you to come pay your respects, but I cannot allow you to tire my husband any longer. Though he is recovering well, I am loath to risk his health unnecessarily."

She stepped away from David to pull the bellcord. Mossley arrived almost immediately; Jocelyn assumed that a close inspection would reveal the shape of a keyhole temporarily imprinted on his ear. "Please show the countess downstairs. I am sorry not to accompany you, Aunt, but my husband and I were discussing something of importance." She went to take David's arm again, making a great show of batting her eyelashes.

In the face of such indifference, the countess turned and brushed by Mossley so quickly her plumes hit him in the face. Jocelyn waited until the footsteps had died away before collapsing into a chair and giving in to whoops of laughter. She gasped, "I know now why you didn't die of your wounds, Major. You were obviously born to be hanged. I have never heard such a string of half-truths in my life. 'We have known each other this age,' indeed!"

"The advantage of legal training, my dear." David laughed from his seat on the bed. "Any lawyer worth his salt can choose words so effectively that he can convince a reasonable man that black is white. Careful analysis of what I said should not show any actual lies." He smiled at her impishly. "If I was born to be hanged, you were born for Drury Lane. You got into the spirit of that play rather quickly."

"It was very bad of me," Jocelyn sighed. "But that Aunt Elvira should speak to me so in my own house!"

"Do you always clash?"

"She married my uncle Willoughby when I was two. When we met, she scooped me up in her arms in an effort to prove her maternal instincts, whereupon I bit her on the nose. Our relationship has been deteriorating ever since."

"Your aunt was right: you are a shameless baggage."

Jocelyn grinned back at him, unabashed. Then a thought occurred to her. "Could she contest my inheritance on the grounds that I am not truly married?"

David shrugged. "On a given day, almost anyone can take almost anyone else to court on almost any charge. I think her chances of winning would be minuscule, but you will want to discuss the whole matter with your own lawyer. Would your uncle wish to take you to court? He could bring a nuisance suit even if he has no chance of winning."

"Willoughby will do what Elvira wishes; he's a pleasant man, but thoroughly under the cat's paw." She wrinkled her nose. "One of the drawbacks of an annulment is that it will give Elvira license to say that no man would have me. While the desire to buy land might have been my strongest reason to retain my fortune, honesty compels me to admit that the desire to thwart my aunt came a close second."

"Ignoble but understandable."

She gazed at him fondly. "Major, not least of your many virtues is your remarkable degree of tolerance." Elvira's visit had made her think of the future, so she asked, "What will you do now, after you are well and free of our improbable marriage?"

He shrugged. "I'm not sure. I may return to the army. Garrison duty is not too appealing, but I'm not sure what else I am qualified to do. It's also possible that the army won't want me; I'm sure there will be troop cutbacks now that Boney's gone."

"It seems so unfair that the men who saved England will be discarded like . . . like old shoes now that they are not needed."

In spite of Jocelyn's earnest look, David had to laugh out loud. "Life is a good deal more comfortable if you don't expect it to be fair."

"I suppose you're right."

A knock sounded at the door, and Mossley entered to say, "Dr. Kinlock to see the major."

Moving with his usual impatience, Kinlock entered on the butler's heels. His busy eyebrows raised at the cozy scene in front of him and he gave a half-smile. "I was through at my surgery early today, but it looks like my concern for your welfare was misplaced."

David had stood at his entrance. "Your prediction about the opium withdrawal was entirely accurate. I may not be ready for riding or twenty-mile marches for another few weeks, but I feel right as a trivet."

"We'll see about that." The doctor glanced at Jocelyn and she quickly rose. Kinlock would want to examine his patient, and she abruptly realized she had spent far more time with the major than she had intended.

"I'll be going along now. Major Lancaster, shall I ask my lawyer to call on us tomorrow?"

"Very well," he agreed. Both he and the doctor admired the elegance of her departing figure as she slipped through the door.

"She's a braw bonnie lassie," the doctor said in one of his stronger descents to a Scots accent before he began poking and prodding his patient. After a thorough examination that included listening to the heart through a rolled tube of heavy paper, Kinlock said, "You have the constitution of an ox, Major. The surgical incision is nearly closed with no sign of infection and you've come through the opium withdrawal without damage, though I'll admit I was worried yesterday."

Replacing the paper tube in his medical case, he continued, "I won't waste my breath on instructions for your convalescence since you will do as you please no matter what I say." With a glare from under the bushy brows the doctor said balefully, "I trust that you have enough common sense to eat well, rest often, and not push yourself beyond your strength?"

The major chuckled. "I have no desire to ruin the splendid job you've done, Dr. Kinlock. I've had considerable experience with wounds and recovery and won't do anything foolish." More seriously, he said, "I owe you my life and health. There are no adequate words of thanks, but I hope you know how much I appreciate what you have done."

"Don't thank me, thank your sister. When everyone else had given up on you, she didn't. I just happened to be the surgeon she found; any competent practitioner could have removed the shrapnel and seen how the opium was affecting you." He snorted, then added dryly, "Unfortunately, the doctors at the York Hospital had already decided you were hopeless."

"As you will, though I think you undervalue your own skills. I presume you won't be calling again?"

"I'll remove the stitches in a few days, but apart from that, you have no need of me, Major." He closed his medical bag with a snap.

David offered his hand. "Again, my most profound thanks."

Kinlock's grasp was quick and firm. "My pleasure, Major Lancaster. Among all the failures of a physician's life, it is rewarding to have a splendid success now and then." He gave a quick, boyish grin. "Besides, Lady Jocelyn has already paid the outrageous bill I sent her. It will keep my free surgery supplied with medicines for the next year. Good day to you." He nodded, then vanished out the door.

David lay back on the bed with his hands tucked

under his head, his eyes absently tracing the geometric moldings of the ceiling. So Lady Jocelyn had even paid the medical bill? The money itself might be insignificant to a woman of great wealth, but it was another sign of her good sportsmanship in the face of the jest fate had played in the matter of her marriage. He thought of the bright mischievous smile, the friendly consideration she showed everyone in her household, then closed his eyes with a sigh, feeling enormously weary.

She was everything he had ever dreamed of in a woman, she was his wife, and he had just given her the means to leave him. When would he ever learn to keep his mouth closed? He mentally shrugged and tried to empty his mind so sleep could claim him. The Lady Jocelyn Kendal, only and wealthy daughter of an earl, was not for a half-pay officer without profession or prospects.

Elias Wildon responded to Lady Cromarty's summons without enthusiasm. While the earl was easy to deal with, the countess insisted on inserting herself into matters that were none of her business, and as the family lawyer, Wildon perforce had to obey her orders if he wished to maintain his extremely comfortable standard of living.

When he reached Charlton, the lawyer was summoned into Lady Cromarty's presence without even a token wait; he surmised that something very important must be on her mind. Her ladyship's eyes were cold and angry as she greeted him, and she did not offer him a chair. Her voice was brusque as she said, "You have heard that my husband's niece, Lady Jocelyn, has married?"

Wildon nodded. "Yes, only a few weeks before her twenty-fifth birthday, but with ample time to fulfill the requirements of the late earl's bequest."

"What if she isn't really married?"

Wildon pursed his lips and looked at his client disapprovingly. "I myself have seen the marriage lines at

Hamilton's office. There is no question that she is married."

"I've no doubt that she went through a ceremony," the countess said with an impatient wave of her hand. "But what if it is just a form marriage? A marriage of convenience?"

"I fail to see the point you are trying to make, Lady Cromarty." Wildon's voice was terse.

"Her father's will specified a real marriage. It was well-known that he wished her to marry and have children. If she and this military jackanapes were to separate, surely she would be failing to fulfill the spirit of the bequest?"

The lawyer paused, his attention reluctantly caught by the intellectual puzzle of the question. "It could be argued that it was no true marriage," he said cautiously.

"Well, then, find me the proof!" the countess said triumphantly.

"I beg your pardon?" Wildon asked in bewilderment.

"You must know how to investigate matters discreetly. Find out when Lady Jocelyn met this so-called major, the circumstances of their marriage, everything!" Her eyes glittered coldly. "Then, if they separate after a few weeks or months, we take her to court."

The lawyer shook his head. "Even if that was to occur, I must tell you that your legal position would be quite weak. And I'm sure you are aware of the potential for scandal."

Lady Cromarty stood, her fists clenching. "You talk to me of scandal? When that jade has made a mockery of marriage to keep a fortune that should be ours? I would wager any sum you choose that within six months her *affaires* will be the talk of the *ton*. Her precious 'major' will disappear and she will start carrying on in a way that will make Caro Lamb look like a nun! Oh, yes, I know Lady Jocelyn. And she will not be permitted to get away with her shameless plans."

Wildon was astonished at the venom in the countess's

voice. He had met Lady Jocelyn and considered her a charming girl, if a trifle too high-spirited; he supposed it was inevitable that a termagant like this one would be jealous of her. Still, if the countess wished to waste her blunt on fruitless investigations and lawsuits, he might as well be the one to benefit. He bowed his head and said, "It shall be as you wish, Lady Cromarty. I will send you regular reports on what is discovered."

It was a pleasure to remove himself from the poisonous confines of Lady Cromarty's morning room. The lawyer could understand perfectly why the earl kept a mistress in London: the countess would be no pleasure to come home to.

## 9

When Sally Lancaster entered her brother's room in midafternoon, she was so delighted to see him up and well that she raced across to his chair and only just refrained from giving him a hug altogether too energetic for an invalid. She settled for grabbing his hands and holding them tightly while she looked him over. "You're really back now, aren't you, David?"

"Yes, Dr. Kinlock thinks there is no more reason for concern. With a few weeks of eating, I should be as good as new. And I owe it all to you, Sally. Everyone else had given up, me included. But you didn't." He stood and embraced her. "I don't know what I have done to deserve you for a sister; all I can do is give thanks."

She blushed and sat down, uncomfortable with accepting compliments. "I did it for my own benefit, David. Who else would put up with me the way you do?"

"Plenty of men would be delighted to do so." He looked at her thoughtfully. "What do you intend to do now, Sally? You have a comfortable income, you no longer need to teach. Have you ever thought of marrying?"

She looked surprised. "I assumed the settlement will be retracted, since dear Lady Jocelyn didn't get what she bargained for, which was a dead husband."

"I discussed that with her just a few minutes ago. First of all, the trust is in your name and she couldn't revoke it if she wanted to. Second, she doesn't want to. The marriage accomplished her goal and she will inherit her fortune. My continued existence is a complication, but not one that was covered in the contract."

"Is that all it means to her, a matter of contract law?" Sally asked indignantly. "That woman has ice in her veins."

David was surprised at his sister's vehemence. "Have you taken her in dislike, Sally?"

"We have had little opportunity to become acquainted," Sally said stiffly as she sat down in one of the chairs by the window. "Lady Jocelyn has been most considerate about the use of her house and her servants. She even sent me a note this morning to let me know that you had fully recovered from the opium withdrawal, or I should have left work earlier to come here."

In spite of her resolution to be high-minded and not burden David with details of Lady Jocelyn's repellent behavior, Sally could not help adding, "But honestly, the thought of being related to her for the rest of my life makes the blood curdle in my veins."

David frowned slightly and had just opened his mouth to reply when a cool voice sounded from the doorway. Lady Jocelyn was entering with two books in her hand, looking every inch the grand lady as she said, "You need have no fears on that score, Miss Lancaster. Your brother and I have already discussed seeking an annulment, so your blood may continue to flow uncurdled."

Sally was sure her face must be beet-red with embarrassment, and with the bravado that comes of having been caught in a faux pas, she said, "Splendid. If an annulment is possible, I presume David is in no danger from you."

"Sally!" David exclaimed, turning his head sharply.

Jocelyn said disdainfully, "Don't worry, Major. It is not the first time your sister has made such accusations. I think it is possible that her concern for you has addled her wits." She placed the books on the table between the Lancasters and turned to leave. "As you can see, I managed to find the volumes of poetry that we had been discussing. I trust you will enjoy them. If you will excuse me . . ."

"One moment, please, Lady Jocelyn." The major's voice had taken on a definite note of command, and her ladyship turned her cool gaze back to her guests.

"Yes, Major Lancaster?" she said with raised eyebrows.

Sally had to admire the haughtiness Lady Jocelyn displayed; one could see invisible ranks of long-dead Kendals lined up behind her, all of them masters of pride and clearly satisfied with their descendant's ability to depress pretensions.

Unintimidated, the major said, "Have you two been at daggers drawn?"

Lady Jocelyn said crisply, "Your sister has taken it into her head that I am a threat either to your continued existence or possibly to her relationship with you. Since she apparently prefers to see dangers where none exist, I doubt you will be able to convince her otherwise."

Sally's precarious hold on her temper snapped. "Threats where none exist! David, I hadn't meant you to know, but I had to force her to let you come here. Having gotten her marriage lines, she was willing—no, eager—to leave you in that ghastly hospital, so you couldn't trouble her selfish existence. She was afraid having a dying man here would 'disrupt the household!' "

"Is that true?" David asked dispassionately.

Jocelyn hesitated, then nodded.

Sally wasn't finished yet. "When she gave me the first quarter's allowance, I asked why it wasn't thirty pieces of silver, and she said that silver was for selling people, and that since she was buying, she paid gold!"

"Did you really say that?" David asked in astonishment.

Jocelyn's face flamed. "I'm afraid so." Suddenly she looked much more like a child caught in mischief than a proud lady with ice in her veins.

David looked at the two of them, then burst into laughter. "Really," he gasped as he attempted to collect himself, "I have never seen two such totty-headed females."

Both pairs of watching eyes grew frosty, and Sally asked, "Just what do you mean by that?"

The major grinned. "You are the two most managing

women I've ever met and I should have known there would be trouble. No doubt you have been busy bringing out each other's worst natures.''

He shook his head in amusement, then added, ''Whoever claimed females were the weaker sex never knew either of you. All a poor male can do is agree quickly and hope to escape unscathed.''

Sally glared at him, then said acidly to her ladyship, ''What a whisker! David is generally quite easygoing, but whenever he has an object in mind, one might as well wave the white flag immediately because he is going to do whatever he wants and the devil take the hindmost.''

''I have seen signs of that,'' Jocelyn agreed. Then her mouth quirked up and she said to Sally, ''Do you realize this is the first time we have ever agreed on anything?''

David reached across and took his sister's hand. ''Sally, I gather that because of the way she met me, you have assumed that Lady Jocelyn is my enemy, but she could not have behaved better had we been married twenty years and been as fond as Romeo and Juliet. If she had wanted to see the last of me, she could have let me pitch over the railing to the foyer last night, which would have made her a widow in earnest.''

Sally gasped and said, ''You almost fell off the gallery?''

''Yes, my wits were wandering and apparently I decided to follow them. Jocelyn pulled me clear and put me to bed. I also recall that she spent a good part of two nights sitting up and holding my hand, feeding me, and generally playing nursemaid, which she was under no obligation to do.''

Sally flushed and tried to withdraw her hand, but David held it firmly. ''Did you really do that, Lady Jocelyn?'' she asked in a low voice.

''Yes, though I'm surprised your brother remembers,'' Jocelyn admitted.

Sally forced herself to meet her sister-in-law's eyes. ''Then I owe you an abject apology. What I said was quite abominable.''

"You had considerable provocation. You were quite right at first, you know," Jocelyn said ruefully. "I thought it a great pity your brother was dying, but it never occurred to me that I could or should do anything to improve his lot. And you have the most magnificent talent for causing me to lose my temper and say dreadful things. If my Aunt Laura had heard me, she would have sent me to bed without any supper for a month. Shall we pretend that the last week never happened and begin over again?"

Sally had been right in her speculation two days previously: when Jocelyn Kendal turned on the full force of her smile, she was impossible to resist. Sally smiled back and offered her hand. "That is an excellent plan. Good day, Lady Jocelyn. My name is Sally Lancaster. I believe you are married to my brother. So pleased to make your acquaintance."

"The pleasure is all mine," her ladyship said, returning the handshake firmly.

"Shall we celebrate the cessation of hostilities with some tea?" David inquired.

"I think that's a lovely idea," Jocelyn agreed. She pulled the bellcord, then seated herself on the nearby sofa.

Any remaining tension between the two ladies vanished in the course of an affable hour of tea, cakes, and conversation. Now that they had decided not to be adversaries, Sally discovered Jocelyn's natural warmth and friendliness, and her ladyship could enjoy her sister-in-law's dry, acerbic humor. While they were still very different in nature, they were each beginning to show a real appreciation of the other's good qualities.

David contributed little to the conversation, content to watch their rapprochement. It was somehow important that Sally like Lady Jocelyn, even though her ladyship would soon be out of his life forever. It would be pleasant to occasionally reminisce with his sister about this short, unusual interlude.

After an hour Lady Jocelyn excused herself, claiming obligations out of the house. Sally stayed with David a while longer, but rose to leave when she saw that he was tiring. As she picked up her reticule, she asked, "Did Dr. Kinlock say when he would come again, David?"

"He'll remove the stitches in a few days, but otherwise he won't come again unless I have a relapse, which I have no intention of doing." David was crossing to the bed and didn't notice the fleeting expression on his sister's face.

"Oh. That is unfortunate. I never properly thanked him."

David glanced at her as he lay down on the wide mattress. "You can be sure that I did. He's an interesting person as well as a fine physician, and I'll be sorry not to see him again, but he's not the man to waste time on healthy people."

"I suppose not." Sally gnawed at her lip a bit. "Perhaps I should stop by his surgery to settle the account with him. He is only a few blocks from the Launcestons'."

"Lady Jocelyn has already taken care of what Dr. Kinlock assures me was an outrageous bill." David found his eyes closing, but they opened again at his sister's reply.

"She paid it already? But that doesn't seem right. We should take care of it." She wrinkled her nose. "Even if it is out of the money Lady Jocelyn gave me."

"I'm inclined to agree with you, but frankly, I'm not up to arguing with her at the moment. If you care to fight her about the bill, feel free."

Sally looked at him with compunction. "I shouldn't be wearing you out with something so trivial. Besides, I find that I object to her ladyship's magnanimity a good deal less now that I have made my peace with her." She kissed her brother on the forehead. "I'll see you tomorrow afternoon."

As Sally left the house, she turned left toward Hyde Park. She would not be needed back at the Launcestons' for the rest of the day; they took the view that during the summer the children should have only half a day of lessons, leaving her with considerable free time. She was really most fortunate in her employers.

As she walked, her mind was not on the park's green expanses but on that sudden pang of regret she had felt when David said that Dr. Kinlock would not be coming back. She had deeply appreciated the skill and compassion that lady under the doctor's gruff exterior, but was there more to it than that?

She repressed the thought. Sally Lancaster was a paragon of the practical virtues, without a romantic bone in her body. To be sure, she kept thinking of the doctor's powerfully muscled figure, the large hands that could move with such delicacy, but that was merely admiration for the surgeon's strength and skill. And while the image of his prematurely white hair and its contrast with his dark, shaggy brows kept recurring to her, that was just because his looks were so striking.

*Just whom do you think you are deceiving?* Sally's steps had led her to the Serpentine, where she found a seat by the edge, staring unseeing over its placid waters. She was not in the habit of hiding from unpleasant truths and now she had to face the fact that Ian Kinlock appealed to her in ways that had nothing to do with his considerable skills. She liked the man—liked his passionate commitment to his work, liked his rough tongue, and deuce take it, liked the way he moved, the quick, impatient strength of him.

She chuckled ruefully. How typical that the first man that had attracted her since her childish infatuation with the vicar should be so ineligible. Ian Kinlock lived for his work, and as David had said, he had no interest in healthy bodies. And if he did, plain brown Sarah Lancaster was not the one to distract him from his serious business of saving London from the Reaper. Was that one of the reasons she had resented Lady Jocelyn, whose beauty and charm even the good doctor had noticed?

Sally fiddled with the buttons of her spencer as she faced the fact that envy of her ladyship must have played a part in Sally's antipathy; how disheartening to admit that one was not really a very nice person. It had

128                          *Mary Jo Putney*

been satisfying to scorn Lady Jocelyn as a cold-blooded
*femme fatale*, but based on the last few days, Lady
Jocelyn was ahead in the character department as well
as in looks. To think of that flawless society beauty
feeding David soup, caring for him in his extremity,
when she hardly even knew the man; it was a sobering
lesson in not being ruled by appearances.

She stood with sudden resolution. Ian Kinlock might
not find a plain brown governess attractive, but surely
now and then he needed a friend? From what she had
seen of his life, he continually gave to others; perhaps he
would appreciate someone doing something for him. As
she walked out of the park, she thought of what she
knew of his schedule. It was one of his days at St. Bart's
and she had seen how exhausting that was for him. She
started to smile; she knew exactly what to do.

When Ian Kinlock returned to the grubby cubicle that
was his home at St. Bart's, he was so depleted he could
barely open the door. It had been a particularly bad
day, with a huge number of general medical patients
followed by tragedy on the cutting ward as one woman
died under surgery and another wouldn't last the night
in spite of his best efforts. Times like these he wondered
why he didn't pursue a fashionable practice that
wouldn't demand such reserves of emotional and
physical strength.

When he entered the room, he headed toward his desk
and the locked whiskey drawer, not noticing that he had
company until the light voice said, "You will be able to
drink more if you eat something first."

He blinked and turned his head to discover Miss
Lancaster sitting in the only other chair. She had been
reading a book, but she set it aside and lifted a basket.
"I thought you would be hungry, so I brought this."

Bemused, he pulled the chair from the desk and sat
down. "I guess I am. At the end of a day at St. Bart's, I
generally can't remember when I ate last."

"Care for some chicken?" She handed him a cold

drumstick and he bit into it automatically. She also pulled out a jug of ale and poured him a tankard full.

"Aren't you going to eat too?" he asked.

"I thought you'd never ask," she said with a smile. The next quarter-hour was taken up with eating and exploring Sally's capacious basket. Besides chicken and ale, she had brought sliced beef, bread, cheese, and gingerbread, picnic foods easily eaten, all of excellent quality.

Ian licked the crumbs of gingerbread from his fingers and replenished his tankard of ale. "Now that I am a rational man again, it occurs to me to wonder what you are doing here."

Sally shrugged and busied herself with packing the leftovers in her basket. "David said you wouldn't be coming back, and I realized that I hadn't properly thanked you."

He chuckled, more relaxed than he had been in weeks. "I like thanks that take a practical form. Though I was just the instrument, you know. I do the best I can, but healing comes from a level beyond my poor skills."

Her eyebrows lifted. "I wouldn't have expected such a mystical statement from a man of science."

He tilted his chair back and put his feet up on his desk with a sigh of relaxation. "I may be a scientist on the surface, but underneath I'm pure wild Celt." He smiled wryly. "A respectable English lady like you wouldn't understand that."

Sally snorted and stood up. "Watch whom you call English, laddie. My mother was Welsh and as wild a Celt as you." She walked over toward the desk with a package. "I've wrapped the bread and cheese in paper and they should keep for several days. It wouldn't hurt your patients if you ate now and then."

She looked for a clear spot on the cluttered desk to put the food, not wanting the cheese to stain his papers. Her eye was caught by an envelope as she moved it away, and she lifted it curiously.

*The Honorable Ian Kinlock.* She showed it to him. "I'm sorry, I couldn't help seeing this. Are you sure you're a wild Celt?"

Ian actually blushed; she wouldn't have believed it possible. "My mother insists on addressing me that way. My father is the Laird of Kintyre, and she periodically writes to suggest I give up this medical nonsense and come home to live like a proper Kinlock."

"So you can slaughter helpless animals and gamble away your fortune?" Sally inquired, remembering what he had said the night he had taken her to the tavern.

"Aye, my brothers are a dab hand at that sort of thing. To be fair, none of them has actually gambled away a fortune, and they are good-enough fellows in their way; two are army officers like your brother. But we're as unlike as chalk and cheese."

"I can well imagine." Sally was fascinated by this unexpected glimpse of the doctor. "I should think you would perish of boredom in a fortnight."

"Exactly." He sighed. "My mother has never understood that. She is also convinced I'll succumb to the charms of some hopelessly ineligible female. Bless her, she assumes that any of her five sons must be irresistible. She has never really accepted that I am out of leading strings, even though I've more white hair than my own father."

Sally smiled. "She sounds rather dear."

"She is. Hopeless, but dear." He pulled a drawer open for the packet of bread and cheese, then stood. "Shall we go outside and find a hackney? I'm too tired to walk you home."

"You needn't concern yourself. It's still light out and I have been living in London for years."

He scowled ferociously. "I may not consider myself an Honorable, but I certainly won't let a lady go home alone in the evening. Besides," he finished practically, "you only live three blocks away from me."

"Yes, Dr. Kinlock," she said demurely, her eyes dancing.

"Call me Ian. Hardly anyone does anymore," he said

as he ushered her outside, then locked the door of his office. "Sometimes I get very tired of being Physician and Surgeon Kinlock, one very long step removed from God."

"Just as I get very weary of being Miss Lancaster, paragon of virtue and governess *extraordinaire*," Sally said feelingly. "By the way, what does a Sally look like?"

He chuckled as they stepped into the mild summer evening.

"Look in the mirror and you'll find out."

He flagged down a hack and handed her into it. As she settled against the dingy seat, Sally felt well-pleased with her evening's expedition. There was nothing the least loverlike in the doctor's attitude—there probably never would be—but he seemed willing to be friends. She glanced sideways at him, admiring the craggy face under the shock of white hair. He might be willing for friendship, but would that be enough for her?

When Jocelyn's lawyer, Stephen Hamilton, called the next day, he refrained from uttering any "I told you so's" about the unexpected results of his client's impetuous marriage since her ladyship was his most valuable client. Besides, she seemed singularly unchastened by the situation. Hamilton was impressed by the quality of Major Lancaster's mind; when he discovered the major had trained for the law, his admiration was explained and justified.

The lawyer and the major spent some time discussing the legal situation and its ramifications while her ladyship listened with interest. At the end of the discussion, Hamilton rose and said, "I shall start the annulment process right away, but it will take several months. You understand, Lady Jocelyn, that while your legal position is secure, an annulment will leave you vulnerable to a nuisance suit from your uncle?"

When she nodded, he said, "I have no doubt you will win, but the legal fees would be considerable and there could be some notoriety attaching to you. You would

not consider remaining married?'' He asked the
question without hope, though he privately considered a
rational man like Major Lancaster to be a perfect choice
for the volatile Lady Jocelyn.

She just laughed at him. "Goodness, Mr. Hamilton,
what do you take me for? It seemed logical enough to
marry at the time, but given the changed circumstances,
we have reconsidered.'' The long lashes fluttered
fetchingly over her hazel eyes, and the lawyer conceded
the point to her. He always did.

"Good day, Lady Jocelyn, Major. I will have the
depositions ready for your signatures within the week.
Nothing more will be required of you.''

After Hamilton left, David said, "I shall need to start
looking for rooms soon.''

"Nonsense, why should you do that?'' Jocelyn asked.
"I have plenty of space here, and from what Mr. Hamilton said, there would be no impropriety in staying together until the marriage is dissolved.'' Seeing the
major's hesitation, she added coaxingly, "Besides, it is
sadly flat living here alone, and I have no idea when
Aunt Laura will forgive me and come back.''

"Is she your usual companion? I have wondered
about an attractive young woman living alone in
London.''

"Cromarty House has always been home to my aunt
and her family when they are in London. Since my
father died, she has stayed with me when it was not
advisable to follow the drum. When she was with her
husband, some other female connection lends me
countenance, but none is so nice as Aunt Laura.''
Jocelyn smiled fondly. "She has been so good to me
over the years. Her own children are sons and she has
treated me like a daughter.''

"Your own mother died when you were young?''

"She . . . went away,'' Jocelyn said shortly. Before he
could ask for clarification, a knock at the door was
followed by Captain Dalton. After greeting him
warmly, Jocelyn excused herself to leave the two
officers together.

After she left, David looked at his friend closely. "You're looking pulled today, Richard. Is your leg acting up again?"

"Yes." The captain grimaced as he lowered himself into a chair and laid his crutches down. "But it's more than that. I went to see Dr. Kinlock at his consulting rooms this morning. He thinks more surgery is indicated. The thigh bone was badly set after the battle and is not healing straight. It needs to be broken and reset."

David whistled soundlessly; his friend was in for a long stretch of heavy weather. "That's unwelcome news. Are you going to do as he recommends?"

"Yes." Richard's face held an expression of calm confidence that David realized he had not had since Waterloo. It was explained when the captain continued, "I can't say that I'm looking forward to it, but Kinlock is the first surgeon to hold out any hope that I might be able to get rid of these damnable crutches someday. Another operation and a few more months on my back are a small price to pay for the chance to live something close to a normal life. Besides, I don't have any better plans for the next few months."

David was shamed at his own lack of perception. Over these last wretched weeks, Richard had always been there with a ready hand, a quip, or undemanding silence as required. Concerned with his own physical state, David had accepted his friend's uncomplaining good nature at face value, never really thinking about the bleak future the captain was facing. Resolving that over the next painful months he would be as good a friend to Richard as Richard had been to him, David said reassuringly, "Based on my experience with the good doctor, your leg will be perfect by the time he gets through with you."

"It needn't be perfect," Dalton said with a trace of a smile. "I'll settle for ninety percent or so." Changing the topic, he said, "What about you? You seem a bit blue-deviled for someone who has just stepped into a fairy tale complete with a miracle and a beautiful princess."

"You always did notice too much, Richard." David laughed shortly. "Fairy tales end with 'happily ever after.' The real world is a good deal more complicated."

"Meaning?"

The major considered a moment, then decided to talk; after all, that's what best friends were for. "Meaning that I find it vastly frustrating to be married to a fairy-tale princess who would like to enlist me as a brother and who is pantingly eager to disengage herself from me as rapidly as possible."

His friend nodded. "I had wondered if you might be falling in love with her; she is a splendid woman."

The major looked at Richard sharply. "What about you? Are you in love with her, too?"

"No." When David looked skeptical, the captain laughed and said, "I realize that shows a lamentable lack of judgment on my part, but while I have enormous esteem for the lady and think the man she loves will be very lucky, she does not inspire me with a desire to lay my heart at her feet."

"From what I have heard about her winter in Spain, you were one of the few single officers who didn't offer for her."

"Probably true." A thoughtful look came into Richard's eyes and he said, "Do you know, that may be why she and I became friends? She seemed to, not exactly despise, but at least not take seriously those who pledged undying passion for her. I actually had more of the lady's company than any of her suitors. Perhaps she dislikes feeling pressured, or perhaps so many men have courted her that she's bored by the process."

"Interesting." David stroked his chin as he thought about the implications of that.

Richard hesitated, then said, "If you remember the wedding toast I made . . . When I said it looked to me as if you belonged together, it was not just rhetoric."

David stared at him. "Good Lord, you have a devious mind! You couldn't possibly have planned this."

"Of course not. You seemed unlikely to survive the week." Richard thought a moment, then clarified. "It just seemed right to bring you together, like one of those battlefield instincts that says when to duck."

"Well, I should have ducked sooner this time." David sighed, running his fingers through his thick hair distractedly. "Lady Jocelyn never bargained for a live husband, and it would be dishonorable to hold her to the marriage. We have already begun proceedings for an annulment."

"Surely that will take a while?"

"Several months."

"That should give you ample time to change her mind."

"Blast it, Richard, look at the disparity in our fortunes! She is rich, I most certainly am not. She's the daughter and niece of an earl, I have no relatives besides Sally I am willing to admit to." The major stared at his friend in exasperation.

The captain refused to be cowed. "Are you going to give up without a fight because of pride? You may not be of equal rank, but you're a gentleman, as the world defines these things."

David snapped back, "She's in love with someone else."

Richard nodded. "She said something about that the first time she came to the hospital. The fact is that the object of her affections has not been interested enough to pursue her. Perhaps she is attracted to him precisely because he refuses to make a cake of himself over her. He may eventually succumb, but it is equally possible she may never bring him up to scratch." He grinned. "While you are available, interested, and based on your past performance, have more than enough address to change her mind. So what are you waiting for?"

David said slowly, "Permission, I suppose. For someone to tell me that it's all right to take advantage of my proximity to try to attach her. But it still seems wrong. She could do so much better than me."

Richard shook his head. "In the worldly sense only."

He absently rubbed his hand along his injured thigh, then added encouragingly, "Lady Jocelyn may be intrigued by someone who hasn't spent his life worrying about the cut of his coat. If you're concerned about being thought a fortune-hunter, no one who knows you would believe such a libel, and who else's opinions count? Would you care if she were penniless?"

"I wish she were!"

"Then give Lady Jocelyn leave to make up her own mind. She is almost twenty-five, intelligent, worldly, and quite capable of sending you packing if she doesn't want you for a husband."

David put his head back and laughed, feeling as if a great weight had been lifted from him. "Thank you for telling me what I wanted to hear. I think I knew that you would, or I would never have raised the subject."

"Good. After all, isn't Lady Jocelyn worth fighting for?"

"That she is." The major's green eyes took on a glint his soldiers would have recognized. "She most certainly is."

# 10

L ady Laura Kirkpatrick stretched luxuriously, then seated herself by the table under her bedroom window. The steaming silver coffeepot shone bright in the sunshine, and she was pleased to see a letter from Jocelyn lying on top of the morning post. As she slit the envelope, she listened to the sounds of her husband washing in the adjoining room and knew that she was smiling like a romantic schoolgirl. Kennington lay just off the Dover-London road, and General Kirkpatrick had arrived very late the night before, no more expecting to find his wife in residence than she had expected him to be free of his military duties so soon. Travel-stained and unshaven though he was, Andrew had wasted no time in joining his wife in her bed for a reunion that made her blush to her toes when she thought of it. Laura scanned the first sheet of jasmine-scented paper, then made an exclamation of pleased surprise.

Andrew Kirkpatrick entered the room, toweling the last moisture from his face. He was a broad, powerful figure in his velvet dressing gown and moved with the vigor of a man much younger than his fifty years. "Good news, love?"

"Wonderful news, Drew. Did you get the letter I wrote you about Jocelyn marrying Major David Lancaster?"

From the startled look on her husband's face, the letter had missed him, and some time was spent in explanations while they drank coffee and ate bread with sweet butter and honey. Having laid the groundwork, Laura finished happily, "Now Jocelyn writes that the major had an operation and will recover fully. I am so glad. David was always one of my favorite officers."

A smile wreathed the general's broad face. "That is

wonderful news. He's a favorite of mine too, and a splendid officer as well. I knew that he had been sent to London, but no one gave him any chance of survival." He sighed, his face shadowed. "A disproportionate number of officers fell at Waterloo. Not that it's any better when common soldiers die, but naturally I have more friends among the officers. So many gone . . ." He forcibly turned his mind to the present; during his thirty years in the army, tragedy had been no stranger.

"So now that your minx of a niece is not going to be a widow, what are her intentions toward Lancaster?"

Laura glanced at the sheet in her hand. "Mm . . . she says that he suggested an annulment, and her lawyer foresees no problems." She sighed. "What a pity. I think he would make a wonderful husband for her. Still, if they think they won't suit, there's no help for it. I suppose I should go back to London to chaperon," she added reluctantly. The idea of staying at Kennington appealed to her more; her husband had several weeks free before he needed to return to London, and a second honeymoon in the country would be delightful.

Andrew snorted. "Why on earth should you have to chaperon a married couple? Besides, if you aren't there, perhaps their acquaintance may progress to the point where they will forget about an annulment."

"Perhaps. But I'm afraid the outrageous way Jocelyn used him may have given the major a disgust of her."

"You think your niece is outrageous? Is this the same Lady Laura Kendal who begged me to carry her off to Gretna Green when her father would not accept my suit?" The general had a devilish gleam in his eye, and Laura could not forebear laughing.

"For heaven's sake," she begged, "don't ever tell Jocelyn that! I have spent years presenting myself as a pattern card of propriety, and she would never let me forget it if she knew how impetuous I had been. Though if my father hadn't relented, it would have been Scotland if I'd had to abduct you myself."

Their eyes caught and held for a moment of intimacy before she continued with more seriousness. "It certainly would be nice if they fell in love with each other. She needs a man who won't try to change her, but won't let her walk over him, either."

"You may take it from me," the general said as he rose and came to stand behind his wife's chair, "that David Lancaster is already in love with her." He wrapped his arms around his wife's waist and started nibbling on her ear, pausing only to say, "The Kendal women are absolutely irresistible to military men, and given another twenty years, Jocelyn might be as beautiful as her aunt. Now, shall we stop talking about your tiresome niece?"

Laura laughed and turned her face up to her husband's. Teasingly, she said, "Tiresome? But you have always been very fond of Jocelyn."

The general accepted his wife's offered lips, murmuring, "I find her distinctly *de trop* at the moment. Now, where did we leave off last night?"

Laura decided that Andrew was quite right: Jocelyn had no need for a chaperon and could be left to her own devices for the next few weeks. Her aunt had better things to do.

Jocelyn felt no need for either chaperonage or company. Major Lancaster was the most delightful of companions; intelligent, amusing, and quite willing to accept her on her own terms. It made her realize what she had missed all these years by being an only child.

If David made a good brother, by extrapolation Sally was her sister and the two women were becoming fast friends. Sally occasionally came by for dinner and military friends of David's often called. They were uniformly polite and admiring, but they neither fawned nor affected the exaggerated air of boredom common to members of the *haut monde*.

Two weeks after his operation Jocelyn judged her husband well enough to go abroad and invited him for a ride in her phaeton. She took a proprietary pride in how healthy he looked; he moved with ease, and while he was still too thin, the look of emaciated fragility had disappeared. He helped her into the phaeton, then watched without anxiety as she sprang her horses down Upper Brook Street.

Jocelyn pulled back a bit when they reached Park Lane, glancing at the major with a quick smile. "Congratulations, David, you have nerves of iron. Most men would be clutching the edge of the carriage and muttering between their teeth about harebrained females."

He laughed. "Anyone who has faced Napoleon's Imperial Guard is inured to lesser hazards. Besides, I had every expectation you would be a good whip; the only surprise is that you don't drive a high-perch phaeton."

"I wanted one, but let Aunt Laura prevail on the point. I feel it is necessary to accede to her wishes occasionally, or she might think that I never listen to her." Jocelyn expertly turned the light carriage south away from Hyde Park.

"Do you listen to her?"

"Oh, always," she assured him. "I listen judiciously, ponder on what she said . . ."

"And then do exactly what you want."

"Nine times out of ten. The tenth time I give in gracefully. I consider it a form of tithing." Jocelyn enjoyed his laughter and the warm look in his eyes as they rested on her. She should have adopted a brother years ago.

It was a sunny August day, and a light breeze blew away the less pleasant scents of the city. They drove for some time and Jocelyn gave the major credit for not demanding to know their destination. They were in the village of Chelsea when she finally pulled the horses up by a livery stable.

"Come, I want to show you my favorite place in the London area."

He helped her alight and they left the horses in the ostler's charge and walked down the street. A faded brass plate set in the tan brick wall read: Hortus Botanicus Societatis Pharmaceuticae Lond. 1686.

The gatekeeper greeted Jocelyn with pleased recognition, and as they walked toward the center of the garden, she explained, "The Chelsea Physic Garden isn't open to the public. It's run by the Worshipful Society of Apothecaries for research into the properties of plants. However, an old friend of my father's is in the Royal Society and he brought us here once. I enjoyed it so much that he secured permission for me to come when I wish."

It was like being in another world, one far removed from London. The garden covered perhaps five acres of land and was full of rare plants from around the world. There was no need to speak and they explored the paths for some time, admiring the two cedars of Lebanon flanking the water gate that opened to the Thames on the other side of the brick wall.

Eventually they settled onto a bench near the center of the garden, within sight of a statue of Sir Hans Sloane, an early benefactor. Jocelyn closed her eyes, inhaling the rich scent of herbs and flowers that blended in a heady perfume. "When I tire of the city I come here to remember the country. This is a working garden. They study plants, trying to understand their properties and how they can serve mankind. The rock garden we passed is said to be the oldest in England. Sir Joseph Banks brought the stones back from Mount Hecla in Iceland."

As David looked down at her lovely face, the long lashes dark against her cheek, he had to fight down an overwhelming urge to take her in his arms. She wouldn't be so relaxed and open if she didn't trust him, and he could destroy that by moving too quickly. It was a delicate balance; he didn't want her to get too used to thinking of him as a brother, but if Richard was right, premature declarations of love might alienate her. He could only hope that there would be a right time and that he would recognize it when it occurred.

On impulse, he reached down and picked a flower with a cluster of tiny blue blossoms. It was some kind of herb, with a tangy scent that reminded him of lavender, and he thought the Physic Garden could spare one from the large clump. He gently tucked the flower behind her ear, admiring the silkiness of her chestnut hair. When her eyes opened with surprise, he said, "Your eyes are that color when you wear blue."

Jocelyn looked at her companion, her heartbeat accelerating strangely. The light brush of David's fingers on her ear had started a tingling that spread in all directions, and she could not imagine why she was reacting so strongly to a casual gesture. She had had no idea that ears possessed such a power of feeling, and as she looked at the major, she vividly remembered the night he had kissed her. The memory of his lips on hers was so intense that she wondered if he could pick it up from her mind, and she could feel a warm flood of color in her face.

She realized that she was leaning slightly toward him, and pulled back abruptly. What on earth was she thinking of? This was her friend, her honorary brother, David, not one of her tiresome suitors and definitely not the man she was in love with, the fascinating and enigmatic Duke of Candover. Apart from a few gallantries when he was ill, the major had shown no signs of being smitten with her; it was one of the things Jocelyn liked about him.

She jumped up nervously. "It's time we were getting back. I tend to forget myself here." When they reached the stable, she said, "Would you care to drive home? I think I am about to have one of my absentminded moods, when I might accidentally drive into Surrey, or the river."

David's green eyes crinkled with amusement. "I can't believe you would do your horses such a disservice, but it would take a stronger man than I to resist the temptation to drive such sweet steppers. Are you sure you trust me not to ruin their mouths?"

She chuckled with a creditable show of casualness. "My faith in your driving skills is equal to yours in mine. And if I am wrong, I will simply snatch the ribbons back."

Her threat was quite unnecessary; as she expected, he was an excellent whip, and she enjoyed watching his light, expert control of the reins. Jocelyn found herself staring at his hands, noticing a thin scar running from the left wrist up to his fingers, remembering how warm and steadying David's touch had been when they had gone through that absurd marriage ceremony. *Till death us do part . . .*

What on earth had gotten into her? Her heart was pounding as if she had been running, and her breathing would not slow down until she fixed her gaze on the sleek sorrel backs of her horses. Candover had chosen them for her; she remembered his teasing comment that he bought them because they matched her hair. She thought of the light that sometimes showed deep in his gray eyes, and felt a wave of longing. "Until September . . ."

It would be at least another month until she would see the duke again and she hoped the summer would pass quickly, before dreaming of him addled her wits. She shook her head sorrowfully. Aunt Elvira was right, Jocelyn was thoroughly shameless. She must be, or she wouldn't be so very aware of the lean strength of the man next to her when she was in love with someone else.

She glanced at David, glad his attention was absorbed with driving. He had a strong profile, but lines of humor were drawn around his mouth and those striking green eyes. In spite of the weeks he had been hospitalized, his face had the weathered tan of a man who had lived outdoors for much of his life. A strong face, remarkably attractive, really . . .

Blast it, she was doing it again. In Candover's absence, Jocelyn's romantic imagination was beginning to focus on David, and if she wasn't careful, she would make some impulsive gesture that would embarrass him. He had been remarkably tolerant of the impetuous action that had landed them in this bumblebroth, but more foolishness on her part might alienate him, and she would be very sorry indeed to lose his friendship. Perhaps she had better not bring him to the Chelsea

Physic Garden again; the place always made her forget herself.

It was a measure of the friendship that had grown between the two women that Sally finally decided to bring her problem to Jocelyn. It was late in the afternoon when she called and her ladyship had just ordered tea in the morning room. She looked up when Sally entered and said, "What wonderful timing. I do hope you will join me for tea. But I'm afraid David isn't here. He's gone to visit Captain Dalton, who just had another operation and is completely immobilized for the next several weeks."

Sally felt tense as she sat down. "I know. Ian Kinlock told me he had broken and reset the leg and the prognosis was promising for Richard." She looked down at her hands and found that she was twisting her gloves nervously. "Actually, I knew that David would be out. It was you I wanted to talk to."

Jocelyn looked at her curiously, busying herself with pouring tea and offering cakes until her visitor was more relaxed. After some minutes had passed in a scintillating discussion of how gray the weather had been for several days, so dismal for mid-August, her ladyship finally said, "Is there something I can help you with? I should be delighted to try."

Sally swallowed hard, the delicious cake in her mouth tasting like sawdust. "I don't suppose you can help, but I don't know who else to ask."

While Jocelyn waited patiently, Sally stared at a large landscape painting as she blurted out, "How does a woman get a man to fall in love with her? I'm sure you've had a great deal of experience in that area, and some advice would be very welcome. Though it might be wasted on me," she added bitterly.

Jocelyn set her delicate Sevres teacup down with a clink. Making a noble effort to contain her astonishment, she said thoughtfully, "I'm not sure if there is any one method. Indeed, I really don't know if many men have fallen in love with me; I think my fortune has been the object of most of the admiration I have received."

Sally still refused to meet her hostess's eye. "I suppose you have had a few fortune-hunters around you, but most of your admirers are genuinely in love with you. Look at David, and Richard Dalton."

"What! Sally, are you feeling well? You can't be sun-touched when the weather has been so gray. Perhaps some out-of-season oysters? I like and admire both your brother and Captain Dalton enormously and hope they feel the same way about me, but no one is in love with anyone."

Sally finally glanced at Jocelyn. "Well, perhaps Richard isn't, though he could be with any encouragement. David is quite besotted with you." Her shoulders sagged. "But if you don't know how you do it, there is no point in asking your advice. Perhaps I had best be going."

David besotted with her? Jocelyn found it an oddly unsettling thought and tabled it for later consideration. Absently she broke off the corner of a cream-filled pastry and offered it to Isis, who had been watching the platter with gimlet eyes. "Sally, please tell me what is the matter. Just talking about it may put your problem in perspective."

Sally appeared on the verge of tears. "If you laugh at me, I shall never forgive you."

Although she was three years Sally's junior, Jocelyn felt much older. "Of course I won't laugh. I gather it is an *affaire de coeur* that isn't prospering?"

Sally looked down at her interlinked fingers. "Exactly. I seem to have fallen quite hopelessly in love with Ian Kinlock. We live near each other and often have dinner at a tavern together, or I'll meet him at St. Bart's sometimes. I've even been to his consulting rooms to help him organize the business end of his practice, which he completely ignores."

She realized her fingers were starting to twist frantically and forced herself to stop. Drawing a deep breath, she continued, "He always appears happy to see me and he seems to enjoy my company, but that is all. I'm not sure he even knows I am a female. If he does, the fact doesn't interest him."

Jocelyn was uncertain what to say, though she could not help but see a certain grim parallel with her own long unrequited passion for the elusive duke. At least he was known to be interested in women and had—finally—shown unmistakable signs of interest in Jocelyn. But would Ian Kinlock ever look up from his work long enough to notice an available female? Doubtfully she said, "I know he is very dedicated to medicine. He might not make a very good husband."

Sally looked up with a crooked smile. "I am aware of his shortcomings. A wife would always come second with him, and I can accept that. I admire his dedication, his selflessness. That kind of passionate caring is unique in my experience. I wouldn't mind being second," she added with a wail, "but I would at least like to be on the list of what is important to him!"

Jocelyn thought of the doctor's muscular body, the startling white hair over the craggy face, the kindness when it was needed, and said tartly, "I hope it is not only his character that you admire. He is really a very attractive man."

"I have noticed," Sally said dryly. Then she chuckled. "If I hadn't, perhaps my admiration would be purely platonic. But it isn't, not at all. What I want to know is how to persuade him to treat me as someone other than a young brother he is fond of."

Jocelyn studied her visitor. Sally was wearing one of her usual dresses, a loose, high-necked, navy gown with not even a ribbon to break up the severeness. Her thick hair was the same rich brown as David's, but it was pulled back into a tight knot from which no curl dared stray. While her features were regular and she had the same wonderful green eyes as her brother, no one would ever mistake her for anything but a governess.

"If you don't want to be treated like a little brother, don't dress like one," she suggested. When Sally bristled, Jocelyn amplified, "Not that I mean to imply you look like a boy. In fact, I have often thought that you might have quite a good figure if you wore a dress with any shape to it. But you seem to be dedicated to looking as respectable and invisible as is humanly possible."

Sally glared at her. "I suppose you think I should cover myself with ribbons and flowers? I would look quite ridiculous. Besides, all that frippery is so, so superficial. A relationship between a man and a woman should be based on respect and mutual affection, not shallow appearances."

Jocelyn firmly told herself not to laugh out loud. "I would not disagree with most of what you are saying. But while affection and respect are the essential foundation, the fact remains that most of life is lived on the surface. For every hour that one discusses ethics or philosophy, there are a good many more spent in dining and driving and the trivia of day-to-day life, and there is no denying that a pleasant appearance adds to one's enjoyment of another person." An image of Candover's handsome, sardonic face appeared in her mind, but curiously it was overlaid with David Lancaster's amused countenance.

Sally said reluctantly, "There might be something to what you say. But can you imagine how foolish I would look rigged out in something like what you are wearing?"

Jocelyn glanced down at her apricot-colored gown with its delicious French lace trim, velvet sash, and appliqué work around the hem. "This may not be just in your style, but there are many other modes available. Tell me," she said as a thought stuck her, "do you dress so plainly because of your principles, or because you are afraid you can't compete?"

She would not have been surprised if Sally had exploded, but her sister-in-law considered the question dispassionately. "Some of both, I think," she finally said. "I do know how to be respectable, and at several posts I held in the past it was a distinct advantage to be

invisible because there were men around who could have
made my life difficult.''

She cast her memory back, casually rubbing Isis' neck
when the cat head-bumped her sympathetically. Sally
reflected on how apt it was that the cat turned out to be
as friendly as her mistress once one got past the aristocratic appearance. ''More than that, after David went
into the army when he was nineteen, it was up to me to
take care of my mother. She was a lovely, sweet lady,
but a dreamer. In fact, a poet. Because I was small, I
tried to look and act older when I was dealing with
tradesmen and the like. Then she died, and I needed to
seek work. I was nineteen, and again it was to my
advantage to look older and more responsible. It is a
habit I developed and saw no need to change, until now.''

Jocelyn was moved by Sally's detached description of
what must have been a hard life of worry and loneliness.
No wonder she was so stern, so protective of her
brother, and no wonder David was so tolerant of her
sometimes sharp tongue. She stood and said, ''I think it
is time you considered a change of style. Come upstairs
and we'll see what is in my closet.''

Sally looked at her in surprise, and with a touch of
anger. ''I didn't come here to beg clothes of you.''

''I know that,'' Jocelyn said, sweeping her sister-in-
law out of the room and up the stairs, ''but I always
adored playing with dolls and haven't had the
opportunity to do so in years.''

Sally had to laugh. As they entered Jocelyn's spacious
suite, her ladyship explained, ''I'm afraid I go through
large quantities of clothes, and my maid Marie is quite
choosy about which of my castoffs she will accept. She
is easily as well dressed as I am, and it costs her next to
nothing. Will you feel better about my frivolity if I tell
you that, pound for pound, I match my wardrobe costs
with contributions to an orphanage? I have other
charities, but this particular one is benefited very
specifically by how much I spend on clothes. It justifies
my extravagance.''

Sally was startled and silenced by Jocelyn's casual explanation. Why had she supposed that her ladyship never noticed anyone outside of the tight little world of the *beau monde*? While she was considering this unexpected aspect of her sister-in-law, Jocelyn rang for her maid.

Marie entered promptly from the next room. She was short, no taller than Sally, but with a more lavishly endowed figure, and as Jocelyn had said, she was very well dressed indeed. The dress might have been altered from one of her mistress's, but it suited the abigail to perfection.

"Marie, we are going to discover what style best suits Miss Lancaster. The hair first, and while you are working on that, consider which of my older dresses would best suit her."

Before she even had time to consider whether she wished to be transformed, Sally was placed in front of the dressing table and Marie was deftly unpinning her bun. It was amusing to see that the maid and mistress discussed her appearance with the ease of equals, and she was gratified when they even consulted their subject about her own preference.

It went without saying that an elaborate coiffure would be unsuitable for the day-to-day life of a governess. Instead, they devised a style where most of Sally's hair was pulled back into a gentle twist that left waves over her ears. With trepidation, Sally also allowed Marie to do some judicious cutting and she soon found herself with a fringe of delicate curls around her face. While it was unexceptionable for a governess, the result was much softer than Sally's usual style, and she was amazed at how much younger and prettier she looked. After some instruction, Sally could achieve the same effect without aid.

By this time getting into the spirit of things, Sally made no objections when Jocelyn and Marie started rooting around in her ladyship's wardrobes. While the ball gowns would be of no immediate use to a governess, a number of the morning and walking dresses were worth considering.

"Let's begin with this one," Jocelyn said, pulling out a simple muslin gown in a shade of dark peach.

"But . . ." Marie started to object that it was brand-new and had never been worn, but she was silenced by a glare from her mistress. The maid hid an inner smile; if Lady Jocelyn wished to give it away, who was her abigail to object? Besides, the color was not one that would have looked good on Marie.

Sally put on the gown and Marie adroitly pinned it at the back and hem to approximate the effect of alterations. All three of the women observed a moment of respectful silence in tribute to the result. Sally's figure had a slim elegance that had heretofore been hidden, and the warm peach tone of the low-necked dress brought out the delicate color of her skin. While she would never be a beauty, she was now a young lady who would draw admiring glances anywhere.

As she stared at her image in the mirror, Sally asked incredulously, "Is that really me?"

"You certainly have been hiding your light most effectively," Jocelyn said with a satisfied smile. "Now, what else would suit you?"

By the end of the afternoon, five more dresses had joined the pile. When Sally had protested at accepting so many valuable gifts, Jocelyn had merely chuckled and said that by the time her sister-in-law had bought new stockings, slippers, and other accessories, she would not think she had received such a honeyfall. Sally did insist on paying Marie for the abigail's alterations and Jocelyn wisely did not object.

While the first of the dresses would not be ready before the next day, Jocelyn insisted Sally accept a cashmere shawl that she could wear to the evening's meeting with Ian Kinlock. It was richly patterned in russet and gold, with a touch of dark blue that made it look good with Sally's navy dress. Sally knew she shouldn't accept the shawl, but she couldn't resist the softness of it under her hand. Marie watched the shawl go with a pang; it would have suited herself to perfection.

The unfortunate and by-now-despised navy dress needed a thorough brushing since Isis had taken up residence on it as she watched the humans with bemusement. As Jocelyn pointed out, the fact that the cat showed such interest in the transformation proved she was a female.

While Marie took the garments away for alteration, Jocelyn helped her sister-in-law to dress. With elaborate casualness, she asked, "By the way, who is Jeannette?"

Sally turned to look at her in surprise. "How did you find out about her?"

"Oh, David mentioned her name when he was out of his head, and I was curious. I thought it best not to ask him since she might be one of the sorts of female men won't talk about."

"No, she was not of the muslin company." Sally laughed as she checked her hair in the mirror. "She is a French Royalist whom David met when he was sent to North America. I really don't know much about her except that she was beautiful and they were thinking about marriage. Then his regiment was pulled back to Belgium for the battle." She twisted a side curl around her finger and checked the effect with satisfaction.

"With so much happening in the last months, I had almost forgotten her existence. I did ask David when he was sent back to London if I should write her." She knit her brow, then finished, "I don't remember his exact words, but he said it was unnecessary. I had the impression someone had already notified her of his wound and expected demise."

"I see. No doubt he has written her himself about his recovery." As Jocelyn brushed the last cat hairs from Sally's dress, she found that her reactions to the news were extremely mixed. So David had plans of his own to marry. That would explain why he had shown no interest in Jocelyn except for that time when he mistook her for Jeannette, and why he was as eager for an annulment as she was. She was glad his affections were engaged—wasn't she?—because she needn't worry about him importuning her.

But why did a man get more attractive as he became more unavailable? How humbling to think one had so much in common with a cow stretching its neck through a gate for better grass.

Before leaving to face the world, Sally took one last glance at herself for courage. Her hair was lovely, improving her looks enormously without looking so different as to appear odd, and over the gorgeous shawl her cheeks glowed pink with excitement.

Jocelyn examined her carefully, then nodded approval. "Perfect. It is really better to do this in two stages rather than hit the good doctor with everything at once. You can wear one of the new dresses next time you meet him." She looked at her sister-in-law seriously. "Remember, fine feathers are only part of what is required. What is more important is to feel that you are attractive, that he *should* want you."

Sally laughed. "So there is a secret to making men fall in love with you, after all, and you have just explained it to me."

"Perhaps I did," Jocelyn said in surprise.

Sally gave Jocelyn a quick hug. "Thank you for everything. Now, wish me luck, and not a word to David unless I am successful!"

# 11

When Sally arrived at Ian's consulting rooms that evening, she saw her hand trembling as she turned the knob. She was not at all sure her improved appearance would attract the notice of someone as high-minded as Dr. Kinlock, but if this didn't work, she had no idea what would.

The front room on the ground floor where patients waited to see the doctor was plain but clean, with a number of wooden chairs around the walls and a battered oak desk at the far end. When Sally had first come here, it had been cluttered and dingy, but she had made arrangements with one of Ian's patients to come and clean regularly. The woman had a number of children and very little money and had been delighted to barter her labor in return for care and medicines for the childish ailments of her brood. Since Ian would have treated them for nothing, Sally thought it reasonable that he received something in return.

Kinlock was talking with his last client of the day, an old woman with knotted arthritic hands. He looked a bit surprised when he saw Sally, then gave her a hard look that was nearly a scowl before returning to instructing the woman on making poultices.

Sally went to the desk at the far end of the room and pulled the account book from the lower drawer where she stored it. Prior to her bringing the ledger in, Ian's accounting system consisted of numbers jotted on scraps of paper that frequently got lost. He treated many of his poor patients for free and Sally knew better than to suggest charging them. However, prosperous merchants and even a few gentry were numbered among his practice and she saw no reason why they should not be reminded to pay their bills.

Sally's current project was entering names, amounts,

and dates from the scraps of paper into the ledger book so that people could be properly invoiced. It was a mixed blessing that Ian had a small independent income from his family; the money kept him solvent, but also permitted him to ignore his business. The man definitely needed a keeper, she decided. The trick was to convince him that she was the best one for the position.

The old woman left a few minutes later, and based on the condition of her clothes and her profuse thanks, she was another one of Ian's charity patients. After seeing her to his front door, the doctor ran one hand through his white hair and sighed. Glancing up, Sally noticed the signs of fatigue with surprise; usually it was St. Bart's that depleted him.

"Was it a particularly difficult day, Ian?" she said, glancing up from the ledger.

"No, not really," he said, crossing the room to sit in one of the wooden chairs, tilting it back and letting his feet rest on the edge of the desk. His look at Sally was searching, and she wondered if she looked any different to him; she had kept the beautiful shawl on to brighten her appearance.

He said abruptly, "I don't know why it has taken me so long to think of this—after all, I was raised as a gentleman, even if I have fallen off from that standard —but it is not at all the thing for you to come here alone."

"Since when has coming to a doctor been scandalous behavior?" Sally said lightly.

"But you aren't here as a patient. You're a young, attractive woman. It could ruin your reputation. What if your employers took exception to your seeing a man without any chaperon? You could lose your position."

"You are sounding positively Gothic," she said. "Besides, the Laucestons are very liberal people and have the radical view that employees are entitled to some privacy. Mrs. Launceston is something of a bluestocking, and her husband is a natural philosopher and essayist. They trust me to do nothing detrimental to the children, and as long as I do my job well, they make no attempt to lock me away from the world." When Ian made no reply, she added, "They were wonderful about David's illness and let me arrange things so that I could spend time with him."

Ian pulled his feet from the desk impatiently, letting the front legs of the chair strike the floor. "Their attitudes are commendable, but the world in general would still think badly of you. I never should have permitted it."

Sally found that she was gripping the pen rather hard. "Do you mean you don't want to see me again? I had thought we were friends." Try as she might to sound calm, there was a slight quaver in her voice. Playing Cinderella was definitely a mixed blessing; she would never have changed her appearance if she had known it might mean exile from Ian's presence. He had never said she was attractive before, just as it had never occurred to him that their behavior was improper.

"We have been friends, and I shall miss you a great deal." His voice was very deep, and the Scots burr was becoming more noticeable, as it always did when he was moved. "But the hospital and the tavern are no place for you. How often have I kept you waiting? Three times out of four?" The question was rhetorical; they both knew the answer. Medical work was unpredictable, and more often than not an emergency or an unexpected number of patients would delay him.

"I'm not sure which is worse, having you wait for me in a tavern or coming here and meeting me privately. Neither is right for a lady."

Ian's blue eyes were troubled and Sally had the horrible feeling that his attack of nobility would take him away from her forever. She blurted out, "There is a time-honored method for a man and woman to be together with complete respectability. It is called marriage." She stopped, utterly aghast at what she had said, and in the silence they both heard the snap of the pen as it broke between her numb fingers.

Ian stared at her incredulously and with a hint of amusement. "Sally, have you just proposed to me?"

She nodded mutely, her green eyes huge and vulnerable. The doctor stood, unable to face the appeal in those eyes. His thoughts were in a turmoil as he crossed to the window and stared into Harley Street, where the oncoming dusk cast long shadows. He should have known something like this would happen. He had known, and hadn't wanted to think of the consequences. It had meant so much to have a friend, a companion, that he had refused to see how much more Sally had become.

"I was married once before," he said abruptly. He could feel the tight pain in his chest. It had been years since Ian had spoken of his marriage, but time had made it no easier.

"Elise and I were childhood playmates. She was the loveliest creature, delicate as a fairy. I had always been interested in medicine, taking care of injured animals, sometimes traveling with the local physician on his rounds. I knew I should study medicine; it was a calling as strong as a priest feels. But it was not the occupation of a gentleman, and Elise deserved better, a husband who would be there, who would live the life of a gentleman. We married after I finished at Cambridge, and we lived in Edinburgh, where I had taken a government post.

"That was fifteen years ago. I was twenty-one, she was twenty. Four months after we married she fell down the stairs. She seemed all right at first, but that afternoon she collapsed. There was a brain hemorrhage. She died twelve hours later."

It was very hard to keep his voice steady. He sensed that Sally was standing behind him, knew the sympathy he would see in her eyes, and he wasn't sure he could bear it.

Without turning from the window he said, "I don't know if any doctor in the world could have saved Elise. Certainly I could do nothing. But I do know that if I hadn't married her, if I had obeyed my instinct and studied medicine, she would never have died. She would have married someone else and been happy. She was born to be happy."

It was becoming dark enough outside to see his own haunted reflection in the window glass, and he turned abruptly away to face Sally's quiet understanding. "So I trained first as a physician, then as a surgeon. I signed on

sailing ships, traveled all over the world, learning and
practicing everywhere. Sometimes I think physicians do
very little good, but there are times when I know I made a
difference. That is what my life has been about. Not
marriage, not money, not ambition as most men know it.''

"And has it also been about loneliness?"

Sally's voice was very gentle as she asked the question,
and she must have seen the answer written on his face.

Nonetheless, he said, "Of course I have been lonely."
He paused, then said very deliberately, "Sometimes there
have been women who have been grateful for what I have
done for them, or for their loved ones, and who have
wanted to express their gratitude in a very personal way.
Most of the time I have refused. As I have said, I was
raised as a gentleman. But other times . . . I am only a
man."

He struggled to control the emotions she had unleashed,
and after a long moment he could say with creditable ease,
"I know you are grateful that I helped your brother. Don't
make the mistake of confusing gratitude with love."

She drew a step closer, looking up at him steadily. She
was so small, almost as small as Elise had been. "Give me
credit for some sense, Ian. Of course I am grateful for
what you did, and I would have cheerfully given you every
penny I had or ever would have to save David. I would
even have given my body if that was what you would have
wanted." She reached up and softly laid her hand on his
arm. "But gratitude alone could never have made me love
you."

Ian pulled sharply away from her, trying to maintain a
scientist's detachment about how his body was reacting to
her touch, but his voice was ragged as he said doggedly,
"I'd make the very devil of a husband, Sally. I become
absorbed in what I'm doing and forget the time, I have no
financial sense whatsoever and will never earn more than a
modest living, I get irritable and bark at everyone around,
and I think about my work sixteen hours a day."

In spite of what he said, she refused to turn her gaze
away. "All of that is not really the point, Ian. I'm
perfectly aware of how important your work is to you and

would never interfere with that. I am not at all fragile, nor am I a schoolroom miss who needs constant attention. Most important, I haven't the least desire to change you. I am simply making a modest proposal: you will continue to be in charge of saving the world, and I will be in charge of saving you.''

He couldn't help laughing even through the ache of emotion. "Sally, you minx, haven't you heard anything I've said?"

"Yes, I've heard it." She stepped within an arm's length of him and raised her eyes to his, challenging him to match her honesty and vulnerability. "The one thing you haven't said is that you don't love me."

Looking down into those clear green eyes, Ian mused as much to himself as to her, "Love is not something I have thought about very often. I do know that when I am with you I am relaxed and happy as I haven't been in more years than I can remember, and that you fill up holes in me that have been empty so long I had forgotten what it felt like not to have them. It would be the greatest of pleasures to come home and know that you would be there, if you're sure you could put up with me."

Almost against his will, he lifted one hand and traced the edge of her face, the smooth skin and the firm jaw, the warm softness of her lips. With the beginning of a smile, he added, "And when I look at you, I think of what a wondrous and beautiful creation the female body is, in a way that has nothing to do with my profession. I hadn't dared put a name to my feelings, but since you will not let me escape with anything less than the truth, I have no choice but to say that I love you."

With a smile that transformed her small face to beauty, Sally said, "Since we seem to be in agreement, why don't we do something about it?"

With a burst of gladness, Ian Kinlock surrendered to his fate, wrapping his arms around Sally in an embrace that nearly lifted her from her feet. For a long, long time they stood in front of the window making a spectacle of themselves for anyone who might be passing by in Harley Street. Dizzily it occurred to Sally that of course one would expect a doctor to kiss with great skill; after all, his knowledge of anatomy was profound.

Finally Ian loosened his hold of her and smiled down reminiscently. "You were so adorable, searching St. Bart's for the mad doctor, finding yourself with that skull in your hand, throwing that gold at me. And brave, the way you helped me with the operation. I kept thinking how lucky your brother was to have earned such loyalty." He sighed. "I just hope to God that you don't live to regret this."

Adorable? Sally thought about that for a moment; it wasn't a word she had ever associated with herself, but she decided she liked it. If he had admired her then, how would he react to the peach dress? She grinned up at him. "I won't regret it. You may think of your work sixteen hours a day, but that still leaves eight hours for me, and I don't expect that you'll be sleeping for all of them."

He burst out laughing, his face boyish under the white hair. "No, I don't suppose I shall." He paused for another long kiss. "I now propose to buy you dinner, then we can go to Cromarty House to break the news to your brother. I have no intention of asking his permission, because if he has any sense at all, he would refuse it."

Slightly breathless from the last kiss, she said, "He'll be glad to have me off his hands before I dwindle to a maiden aunt." She fluttered her lashes. "Shall I draw up a lineage chart for your mother's approval? I am not without respectable connections, and I also have five hundred pounds a year."

"Really?" Ian asked with interest as he opened the door for her. "If you had told me you were a wealthy woman, I would have proposed earlier."

"I proposed to you, remember? And don't worry, by the time I have your office in hand, you'll be making quite a good living. After all, aren't you the finest physician in London?"

On the steps outside the door he stopped and lifted one hand to her cheek. "Not the finest, perhaps," he said, his voice very tender and Scottish. "But certainly the luckiest."

Regardless of who might be watching, Miss Sarah

Lancaster, former prim governess, pulled her fiancé's head down and kissed him with great thoroughness.

Jocelyn and David had lunch in the garden to take advantage of the welcome sunny weather. It was mid-August and summer was drawing to a close; soon the birds would be flying south and the *ton* would be returning to London. They had both agreed it would be foolish to go out socially together; far better not to be queried about their relationship. Though Jocelyn continued to receive invitations, she found herself declining them as she preferred keeping David company to going out alone. For weeks they had been living in an enchanted bubble, untroubled by the normal cares of the world.

It was pleasant in the garden of Cromarty House, where an artful design of paths, flowers, trees, and shrubs made it appear much larger than it was. They lingered in the shade of the belvedere, discussing Sally's news of the night before. Jocelyn had rung for champagne when the happy couple had made their announcement and they had all gotten rather merry. She hadn't believed the intense doctor could be so relaxed and happy, and Sally had looked lovely even in her old navy-blue dress.

"More coffee, David?" Jocelyn poured a cup for each of them, then stirred sugar into her own. "In the excitement last night, I forgot to ask when they intend to get married. Did Sally mention anything to you?"

"Fairly soon, I think. Sally won't leave the Launcestons until they find a satisfactory replacement for her, but apart from that, there is no reason for a long engagement." He blew on the coffee, then swallowed a mouthful. "I can't quite get over how she managed this right under my nose without my noticing, but she always was a determined miss. Kinlock never had a chance once she made up her mind."

"He didn't appear to have any desire to escape the parson's mousetrap." Jocelyn laughed. She felt pleased to have contributed her mite to the romance. Admittedly the peach dress hadn't been needed, but apparently the new hairstyle and shawl had precipitated a happy outcome.

As she sipped her coffee, she saw Mossley coming down the garden path with a tall, serious-faced man who looked like he might be something important in the City. Mossley looked disapproving; there had been too many unusual visitors in the house lately for his taste.

"Excuse me, Lady Jocelyn, but this person claims to have extremely urgent business with Major Lancaster."

"Indeed?" she said, her voice cool. The visitor must be very persuasive to have talked Mossley around.

The man stepped forward and bowed to them both. "I am sorry to disturb you at your lunch, but I have been searching for Major Lancaster for some time." He glanced at David. "You are indeed David Lancaster, born at Westholme in the county of Hereford?"

David stood and looked very hard at the man. "I am. And if you will forgive my rudeness, what business is it of yours?"

The man said, "Permit me to introduce myself. I am James Rowley. You may not remember my name, but the Rowleys have represented the Lancaster family for three generations."

David's voice was so cold that Jocelyn would not have recognized it. "I think I understand. My brothers heard I was near death and sent you to confirm the happy event. You may inform them they are out of luck. My health is now excellent and I have no intention of gratifying them by dying any time soon. May I look forward to being ignored by them for another twenty years?"

"That is not why I am here. May I say how delighted I am to find you recovered"—Rowley paused, then said with heavy emphasis—"Lord Presteyne?"

Jocelyn gasped slightly in shock, unable to miss the implication of Rowley's statement. David's face was absolutely expressionless. After a long moment, he said, "Perhaps you should sit down and explain yourself, Mr. Rowley."

The lawyer stepped into the belvedere and seated himself, leaning his leather portfolio against the chair leg.

"It is quite simple. Your three brothers are all dead without heirs," he said with dry precision. "For the last several weeks you have been the ninth Baron Presteyne.''

David's eyes were still hooded. "All three of those healthy louts met their maker at once? Did someone burn the house down with them in it?''

The lawyer cleared his throat. "Not quite so dramatic. The middle brother, Roger, drowned five years ago. Last month the remaining two brothers, Wilfrid and Timothy, got into a drunken brawl.'' He glanced at Jocelyn, who was listening in fascination. "The cause is unimportant. They decided to duel on the South Lawn to settle the matter immediately. Whatever their defects of character, they were both good marksmen. Timothy was killed outright. Wilfrid lingered for some days before succumbing.''

"Dare one hope that he suffered a great deal?'' David's voice was so bitter and unlike him that Jocelyn was shocked, and she reached under the table to him. He caught and held her hand so tightly that she knew her fingers would be numb, but she made no attempt to pull away. It was obvious from his expression that he was experiencing powerful emotions, and she remembered how he had described his brothers, how they had abused him and Sally and thrown his mother out of her own home.

Rowley sighed. "Lord Presteyne, you have every right to be angry with them. Wilfrid in particular acted abominably. It was most unfortunate your father did not make clearer provisions for his second family, but he was too trusting.

"Be that as it may, they are dead and you are alive. You are now Lord Presteyne, with everything that implies.''

David's voice was a little more relaxed as he said dryly, "From what I remember of Wilfrid, that would imply a large number of debts. Will there be anything left after settling them?''

"The estates are encumbered, but not hopelessly so,'' Rowley admitted. "The trustees, of which I am one, would not let your brother dip as deeply as he would have liked.'' He caught and held David's eye. "I would not go so far as to say I wished for your brothers' deaths, but I cannot regret that you have inherited. I stayed in contact with your mother after she left Westholme, and I followed your army career. You and your sister are cut from very different cloth than your half-brothers."

He hesitated, then said, "Would it make any difference if I told you there was madness in their mother's family? They were more than just disagreeable; I think they were afflicted."

David sighed and released Jocelyn's grasp, then lay his left hand on the table palm down. "I have no trouble believing that." He pulled his left sleeve up slightly. Besides the thin scar that Jocelyn had once noticed on the back of his hand, she saw several other marks parallel to it on the wrist. Pointing to the scars, David said, "Timothy made those with an Italian stiletto he was very proud of. He said he would keep cutting until I would say my mother was a whore. I was six years old."

Jocelyn gasped, seeing her own horror and revulsion reflected in Rowley's face. She swallowed hard and asked, "What happened?"

He smiled without humor. "When I managed to break free of his grip, I attacked him. He was sixteen and about three times my size, so my chances of winning weren't great, but the noise attracted two footmen, who separated us."

"Was he punished?" Jocelyn's voice was hushed.

"Wilfrid told him not to play childish pranks."

Jocelyn felt that she might choke. "Childish pranks . . . !"

"My feeling exactly. Timothy was the most dangerous on a daily level and Wilfrid was the most cold-blooded; he told my mother she must leave on the day of my father's funeral. While Roger was not especially likable, he usually ignored us."

The lawyer shook his head in amazement. "I had no idea it was that bad."

David looked at him with a wry smile. "I'm sorry to have given you nightmares. That is all ancient history, and for obvious reasons not something I dwell on. Mother and

Sally and I were much happier in a cottage than we would have been at Westholme, and I can't complain about my life."

Rowley leaned forward earnestly. "I can understand that you might not wish to return to the scene of so much unpleasantness. Nonetheless, Westholme needs you. The estates are mortgaged and have been neglected, the tenants are demoralized. I am here today not just to tell you of your inheritance, but to urge you to take control of it as soon as possible. It took time to locate you after Waterloo, and the sooner something is done about the estate, the better. If you take over, the other trustees and I will release some money toward immediate improvements."

David stood. "You need have no fears on that head. It was my brothers I hated. Westholme . . . Westholme I have always loved. If you will give me your direction, I will call on you tomorrow to discuss the condition of the properties, but for the moment you have given me quite enough to think on."

Rowley stood and gave a rare smile. "On behalf of the tenants and employees of the Westholme estate, may I congratulate you on your new honors, Lord Presteyne?"

David smiled faintly and offered his hand. "You may."

After shaking hands and nodding to Jocelyn, the lawyer made his way up the garden path. David sat down again, then turned to Jocelyn. "Now you know my guilty secret."

"That all of these years you were 'honorable' but hiding the fact?" she asked teasingly. She laid her hand over his and asked quietly, "How do you feel about this, David? Are you sorry?"

He shook his head. "Stunned, but not sorry. It quite literally never occurred to me that I would ever inherit, not with three older brothers. I guess it disproves the old saying that only the good die young."

"That morning when you were just recovering from the opium withdrawal you said you had been heading toward Hereford. Will you be happy to return there?"

"Yes, I will. In spite of everything, I will."

His face had been remote with thought, but now he turned and said slowly, his green eyes holding hers, "I must go to Westholme as soon as possible to determine what needs to be done."

Jocelyn felt a pang of regret at the thought; she had known this lazy, pleasant summer would not last forever, but she had not thought it would end so soon. But there was no reason for David to stay with her now that he had his own country estate, possibly a town house as well. He certainly didn't need nursing; a few more pounds on his tall frame would not go amiss, but he looked so strong and healthy that it was impossible to remember the skeletal wraith he had been when first they met. Still, she would miss him; he was the best companion she had ever had.

Some of her feelings must have been reflected in her face because he smiled warmly and laid his hand over hers. "Would you like to come with me? Things are very quiet here in town and I would value your opinions on the estate. I imagine you have a great deal more experience with land management than I do."

"Would you really like me to come?" A warning bell went off at the mixed wave of pleasure and trepidation the invitation produced, and a small voice said, You are asking for trouble. She firmly told the small voice, Stubble it! Then she said aloud, "I would love to."

He squeezed her hand, producing a most agreeable spreading warmth, then stood. "I think I will go tell Sally the news. It may be a while before the money is available, but she will eventually have the portion she should have inherited when my father died." He hesitated, then said, "Would you mind terribly if I went to call on Richard myself? I know we had planned to go together, but there are some things I would like to discuss with him privately."

She felt a little hurt by the exclusion. Was she really envious of the fact that Captain Dalton was David's best friend? It was an unworthy thought, quickly suppressed. She rose and gave a sunny smile. "Of course not. Let me get the basket they prepared in the kitchen. I think it is time to supplement the hospital diet again.'' She shook her head. "I do wish he had come here to convalesce from the operation. It would have been no trouble.''

"He had his reasons, I'm sure. I shall see you at dinner.''

David chose to walk rather than take one of the carriages, partly to build his strength but more to give himself time to think about this unexpected new development. Lord Presteyne . . . Who would have ever imagined?

Sally had just finished her day's work at the Launcestons' and they had a long discussion about Rowley's news. She was no more upset to hear of their brothers' demise than David himself had been; in all the world, only the two of them would ever know the whole wretched story of abuse. Their parents had prevented the worst excesses, but were not really aware of the small daily humiliations Sally and David had experienced, and that shared persecution was the basis of their unusual closeness. Someday it might be possible to pity the three older Lancasters, but for the moment neither of the younger ones had any desire to try.

Sally was not averse to receiving the inheritance she was entitled to; already she was thinking in terms of raising a family and building security for old age. She also revealed that Ian Kinlock was the son of a baron himself, so the news that Sally was the sister of Lord Presteyne should be well received by Ian's mother. David thought of pointing out that she had always been the sister of Lord Presteyne but refrained; Wilfrid was not a connection either of them had wished to claim.

Richard Dalton had a drawn look that implied considerable pain, but his greeting was cheerful. His injured leg had been splinted and bound and it would be at least two months before the rebroken bone knit to the point where he could use crutches again. The dismal hospital room benefited by the flowers that Jocelyn sent daily, and there were other small comforts that most patients lacked. But even so, David wished he had overcome his friend's scruples about intruding in Cromarty House.

David found himself unexpectedly tongue-tied when it

came time to break his news. Moving the chair to a spot where Richard could see him without straining, he said hesitantly, "I'm going to be selling out, after all. I've found another situation outside the army. Or perhaps I should say it found me."

"Yes?"

The major brushed his fingers through his hair and said, "I had told you I had three half-brothers that I didn't get on with. What I didn't mention was that my father was Lord Presteyne. This morning I learned that all three brothers have shuffled off this mortal coil." He stopped, then said baldly, "It appears that I am now a baron."

"Good God!" Richard said in blank astonishment. Attempting lightness, he added, "Will you still talk to us commoners?"

David glanced up with a flash of real anger. "Richard, don't *ever* say anything like that again, even in jest."

"I'm sorry," his friend said quietly. "That wasn't particularly funny. I know you would never drop your old friends for such a reason." He studied David's face, then said, "You look like you've been struck by lightning."

"That is how I feel. My whole view of my future has changed." He gave a wry half-smile. "I'm not unhappy about inheriting, but the idea takes some getting used to."

"I can well imagine." Richard laughed. "Thank heavens my father was an itinerant fencing master; being a lord strikes me as a very confining occupation. Better you than me." He studied the major's face and said more seriously, "I assume this eliminates your worries about your station being too far beneath Lady Jocelyn's?"

"It does." David stared down at his linked fingers. "Her rank and fortune are still greater than mine, but not impossibly so. What bothers me now is that she has a passion for land. She might want to stay married to me for my estate."

Richard stared at him. "Do you really believe that?"

David shook his head. "I don't know. Sentimental fool that I am, I'm not sure I would want her to stay for such a reason."

"You are making large bricks with precious little

straw," Richard said robustly. "Lady Jocelyn is as romantic as you are; if she stays with you, it will be for the right reasons."

"I hope so," David said slowly. He realized now that this was the source of his uneasiness about his inheritance. No wonder Jocelyn had despised the fortune-hunters who courted her for her inheritance; the idea that he might keep the wife of his dreams solely because of her land hunger repelled him. He shook the worries from his head; Jocelyn was too loving and honest to go where her heart didn't lead her. He glanced at Richard and said, "She's going to Hereford with me. The next two or three weeks should tell the tale."

The captain smiled encouragingly. "You'll carry the day. You've always been a first-class campaigner."

"I wish I had your confidence." A gleam of determination lit David's eyes. "But if I fail, it won't be for lack of trying."

## 12

Three days later they left for Hereford. Rhys Morgan rode on the box with the driver and acted as guard, an excellent use of his military experience. Though it would be a while before an artificial limb could be fitted, he had already made a place for himself in Jocelyn's stables, working with the harness and horses.

Jocelyn's maid nearly purred when she found that she would be sitting next to Hugh Morgan for two days. Hugh had easily shifted from being the major's nursemaid to his valet; though his skills were still imperfect, his enthusiasm for the situation more than compensated for any shortcomings. All in all, it was a happy expedition. The only discontent was manifested by Isis, who was not invited along for the journey.

They took an indirect route, swinging west into Wales to drop the Morgan brothers off at their family's home. It had been years since Rhys had seen his parents, and he planned on staying with them at least a fortnight. Hugh was to spend a week, then travel to Westholme to join his master.

Jocelyn had never visited Wales before and was delighted by the dramatic scenery. The Morgans' cottage was high above the market town of Abergavenny, on the side of a mountain called Ysgyryd Fawr. Hugh patiently attempted to teach her and Marie the correct pronunciation, with a notable lack of success.

David had watched the language lesson with amusement. When his wife and her maid dissolved in laughter, Hugh murmured something under his breath in Welsh that elicited a response from David in equally fluent Welsh. The valet's eyes nearly bulged and he gasped, "You speak Cymraeg, my lord?"

David laughed and answered in Welsh while a look of horror crossed Hugh's face. "I should have suspected you were Welsh when I found your Christian name was David," the valet murmured with chagrin.

"My mother was Welsh, and I was raised speaking both languages." The major took pity on him and added, "Don't worry, you never said anything that I might take offense to."

Jocelyn watched the byplay with amusement; it was still another unexpected facet of the major. How many more surprises might he have in store for her? Fortunately for her train of thought and Hugh Morgan's peace of mind, the carriage now pulled into the yard in front of his family's cottage.

A scene of happy uproar ensued, with Rhys grabbing his crutches and swinging off the box, Hugh forgetting his manners and diving out of the carriage, and a solidly built woman with apple cheeks rushing out of the house and attempting to hug both her tall sons at once. Within moments there were three younger children and a man who must be their father contributing to the uproar, along with two dogs and several chickens whose main interest lay in escape.

Jocelyn felt a little embarrassed to be witness to such an emotional family reunion; it underlined how different the Welsh were from the English. David helped her from the carriage and she spent some moments admiring a glorious view of the Brecon Beacon mountains to the west and the Usk river valley below. She said musingly, "It must be very hard to leave here. There can be few more beautiful spots in Britain."

David's reply was pragmatic. "Beautiful, yes, but there is little work. All the Celtic lands are poor. Sometimes it seemed that the army was made up of Irishmen, Scots, and Welshmen. Hugh and Rhys probably count themselves lucky to have good jobs now, and I imagine both of them have been sending part of their salaries home for years."

She looked at him apologetically. "I'm afraid that I never think of such things. Sometimes I feel ashamed to have been as lucky as I am."

"There is nothing wrong with enjoying good fortune as long as one is generous to those less fortunate. And from what I have seen, you have been very generous."

There was a warm look in David's eyes as he spoke and she had the uneasy feeling that he might be giving her more credit than she deserved. Luckily Mrs. Morgan came up to them and shyly asked in a musical, Welsh-accented voice if Lord and Lady Presteyne would honor them by taking tea before they departed.

It was a delightful meal, with fresh bread, pickled onions, crumbly cheese, and delicious flat currant cakes that had been fried on the griddle. Jocelyn noticed that Hugh took great care introducing Marie to his mother, and that lady looked the girl up and down very carefully before giving a hug of approval. Rhys was full of laughter, as a young man should be, the silent, depressed soldier of the hospital no more than a memory. The youngest Morgan, a little girl about five, hid shyly behind her mother but peeked at the beautiful highborn lady.

When it came time to leave, the elder Morgans thanked Jocelyn humbly for what she had done for their sons. Once more she was embarrassed. It had been so little from her point of view, and yet they were so grateful. She was well-skilled at being gracious, however, and escaped to the carriage without succumbing to blushes.

As she settled in the carriage, she heard Hugh's voice saying worriedly, "Are you sure you don't want me to accompany you to Hereford, my lord? There are highwaymen in the Black Mountains, they say."

David replied easily, "No need to abandon your family. We've scarcely thirty miles to Westholme, and should arrive before full dark."

"Very well, my lord."

David swung into the carriage by Jocelyn. "I'm going to have to teach him not to say 'my lord' with every breath. I think he is taking my elevation more seriously than I am."

"Well, of course he is!" Jocelyn laughed. "After all, a servant's consequence is dependent on his master's. Isn't that true, Marie?"

The abigail, now sitting alone on the facing seat, nodded vigorously. "*Mais oui*, my lord. You are a credit to us."

David had to laugh. "You never met my brother, or you

would realize that a title alone never made anyone worthy.''

The weather was dry, the road was good, and they made excellent speed on the next stage toward Hereford. They had changed horses for the last time and Jocelyn was drowsing, tired from the two-day journey, when the highwaymen struck.

"Stand and deliver!" The hoarse shout outside was accompanied by shots and the neighing of terrified horses as the carriage shuddered to a stop and nearly tipped over. Marie was thrown across the carriage and David just barely caught her before she could crash into Jocelyn.

The major glanced outside and evaluated the attack with lightning speed. Two horsemen with black scarves tied over their lower faces were waving pistols, and from the sounds he surmised another man was in front of the carriage. The horses were screaming and plunging in their traces, fully occupying the attention of the driver as well as the highwaymen.

David had learned well the lesson that in combat every second counts and he exploded into action. "Get down!" he barked, pushing both Marie and Jocelyn to the floor of the carriage. Drawing his pistol from a pocket in the door, he vaulted over them and out the far door while both the women were still trying to absorb what was happening.

Once out of the carriage, David immediately dropped to the ground and crawled under the rocking vehicle. Ignoring the possibility that a wheel might roll over him, he braced the multishot pepperbox pistol with both hands to steady his aim and calmly put a bullet through the shoulder of the bandit moving toward the carriage door. The man screamed and nearly fell from his horse, his gun flying from his hand. Ignoring him, David shifted his aim, rotated the barrel, and put his second bullet into the next robber.

The second man spun out of his saddle and crashed to the ground when his horse reared and bolted up the road. Rotating the pepperbox once more, the major brought it to bear on the last of the highwaymen. It was a difficult shot because of the angle, but David was spared the

necessity of firing when both of the bandits still mounted
fled up the road after the runaway horse.

Crawling out from under the carriage and jumping
lithely to his feet, the major crossed to the wounded highwayman and knelt beside him, pulling the mask off. The
rough, youngish-looking man was unconscious from his
fall and bleeding from a shoulder wound, but his breathing was strong. As their driver regained control over the
horses, David turned his head to see his wife emerging
from the carriage, her hazel eyes wide with shock and her
dress crumpled from crouching on the floor.

When Jocelyn touched the ground, she clung to the
door for a moment to steady herself while she stared at the
major kneeling by the fallen bandit. In a triumph of
curiosity over good sense, she had watched the whole
brief, bloody encounter through the carriage window. She
had known soldiers all her life, been dandled on her
military uncle's knee, had danced and flirted with officers
and listened to their war stories, but never before had she
seen a soldier in action and she was stunned by David's
swift, precise application of violence. For the first time she
truly realized that her friend of the laughing green eyes and
quiet understanding was a warrior, capable of moving
with the strength and speed of a striking leopard.

She drew a deep breath and walked over to David with a
creditable show of calm. "I had wondered what other
surprises you might hold, Major, but I hadn't anticipated
this one. This whole skirmish must have lasted under
ninety seconds." She swallowed, then said, "No wonder
Wellington defeated Bonaparte."

He laughed and stood up, brushing dust from his dark
blue coat. "Well, the odds were three-to-one. That is what
we often faced on the Peninsula."

Jocelyn stopped two steps away from him, trying to
reconcile his relaxed air with what she had just seen. David
looked no different than he had before, but her perception
had utterly changed. She saw not the casually elegant
gentleman but the sinewy body, the perfectly controlled
strength. It had always been there, and she marveled that
she had never truly seen it.

As she stared at him, David became very still, holding her gaze with one equally intent. Then with one long step he closed the distance between them, lifting her chin lightly and bending his mouth to hers. Though only his hand and lips touched her, the current of energy between them was so powerful that Jocelyn dizzily thought the watching servants could have warmed their hands at it. She had wondered how he would kiss when he was fully conscious. Now she knew, and the knowledge was shattering.

She was intensely aware of the pure masculine power of him, and had never been so aware that she was a woman. Her eyes had closed as he kissed her, but after an eternal moment she opened them again, needing to escape from the frightening intimacy his touch induced. He lifted his head but his eyes still held hers, searching. Jocelyn had no idea which of her tumultous feelings showed in her face, but what he saw made him step back, his eyes once more calm and detached.

As if the kiss had never happened, he asked, "Do you have a handkerchief I could use on his shoulder?" She nodded wordlessly, then went to get one from her reticule. Marie was just emerging from the carriage, her white face a reflection of Jocelyn's own.

When Jocelyn gave David the handkerchief, he folded it into a pad and tied it over the wound with his cravat. "Will he survive?" Jocelyn asked.

"Yes, unless it mortifies. Since he will probably be hanged, it might have been kinder to shoot him in the heart, but I prefer not to kill unless absolutely necessary."

"An admirable philosophy," Jocelyn said faintly.

David looked up at her, his expression for once devoid of all traces of amusement. "Not admirable, perhaps, but the best I have been able to do."

With the help of the driver, David wrestled the bandit's dead weight into the carriage and they resumed their trip. The major had reloaded his pistol and kept a close watch on his prisoner, leaving Jocelyn to ponder what had happened.

Was there any significance to that kiss? She was inclined

to think not. No doubt he would have done the same to Marie if the maid had gotten out of the carriage first. Jocelyn was dimly aware that there was some kind of connection between violence and passion, though she had had little experience of either. After the seige of Badajoz, an Aunt Laura exhausted from nursing had written her a long letter, pouring out ideas and feelings she would ordinarily not have mentioned to an unmarried woman.

Laura had explained that if a city gave in to an attacking army easily, it was usually treated mercifully. But if the attackers had been forced to fight a long and bloody seige, by the barbarous logic of war the city would be sacked when it fell, its buildings looted and burned, its citizens slaughtered and raped. Badajoz had been just such a bloody victory for the British, and Wellington himself had stayed his hand for two days and nights as his men avenged themselves for their losses.

The brush with danger Jocelyn's party had just experienced was a faint echo of the eternal struggle between the threat of death and the passion for life. David had singlehandedly overcome three armed bandits, and in the aftermath he kissed her. Of course he would have no idea how that affected her; for him it was a fleeting masculine impulse, indulged and immediately forgotten. For Jocelyn, it created an intense physical awareness of the man who happened to be her husband. She was burningly conscious of David's shoulder against hers, and she felt herself wanting him in the most ancient and primal of ways. She closed her eyes as if overcome by the attack, and prayed that she would be under control by the time they reached their destination.

When they reached the town of Hereford, David left the two women in a private parlor at the Green Dragon while the horses were changed and the prisoner was turned over to the law. Jocelyn and Marie shared a bracing pot of tea and Jocelyn was tolerably composed by the time David joined them. As he automatically sipped the tea she poured, Jocelyn asked, "What will happen to the highwayman?"

David said, "The Assizes are meeting in Hereford at the moment and he will be brought to trial a week from today."

"How serious is his injury?"

"Based on my all-too-comprehensive experience with bullet wounds, I think he will survive. A surgeon has already been called to remove the bullet." David's voice was businesslike and detached.

"Will we all be called as witnesses to the attack?"

He shook his head. "That shouldn't be necessary. Your driver and I can testify to the events better than you and Marie. Since the man is not known to have a prior record of violence, I will ask the court for clemency. Highway robbery is a capital offense, of course, but because of my exalted rank he will probably be transported instead of hanged."

"I'm glad," Jocelyn said, staring into the dregs of her cup. "No doubt he deserves to die, but I have no desire to see that happen. After all, none of us was injured, thanks to you."

"Exactly." As David stood, she realized he was avoiding her eye as much as she was avoiding his, but his voice was calm as he continued, "It is time we were on our way. I would like to reach Westholme before dark."

"Of course."

The rest of the journey was less stressful, with only a couple of small bloodstains on the opposite seat to remind them of the highwayman. Forty-five minutes beyond the town of Hereford, David was showing unmistakable signs of tension, and Jocelyn asked, "Do you recognize landmarks?"

"Yes, we're almost there. Most of the old estate lies within a loop of the Wye River, though over the years land has been added all around."

As he spoke, the carriage slowed, then turned between a stone pillar and an empty gatehouse. In the fading light, the drive stretched away through a long aisle of thick, gnarled trees.

"What are the trees, David? I don't recognize them."

Without turning from the window, he said, "Spanish

chestnuts, over two hundred years old. This drive is almost half a mile long."

She could see the tightness of his body, and a day earlier she would have laid her hand on his to show her sympathy at what he must be feeling on this return to a long-lost home. Now, she daren't touch him for fear of her reaction.

After the carriage pulled to a halt in the circular drive, David slowly climbed out, his eyes distant with memory. Jocelyn studied the long, rambling brick facade as she went to his side. While the house was sizable and not unattractive, the architecture was unassuming, a product of several centuries of growth. The grounds had suffered considerable neglect, and when she glimpsed a slight movement and turned her head, she saw several ornamental deer that had escaped from the park and were now happily nibbling on the shrubs.

David's face was remote and Jocelyn could only guess at his thoughts. With the lightest of touches on his sleeve, she said, "Shall we go in?"

His mood broken, he smiled at her and they climbed the broad stairs together. David rapped the lion's-head knocker sharply and they could hear the sound echoing inside. While they waited for a response, Jocelyn asked, "Were you expected today?"

"I sent a message, but by the look of the place, Westholme is understaffed."

After several minutes of waiting, the door swung open to reveal a balding man of middle years. Instead of maintaining a butlerly demeanor, his face broke into a wide smile and he said, "Master David! Welcome home." He executed a low bow, then said, "Forgive me, Lord Presteyne, but everyone in the household has been eagerly awaiting your return."

As they stepped into a high, paneled hall, David stared at the man for a moment, then exclaimed, "Stretton, by all that's holy! Are you the butler now?" Turning to Jocelyn, he said, "Remember the fight I told you about with my brother? Stretton was one of the footmen who rescued me."

Glancing at the butler, he added, "It's a pleasure to see a familiar face. I didn't anticipate that anyone would remember me. I'm glad to see you have advanced in the world." He offered his hand, and after a moment's hesitation the butler reached out to shake it firmly. "This is my wife, Lady Jocelyn, and her maid, Marie. I trust rooms have been prepared for all of us?"

Stretton said diffidently, "Yes, my lord, but I'm afraid you will not find things as they should be. Your brother, the late lord, was loath to spend money on the household. Also"—he coughed delicately—"because of the, err, proclivities of Lord Presteyne and Mr. Timothy, it was difficult to get decent young girls to take positions here."

Jocelyn looked around, seeing the dullness of the woodwork and the shabbiness of the furnishings; it was enough to make any self-respecting butler apologetic.

Beside her, David said briskly, "Well, that will change now. Jocelyn, would you like an hour to rest and freshen up before dinner?"

She nodded and they all trailed up the carved stairway. The room Stretton showed her to was as shabby as the rest of the house, but attempts had been made to clean it; she had stayed at inns that were worse. Marie was less charitable, surveying her surroundings with an audible sniff and muttering under her breath in French as she unpacked for her mistress. Jocelyn explored, finding a dressing room with several wardrobes before opening a door in the middle of the wall to discover another bedchamber.

With a blush, she closed the door quickly. David's bags were by the bed, though luckily he was not in the room himself. Of course they would have been given the master and mistress's suite. She thought of checking the door to see if it had a lock, but she told herself firmly not to be such a lackwit; she would be as safe from David here as she had been in her own house. The question was, as she found herself glancing at the door, Would he be safe from her?

An hour's rest served to clear the fatigue and fancies from her mind, and she greeted David with a smile when they met in the small salon outside the family dining room. As they sat down to eat, he said apologetically, "If I had realized what case things were in, I wouldn't have asked you to come with me."

"Oh, surely it is not so bad as all that!" Jocelyn laughed. "This is a palace compared to the house I shared with my aunt and uncle in Fuente Guinaldo."

"That's right. I had forgotten you are a hardened veteran of the Peninsula," he said with amusement.

They applied themselves in silence to the simple but competently cooked meal. As the platters were removed, Jocelyn remarked, "The wines at least are excellent."

"I'm not surprised," David responded dryly. "I imagine the horses will be equally good. Beyond that, who knows what we'll find?"

"Has the house had no mistress since your mother left?"

"Not for some years. My middle brother, Roger, had married, but he lived in London rather than at Westholme. The marriage was childless and his widow has since remarried. Wilfrid had a wife also, but she died in childbirth some six years ago and he couldn't find another female desperate enough to take him." He swirled his glass of burgundy, then shrugged.

"Or perhaps he didn't wish to have a wife trying to curtail his activities. Strange to think that all three of them are gone, with no legitimate heirs. No doubt I will be hearing from some of the other kind."

"I suppose that is one of the many things you will be expected to deal with. Is there enough money to take care of what needs to be done?"

"Rowley says so, though it will take years to return everything to order." He looked up from his wineglass and said softly, "I can't think of a task I would enjoy more." More briskly, he asked, "Would you care to join me in the morning for a ride around the estate? Your experience will be useful."

"Splendid!" Jocelyn leaned forward in her seat with enthusiasm. "Also, shall I hire some housemaids for you? With Wilfrid and Timothy gone there will be no shortage of applicants to work in the great house of the district."

"You're sure you don't mind?" David asked. "It would be a great help."

"I love hiring people and giving orders," Jocelyn said with a chuckle. "Remember, you yourself said I was one of the most managing females you had ever met."

His gaze on her was very warm. "It was rather a compliment, you know."

Her eyes slid away from his and she said randomly, "This is the strangest birthday I have ever had."

"Good Lord, is this the infamous twenty-fifth birthday? Why didn't you tell me?" David demanded. "I knew it must be around this time but I don't recall ever hearing the exact date. August twentieth. I shall have to remember for the future. In the meantime, let us see if the cellars run to champagne. That's a better way to celebrate than with bullets and bandits."

As he gave the order to Stretton, Jocelyn looked at him a little sadly. There was hardly any point in his noting her birthdate when their marriage would soon vanish like the morning mist. Would they see each other in London and nod politely, or perhaps exchange notes once a year?

But when the champagne arrived, she shook off her dark mood and laughed gaily as David proposed absurd toasts to her. Soon she was feeling quite wonderfully relaxed, and they chatted about all manner of things as the level of the bottle diminished.

With the champagne gone, Jocelyn rose and said, "If we are to be riding about all day tomorrow, I'd best retire early. It has been a very long day."

David stood also, and from the warm look in his eye, she wondered if he was about to give her a birthday kiss. She smiled brightly and said, "I shall see you in the morning then," and left the room before he could draw near her.

David watched her depart, then slowly sat down again. His wife was acting as skittishly as he felt. Had it been a mistake to give in to impulse and kiss her earlier in the day? Her response had been as direct and uncomplicated as his own, and he had been shaken at the strength of his own feelings. All the rest of the day he had deliberately kept his distance, afraid he might throw caution to the winds and make love to her.

He toyed with a silver spoon, seeing not the reflections of candles but Jocelyn's face shifting through its moods, from laughter to warmth to the occasional hints of waiflike vulnerability. As an officer, David's special strength had always been in strategy and tactics, analyzing the available data and deciding on the best course.

With Jocelyn, he had the maddening sense that a vital piece of data was missing, and he was reluctant to make a move that might be the wrong one. For all her apparent openness, he sensed uncertainty and fear beneath her sparkling charm, but had no idea what lay at the root of it. Something to do with her unrequited love for the London gallant? Or perhaps it lay deeper. She was so forthright about most things that her few areas of reticence stood out. His mind reviewed their conversations, remembering how she had spoken of her friends, her father, and her aunts and uncles and cousins. She had made only one comment when he asked about her mother. *She went away*. Was there a clue in that?

He sighed, suddenly exhausted by the day's travel and events. It would behoove him to remember that he had been on his deathbed a short month ago. As he snuffed the candles and headed toward his chamber, he knew only one thing was certain: his time was running out to unravel the mystery of Lady Jocelyn.

# 13

Jocelyn awoke early the next morning and went to her window to admire the view. Down toward the Wye River she could see veils of mist, but the sky was clear, perfect for exploring an unknown estate. She lifted the sash and was inhaling the morning air when her maid came in with a cup of hot chocolate. "Good morning, Marie, how is your room in the attic?"

Bad question. Marie gave her a speaking look that said more than a torrent of criticism would have. As Jocelyn sipped the chocolate, she said teasingly, "Cheer up, in a week your Welshman will be here to share your exile from civilization."

"Ha! Where was he when I needed him, when I was attacked by wild bandits?"

"Well," Jocelyn said reasonably, "Lord Presteyne did quite a capable job of protecting all of us. Besides, if it is military prowess you require, surely Rhys would be a better choice?"

Marie sniffed in a manner designed to indicate that reason had nothing to do with it. Loftily she said, "It would be much more romantic to be rescued by my own man than by yours, *n'est-ce pas?*"

Jocelyn choked on her chocolate. "He is not my man."

"He is your husband, is he not? And if you let him go, you will be of a stupidity unparalleled." Marie's brown eyes were regarding her mistress with the expression of a stern nanny.

"That is quite enough from you, mademoiselle!" Jocelyn banged her cup into the saucer, her voice icy. There were times she regretted being on informal terms with her abigail, and this was one of them. "Get out my blue riding habit."

Jocelyn was a little disappointed to have no audience when she swept down the main staircase; the carved banisters might be in dire need of beeswax and elbow grease, but the stairs were admirably designed for grand entrances. When she reached the bottom, she examined her surroundings, seeing them clearly in the bright morning light. A great deal would have to be done in the way of cleaning and polishing, and carpet and draperies needed replacing. However, the proportions were good and every window in the house seemed to face a beautiful prospect. Her eyes gleamed as she studied the room. Yes, the house had possibilities, definite possibilities.

Before she could get into serious mental list-making, David came in from outside. Whatever odd mood had been on him the day before was gone and his smile held its usual teasing charm. "Good morning, Jocelyn. That is a particularly dashing habit. Surely modeled on the uniform of the Tenth Royal Hussars?"

"But of course." She laughed. "So much gold braid was irresistible!"

"Would it be *lèse-majesté* to say that it looks better on you than it does on Prinny?"

"Not *lèse-majesté*, my lord—treason! However, I shan't report you," she said magnanimously, sweeping by him as he held the door open for her.

As David had predicted, the stables were well-stocked and maintained, much more so than the house, and they had no trouble finding suitable mounts for their expedition. Though David had been only twelve when he left, he remembered a great deal about the estate and found that the principal products had not changed. Westholme was agriculturally mixed, with hops, cider apples, and a variety of livestock that included sheep, pigs, and a herd of the white-faced beef cattle that were named for the county of Hereford. David frowned at the sight of the cattle; the stock had been allowed to deteriorate in both quality and quantity, and Jocelyn could see his mind tallying and analyzing what needed to be done. He asked her opinion often and listened to it with flattering interest.

When noon came, they were some distance from the house and David suggested they picnic on the hill that was the highest point of the estate, with a glorious view across the Wye valley.

"I should have known a seasoned trooper would come equipped with provisions," Jocelyn said admiringly as he reached up to help her dismount. His hands on her waist were disturbingly warm and she stepped away from him as soon as her feet were on the ground. "Such a beautiful, peaceful place," she said, pretending it was the scenery that lured her away from his touch.

"Yes, it is. In spring, this orchard we're in is a paradise of blossoms; in the summer, it produces the apples that made the cider in this jug; and in the autumn, it will be bright with mistletoe berries. Our lunch is entirely local," David said as he unpacked his saddlebag. "It seemed appropriate. The cheese and ham are from the estate, the bread was fresh-baked this morning, even the onions were grown and pickled here."

They spread the food on a linen cloth beneath one of the trees and indulged themselves with country appetites.

"Utterly perfect," Jocelyn sighed after she had finished her meal. "To be riding the land, eating the food grown here—nothing could be more satisfying. My father always said the strength of England was that we are country folk at heart, not like the French aristocrats who lived at court and lost touch with their roots."

"Don't limit it to England; say, rather, the strength of the British," David suggested as he finished the last of the cheese.

"I'm sorry," she said with an apologetic glance. "With true English arrogance, I'm afraid I tend to overlook the other peoples of Britain."

"If you had grown up here, you wouldn't," David said lazily, leaning against the trunk of a tree. "These are the Welsh Marches, the border zones that the English Marcher lords held against the wild raiding Celts. It is only a few miles to Wales and this country was fought over for centuries."

"I keep forgetting that you are half-Welsh. Was your mother from near here?"

"She was from Caerphilly and her father was a mere

schoolmaster. He and my father had a scholarly correspondence for years. They shared a passion for classifying wildflowers. My parents met when my father was near Caerphilly and wanted to show his coenthusiast a new species of wild orchid.''

David chuckled. "The orchid turned out to have already been classified, so my father collected my mother instead. He was quite unworldly, and perfectly happy to fall in love with someone beneath his station. His sons, however, were less accepting. They despised my mother for her birth and 'inferior' Welsh blood. Their mother was the grand-daughter of a duke, as I heard many times.''

Jocelyn was glad there was no bitterness in his voice; there had been none after that first day when Rowley had sprung the news of David's inheritance. Lazily she asked, "Do you feel more Welsh or English?"

He considered that as he took a pull of cider from the stone jug. Finally he said, "On the outside, certainly English, a product of where I grew up and how I was educated. But on the inside . . ." His green eyes crinkled with amusement. "The Jesuits say that if they have a boy until he is seven years old, he is theirs for life. Most of us have mothers, not Jesuits, so by that measure I'm a fey Welshman under the facade of an English officer and gentleman.''

Jocelyn turned her face away, unexpectedly jolted by what he had said. *If that is true, what did my mother make me?* But then, she had not had seven years of her mother. She counted the distant green and gold squares of late-summer fields, using that simple task to push down her unwelcome thoughts. She had gotten very good at burying such things, and it was only a few long moments before she was able to turn back and ask teasingly, "Does that mean you are addicted to daffodils and leeks?"

"Of course! All the people of Cymru are. In the spring, Westholme seems covered with a blanket of daffodils. Sally and I helped my mother plant the bulbs when we were children.''

Jocelyn asked softly, "How does it feel to be back?"

He was silent for so long that she wondered if he had

heard the question. Finally, he said, "There is no other place on earth that would feel as much like home."

"You are very lucky." Her voice very low.

"I'm sorry," he said gently. "I know that you feel the same way about Charlton. But there can't be a happy ending for you, as there has been for me."

She made herself smile, though there was a prickling of tears under her eyelids. He saw too much. "It is the way of the world for women to be taken from their homes and have to establish new ones. Someday I will find another home."

"This one could be yours."

His green eyes were holding hers with an expression she couldn't read. Was he proposing that they combine her fortune and his land permanently, and each of them give up the love they had for someone else? The thought made her throat ache and she broke her gaze away from his. She could feel the presence of the Duke of Candover as sharply as if he had sat down between them to share their picnic. "The price would be too high."

"I see."

He said nothing else, simply stood and started packing the remnants of their meal. They rode back to the house in silence, without the easy camaraderie of the morning. At the stables David excused himself to spend the afternoon with his agent, and Jocelyn watched him go with the frustrating blend of emotions that was becoming constant in her. What if there had been no Jeannette, no Candover? Would they have been content to explore the bounds of their marriage, to see if it was worth keeping? She shook her head. She had no idea—simply no idea at all.

In spite of odd moments of tension between Jocelyn and David, the next five days passed quickly and pleasantly. He spent much of his time with his agent but still rode with Jocelyn every day, introducing her to the tenant farmers on one occasion. She felt odd when they bowed and called her "Lady Presteyne"; she didn't think of herself by that name. She also wondered how David would explain the wife that never came again. Or would he simply marry his

Jeannette and defy anyone to ask him what had happened to the first Lady Presteyne, the English one?

Restructuring the household kept Jocelyn fully occupied and she found Stretton a capable and enthusiastic ally. Within three days they had tripled the number of inside servants and it seemed impossible to enter a room without finding a housemaid busily scrubbing away. The attics produced some rather nice furniture and gorgeous Oriental carpets that had been rolled and put away for some incomprehensible reason. Jocelyn was in her glory; a complete transformation would take years, but already the house looked loved and lived in, and every evening David complimented her on her progress.

On the fourth day Hugh Morgan arrived; from the satisfied look on Marie's face, it was her presence that had caused him to cut his holiday short by three days.

On the fifth day, Jocelyn was just finishing her morning strategy session with the butler when that gentleman cleared his throat in the way that meant he wished to raise a different, possibly questionable, topic.

"Yes, Stretton?"

"It occurs to me, Lady Presteyne, being newlyweds and all, you might not realize that tomorrow is his lordship's birthday."

"Why, the wretch never mentioned it, and he chastised *me* for not telling him about *my* birthday! August twenty-sixth, then?" She stopped a moment, then said, "I am ashamed to admit it, but I am not even sure how old he is." At Stretton's odd look, she said defensively, "It never seemed important."

"Yes, my lady. He will be thirty-two."

"Well, we shall certainly have to do something special for dinner tomorrow night. I trust there is some of that excellent champagne left?"

"Easily enough for the next twenty years, my lady. The late lord had his own priorities."

"Obviously," Jocelyn said dryly. She was thinking about the menu when Stretton cleared his throat again. "Yes?"

"There is something that might be appropriate for

tomorrow," the butler said. "If you wouldn't mind descending to the kitchens . . . ?"

He led Jocelyn deep into the servants' quarters, ending in the butler's own sitting room. He stood aside as she entered, then gestured at a medium-sized painting on the wall. It showed an austerely handsome man in late middle age, a much younger woman, and two children about two and six years old. As she studied the portrait, she realized that all of them except the man had eyes of the same bright, clear green.

"David's family!" she said in surprise. "But how did it come to be here?"

"When the old lord died, Master Wilfrid told me to take the painting and burn it. It didn't seem right to me, my lady, so I put it in one of the kitchen storerooms, knowing the young lord would never come into the servants' quarters. When I eventually rose to be butler, I moved it in here."

They looked like a happy family. David's father had a scholarly mien, a man who might not be too attentive to daily life. His mother was a small, serene woman with dark hair and rosy cheeks like Mrs. Morgan's; it must be a Welsh face. Even at the age of two, Sally had an air of stubborn determination about her, while David looked absolutely adorable. Would a son of his have that same look of good-natured mischief?

She drew a deep breath. "It was very good of you to save this, Stretton. It will mean a great deal to Lord Presteyne." She glanced curiously at the butler. "Why on earth didn't you leave? Wilfrid sounds absolutely dreadful."

"He was, but this is my home. Strettons have always served Lancasters." His voice was unmistakably ironic when he added, "It is quite unnecessary that we should like them."

"You seem to like David."

"Who would not? He was always quite unlike his brothers. Very protective he was of his sister. Neither of them had a trace of snobbery. His mother's influence, of course. The stories I could tell you . . ." He shook his head reminiscently.

Jocelyn decided it would be poor policy to encourage Stretton in his reminiscences, fascinating though they sounded. She said briskly, "If you will have this brought upstairs, I will decide where to hang it."

After much thought, Jocelyn decided the painting would look best in the small salon that adjoined the dining room, and she arranged with Stretton to hang it during dinner the next night. Until then, the butler was to keep it hidden away.

The next afternoon's post brought a letter from Aunt Elvira, the earl's frank scrawled across the corner. Jocelyn wrinkled her nose when she picked it up, then dropped the letter back on her desk without reading it, unwilling to investigate her aunt's latest exercise in malice. For the last weeks she had been ignoring all threats to her peace of mind, and she preferred to continue that way, at least until after David's birthday. She wanted to make the day special for him, and she took extra pains dressing for dinner, donning a gold-colored satin dress with a standing frill collar, very low décolletage, and black piping.

Jocelyn nodded with approval as she checked her appearance in the long mirror. She had decided against her formal jewelry and wore only a simple gold filigree heart on a black velvet ribbon around her neck. Marie had dressed her hair in a cluster of chestnut ringlets, and Jocelyn knew she looked her best even before seeing the admiration in David's eyes when she joined him in the small salon.

"You are looking particularly lovely tonight, Jocelyn," he said with a smile that warmed his eyes. "Is it a special occasion?"

"It is indeed, my mysterious friend. After chastising me for not telling you of my birthday, you neglected to tell me that today is yours."

"Good Lord, so it is," he said as he escorted her into the dining room and held her chair out. "To be honest, I

had overlooked it myself. It has been years since I have
taken any special note of adding another year to my dish. I
suppose Stretton told you?''

"Of course. Old family retainers always know everything. You are the center of this particular world, and if I
had had more time, I would have organized a feast so all
your tenants could have celebrated your birthday with
you. You know the sort of thing—a roast ox, barrels of
ale, games.''

He eyed her with misgiving. "I'm glad you didn't. It is
going to take a little time to become accustomed to playing
the role of lord of the manor.''

Jocelyn smiled and raised her glass to him. "It is a task
you will accomplish to perfection, Lord Presteyne.''

He raised his glass in reply. "I hope so, Lady
Presteyne.''

The leisurely meal was more elaborate than usual, with
two removes and a variety of wines. By the time they had
finished eating and consumed a bottle of champagne, the
evening was well-advanced and Jocelyn felt as bubbly as
the wine. As she studied how the candlelight defined the
planes of David's face, she wondered at what point he had
become so handsome. He had been painfully thin when
she had first met him, the tan skin almost transparent over
the high cheekbones. Now he was a man in the fullness of
his strength, radiating a quiet control and virility that were
nearly irresistible. Her gaze lingered on his well-cut mouth,
remembering the taste of his lips, then lifted to find him
watching her as intently as she did him.

Jocelyn realized that she had lost track of their discussion and that she was drifting into a state of dangerous
dreams. She stood, making an effort to appear natural and
relaxed rather than like a woman running from her desires.
"I hadn't realized how late it was, but I see it is after ten. It
has been a long day. Suddenly I'm so tired I can scarcely
keep up a conversation.''

"It is late," he agreed. "I have to go into Hereford early
tomorrow for the highwayman's trial. Sweet dreams,
Jocelyn.'' David stood, his eyes hooded in shadow as she
left the room, but he made no move to follow her. Instead,

he slowly sank back into the chair as he tried to understand his wife's contradictory signals. He sensed doubt and confusion under her sweet laughter and beckoning eyes. While it was possible she might welcome an advance on his part, his instinct still said, Wait. After all, he wanted to win her not for a night, but a lifetime.

With a sigh, the major rang for brandy. Though he would have to rise early the next morning, he knew from the experience of the last week how difficult it would be to sleep knowing Jocelyn lay on the other side of an unlocked door. It promised to be another long night.

Upstairs, a yawning Marie undressed her mistress, brushed out her hair, and put her to bed in the usual fashion, but Jocelyn tossed and turned, unable to sleep. A full moon poured its silver light in the window and she felt intolerably restless, her mind and body alive with longings. She considered pulling the draperies in the hope that dark would still her unrest so she could sleep. She was deeply aware of her body, of the sheer softness of the thin muslin nightdress against her skin, the light weight of a sheet holding her to the width of the bed.

The moon was only the symptom, a primitive goddess of femininity that her body cried out to worship. She was acutely aware that she was a woman, and that for too long she had held herself apart from men. Was it because she was looking for the perfect man, or because of her fears, fears she could not even name? She finally slipped out of bed and walked to the window, seeing the silver face of the moon smiling benignly down on the earth. From deep in the house she heard a clock striking and counted twelve strokes. Midnight, the witching hour.

She remembered suddenly that she hadn't shown David the family portrait. He hadn't come up to bed yet or she would have heard him through the door that connected their chambers. On an impulse she refused to identify, Jocelyn tied a blue silk wrapper over her nightdress and left the room, picking up a three-branched candelabrum in the hall to light her way down the stairs. Fantastic shadows accompanied her through the silent house, adding to her sense of unreality.

David still sat where she'd left him, his cravat loosened and his tailored coat thrown casually over a chair in the warm August night. His hair was tousled as if he had been running his hands through it, and a half-filled glass of brandy sat in front of him. His distant gaze focused in surprise as she entered the room. "Jocelyn, is there something wrong?"

She shook her head, feeling the weight of her hair heavy over her shoulders. "Not really. I wasn't able to sleep, and then I remembered something I forgot to show you. It is a present to you from Stretton, or perhaps from the house."

Jocelyn led the way next door to the small salon. Stretton had not failed her and the painting of David's family now hung above the fireplace. Wordlessly she lifted the candelabrum high and waited for David's reaction. He stepped forward, then stood stock-still and examined the picture, his eyes moving from figure to figure. When he finally spoke, his voice was husky. "I had no idea this painting still existed. I would have thought Wilfrid or Timothy had destroyed it."

"Wilfrid wanted to, but Stretton hid it away." Jocelyn glanced at the painting, then said, "It's a beautiful portrait. Was your family happy then?"

David turned to face her, his eyes green even in the candlelight. "Yes, particularly when the older boys were away. My father took more pleasure in his second family than his first. I don't think he ever knew the malice his older sons were capable of." He glanced at the portrait again. "Or perhaps he didn't wish to know. He was a kind man, but not a strong one."

"Did your strength come from your mother?"

"It must have. She was able to build a new life for her children, and I never knew her to feel self-pity for what she had lost. Perhaps she was happy not to be the lady of the manor anymore." He paused, then said, "Did you know that this is where the picture used to hang?"

"Why, no. It just seemed a good place." Her words were automatic while the rest of her attention was fastened on David. Their eyes locked and she could not have turned away for all the treasures of Araby. She asked softly, "Why were you sitting alone so long?"

"I was thinking of you." The deep tones of his voice seemed to reach out and caress her. "How beautiful you are, how very difficult it is to be so close without touching you."

She drew a step closer, her breasts almost brushing him, her head tilted back to hold his gaze. "Why won't you touch me?"

He stood absolutely still, making no attempt to either withdraw or reach out to her. "I promised you your freedom, and the promise binds me."

"We have signed the papers for the annulment and we will both have our freedom. But what of now? Who will know or care what happens between us?"

"I care. And I hope that you would." David tried to keep his voice calm, but he could feel the tension vibrating in his body. She was so close that he could feel the warmth radiating from her, see her vulnerability and yearning.

"I know that I want you to hold me." Her voice was husky with longing. David wasn't sure whether it was instinct or treacherous desire that whispered to him, *Now.* He made one last attempt, not knowing if he would have the will to leave her if she changed her mind.

"Are you sure?"

"As sure as one can be in this imperfect world."

David's hand was steady as he took the candelabrum from her hand and placed it on the mantel, but all vestiges of control vanished as he embraced Jocelyn, his mouth crushing down on hers. He had kissed her twice before with skill and passion, but this was much, much more. She could feel his heart pounding against her breasts, the shape of his buttons pressing into her body as he held her close against him. There was passion beyond anything she had ever experienced, but at the heart was a gentleness and caring that made her want to weep with gratitude.

The intensity of feeling both had been suppressing exploded into a hunger that would not be satisfied with mere kisses. David lifted her into his arms and carried her from the room and up the stairs as if she were no heavier than a child. She kept her hands tight around his neck, loath to loosen her grip for even the moment necessary to turn the knob to her room. The door swung shut and latched as he laid her on the bed in moonlight so bright she could see the expression in his eyes before he lay down beside her, his warm hands and lips exploring the mysteries of her body.

The moonlight seemed to bring a madness. Jocelyn should have felt shy as he slipped off her robe and gown, exposing to his view what no man had ever seen before, but it was right for this night, and she reached out to help him remove his own garments, admiring the play of muscles in the bright cool light, glorying in the textures of smooth skin and lightly tickling hair. There was no time, only sensation, and the sharp moment of discomfort Jocelyn felt when they joined was washed away by a certainty beyond words: this was the closeness she had yearned for, the archetypal fusion of male and female that was the ancient ritual of the night.

She wished the morning would never come. For these few hours, her mind was beyond questions and she felt no doubts as David held her in his arms, his own feelings too profound for words. They dozed together, then made love again after the moon had set. This time Jocelyn discovered her own capacity for passion, an experience both sublime and disturbing.

And finally, her head cradled on David's shoulder, Jocelyn slept with the utter relaxation of a child.

## 14

It was very early when David woke, the room still shadowy in the half-light. Outside, the birds sang their dawn chorus and he felt an absurd desire to join them from his own sense of joy. Jocelyn lay curled under his arm, looking more like a girl of seventeen than a worldly lady of twenty-five.

He kissed her lightly on the forehead and she turned against him without wakening. She looked delectable with her chestnut hair spread around her, but also curiously vulnerable, and he resisted the temptation to waken her. For all the magic of the night just past, David suspected that by daylight Jocelyn might feel a certain awkwardness, and perhaps it was fortunate that he had to go to Hereford for the Assizes. While he held no brief for highwaymen, he had seen too much of death to stand by and let a man be executed needlessly. And his absence would give Jocelyn time to adjust to the change in their relationship, perhaps to start planning for their life together.

He slipped quietly out of the bed, tenderly pulling the covers up around her shoulders and brushing her hair from her face. She was still sleeping soundly, so he restricted himself to the lightest of kisses before leaving for his own room, impatient for the day to pass so he could see her again.

Jocelyn awoke slowly, her body a combination of delicious languor and unexpected soreness. Her cheek was tender, as if it had been scraped by something bristly, and as she absently touched it, a flood of memory returned. Of course, David's face against hers, his soft words in her ear . . . She reached out a bit apprehensively but discovered she was alone in the bed. Pushing herself upright, she pulled the covers around herself with a modesty she hadn't felt the night before.

The pillow still showed the impression of David's head and on it lay a red rose, its stem wrapped with a note. The flower had been plucked at the perfect moment, the petals slightly opened, a few droplets of dew lying jewel-like against the deep-crimson surface. She hesitated before picking it up, afraid that somehow the message it contained would change things irrevocably.

Red for passion . . . She inhaled the delicate scent, then unwrapped the note. "Jocelyn, To my infinite regret, I must go to Hereford for the Assizes and will not see you until evening. I love you. David."

Jocelyn stared at the note, then found herself dissolving with a grief as devastating as it was inexplicable. Paroxysms of sobs shaking her body, she buried her face in her hands, the rose clenched in her right fist. She had no idea why she cried and in the depths of her misery there was no room for understanding.

Her tears were exhausted by the time Marie entered with her morning chocolate. The maid said cheerily, "Good morning, my lady. It is another fine day." Then she stopped as she saw her mistress's tearstained face. "Lady Jocelyn! What is wrong?" She set the tray down on a table and wordlessly lifted the blue silk wrapper from the floor, draping it around Jocelyn's bare shoulders as she struggled upright in the bed.

Jocelyn shook her head, realizing dumbly that bright drops of blood were dripping from her right hand where thorns had pierced it. As she stared at the spreading stains, Jocelyn found her voice, saying huskily, "We must leave this morning to return to London."

"But . . . Lord Presteyne will be in Hereford all day."

"He will not be coming with us. Draw a bath for me and tell the coachman to get my carriage ready. The packing shouldn't take long. I want to leave by mid-morning."

Marie stepped forward, concern written on her face. "My lady, are you sure? If there has been some quarrel, would it not be better to wait and discuss it with his lordship?'' The maid's astute eye had easily interpreted the dishevelment of the room. There was some mystery here; it seemed unlikely either that the major would have turned bestial or that Lady Jocelyn would succumb to vapors at the routine loss of her maidenhood.

"Do as I say.'' Jocelyn's voice was devoid of feeling, but something in it made Marie cease arguing and leave to inform the coachman of their upcoming journey.

Jocelyn slowly stood, tying the wrapper around her waist and carrying the chocolate to her desk, where she sat down and sipped it. The hot drink brought a little life to her and she tried to understand why David's note had triggered such a drastic, incomprehensible reaction in her. Was it guilt that he should have fallen in love with her when she could not return his feelings because she was in love with another man? At the moment, she had no idea what love meant or if she knew how to love anyone. Was she ashamed of her own wanton behavior? She had felt no shame last night. . . .

When a new bout of tears threatened, she gave up her attempt at analysis and resolutely started to gather her belongings from the desk. There would be time enough to think on the two-day coach trip. As she cleared the desk, she found the letter from Aunt Elvira that had arrived the day before. She stared at it for a moment, decided it couldn't possibly make her feel any worse, and slit it open to draw out the single sheet. Her aunt's florid script said:

> My dear niece,
>
> Investigation has proved that you never met Major David Lancaster in Spain and that your "long-standing attachment" consisted of a cynical marriage of convenience. My lawyer has also discovered that you have filed for an annulment. Neither of these things is what your dear father had in mind for his only daughter, and I am assured that

a court will take an exceedingly dim view of
your attempt to circumvent the conditions of
your father's last will and testament. While I
have no doubt that we could win a lawsuit, it
would grieve us to have to go to such
unpleasant lengths. Also, I am confident
that you have no desire to disgrace your
family as your mother did.

Therefore, Willoughby and I are prepared
to divide the Kendal fortune, with you
receiving twenty percent and the balance
reverting to my husband, who should by
rights have inherited in the first place. You
will be left very comfortably situated, so I
am confident you will see the justice and
generosity of our proposal. However, should
you refuse this compromise, I fear that we
shall have no choice but to file suit against
you.

I shall expect your response by the first of
September.

Elvira Kendal, Countess of Cromarty

Jocelyn felt a cleansing burst of rage after she read
the letter. Obviously Elvira knew she had no case and
hoped to intimidate Jocelyn into signing away most of
her inheritance. Jocelyn's lawyer had confirmed
David's opinion that her father's will stipulated only
marriage, with no conditions attached. Given the
grounds for the annulment that had been filed, any
lawsuit against her would be doomed to failure.

"Do you want to fight, then? We'll see who has the
most to lose!" Elvira had her brood of children to
establish and they would be injured by scandal far more
than Jocelyn; she doubted her aunt would risk their
futures by bringing a lawsuit she had so little chance of
winning. Crumpling the note in her hand, Jocelyn flung
it across the room in disgust. A pity there was no fire in
the grate at this time of year.

Her brief flare of anger faded, leaving behind the

greatest desolation she had ever known. She did not know if she grieved more for David or for herself; she knew only that she must leave as soon as possible. The entrance of two chambermaids with coppers of hot water encouraged her to push herself upright, and soon Jocelyn was soaking away her aches. Marie returned and started packing and within the hour they were ready to leave. Jocelyn took a last survey of the room. She had been here such a short time—scarcely a week—yet it had begun to feel like home.

Her musings were interrupted by Marie. "Lady Jocelyn, about Hugh Morgan."

"Yes?" Her mistress's voice was remote, but the maid persisted.

"Does he work for you or for Lord Presteyne?"

"Oh. I hadn't thought of that." It was careless of Jocelyn not to have considered. She had been paying Morgan's salary, but he was now David's personal servant. "Ask him to come here."

Marie bustled out of the room, returning in a few moments with her sweetheart. Jocelyn had just finished composing a note to David when the Welshman approached her. She looked up and said, "Since you have been acting as valet to Lord Presteyne, it seems appropriate that you continue with him. If, however, he wishes to dismiss you because of your past association with me, you may return to my household. The same is true for your brother, Rhys."

She handed Morgan a small purse. "I assume that Rhys would find the stables here more interesting than mine. However, I leave the decision on your futures to you and Lord Presteyne. This should cover the fare to London if one or both of you prefer my employment."

Hugh looked down at the purse, then glanced back at Jocelyn with a confused expression on his face. He blurted, "Lady Jocelyn, has his lordship hurt you in some way? If he has . . ."

He looked so protective on her behalf that Jocelyn had to swallow a lump in her throat before she could reply. "On the contrary, it is I who have injured him."

She pushed her chair back and stood, continuing, "Lord Presteyne has been very pleased with your work and I am sure he will wish to retain your services. Please accept my best wishes for your future." She nodded stiffly, then walked from the room, leaving Marie and Hugh to stare after her.

The Welshman opened his arms to give the maid a hug. "What's happened, lass? Her ladyship looks like someone has walked on her grave."

Marie shook her head distractedly. "I don't know. You know how they've been smelling of April and May, then this morning she was crying fit to break your heart." She considered telling Hugh that the lord and lady finally had a real marriage but could not bear to expose Jocelyn's vulnerability and confusion.

"If I know Lord Presteyne, he'll be coming after her as soon as he gets home." He kissed her fiercely. "And even if he doesn't, I'll be coming for you."

"Please, Hugh, let me stay with you now," Marie begged, the tears bright in her eyes.

"Nay, lass, you saw her face. For the moment Lady Jocelyn needs you." He kissed her again, loath to let the girl free to follow her mistress. "But just remember, I need you more. I'll come for you as soon as I can."

With a last look over her shoulder, Marie took her mistress's jewel case and went downstairs to the waiting carriage.

It was late afternoon when David returned home, impatiently pushing the front door open without waiting for one of his servants. As he entered the hall, Stretton approached and the major asked, "Where is Lady Jocelyn? I presume she wouldn't be riding at this hour."

Stretton's face was grave as he replied, "Her ladyship left for London this morning, my lord."

The news hit with the force of a physical blow. David had hardly been able to concentrate on the business of the day for thinking of Jocelyn, her warmth and openness, the magical closeness they had shared. And now . . . "Did she leave any message for me?" he asked flatly.

"Yes, my lord." The butler handed him a sealed note. He ripped it open and read: "David—I'm sorry. I never meant to hurt you. It is best we not see each other again." It was signed simply with a "J." He reread the note twice, trying to make sense of it, then pushed past the butler to climb the stairs.

It was incomprehensible that she was gone, but her chamber showed no trace of its recent occupant. The elegant clutter of perfumes and brushes was gone from the dressing table, leaving only a lingering scent of jasmine. He touched the crisply made bed, as if to find some warmth left from the night before, but there was no remnant of the joy they had shared—the joy he thought they had shared.

He moved through the room numbly, but the only sign of her passing was a crumpled ball of paper in the cold fireplace. Automatically he picked it up, wondering if it might be a preliminary good-bye note that would say more than the one she had left with Stretton.

David almost threw it away when he saw that it was not in her hand, but when he glanced down, he started reading and couldn't stop. A sick knot formed in the pit of his stomach and spread through his body, and only the most ferocious act of will enabled him to maintain a cool detachment.

He had wanted a reason why Jocelyn had left and now he had one. It seemed obvious that her apparent passion had stemmed from her desire to lose her virginity. Last night, had she not mentioned the depositions they had already signed for the annulment? Perhaps she wanted it both ways: she would present her aunt with a doctor's warranty that she was not a virgin so the countess would give up the idea of the lawsuit. While her aunt had no real chance of winning, it was understandable that Jocelyn would prefer to avoid the notoriety of a court case. Meanwhile, the annulment would proceed based on the papers already filed.

Another possibility, not contradicting the first: Hugh Morgan had once mentioned that the Duke of Candover had been a regular caller and the staff had thought Jocelyn was in love with him. David had made a point of learning what he could of the man, and it seemed likely the duke was the sort of aristocrat who preferred his mistresses to be women of experience, with willing flesh and no missishness. Perhaps Jocelyn had decided the duke might not want a virgin mistress, even a virgin who was in some sense married. Who better to relieve her of an unwanted maidenhead than a convenient, easily persuaded temporary husband? He had certainly been happy to cooperate.

David's cold-blooded analysis made sense, but was quite impossible to reconcile with his image of Jocelyn, her generosity, her honesty, her bubbling humor. Had she thought he would be content to make love to her for the moment's pleasure, with no emotions involved? That would explain her apology.

"I never meant to hurt you." He had thought there was warmth and vulnerability beneath her highly polished exterior, but perhaps he was wrong; perhaps she was no more than the heartless social butterfly others had accused her of being. She had grown up in a different world than his, where lords and ladies behaved in ways incomprehensible to common people.

It was an irony he didn't appreciate: traditionally men were blamed for using and abandoning women, while in this case the reverse appeared to be true. Perhaps Jocelyn had not dreamed how his feelings were engaged and was distressed by his foolish, romantic assumption that she must care for him. Would matters have been different if he had spoken sooner?

David was no longer sure if his thoughts were logical. The only incontestable facts were her note saying they shouldn't see each other again, and the letter from her aunt that turned an act of love into a handful of ashes. He was staring blindly out the window when his valet entered the room and said hesitantly, "My lord, I wanted to talk to you about Lady Jocelyn."

"There isn't very much to talk about," David said with brittle precision. "I have apparently offended the lady and she has decided it is time to return to London. The annulment will be final soon." He swallowed before adding, "It was kind of her to come and help organize the household here."

Hugh refused to drop the subject. "Marie said she was distraught this morning. When I asked her ladyship if you had wronged her, she said that on the contrary, *she* had injured *you*." He flushed under David's level gaze and said defensively, "I meant no disloyalty to you, my lord, but she will always have my first allegiance for what she did for my brother."

"Quite proper of you," David murmured, his attention lost in his own internal struggle between English logic and Welsh emotions. His intuition had warned that Jocelyn had hidden depths very different from her bright, confident exterior, and invisible scars might cause her inexplicable behavior. That same intuition believed in her warmth and capacity to love, and it had never misled him about anything important in his life. His chaotic thoughts were interrupted by Hugh's determined voice.

"Marie says Lady Jocelyn is in love with you. Everyone in the house could see it."

Morgan's words broke David's paralysis and he realized he must have been mad to consider abiding by Jocelyn's brief, senseless note. The only way he would let her go was if she would look him in the eye and swear she didn't love him.

He strode to the door and said, "Throw a few of my things in a bag. I'm leaving for London immediately."

"I'm coming, too, Lord Presteyne." As David paused, Hugh said, "I promised Marie I would come for her as soon as I could."

David looked at the valet and smiled faintly. "Then I guess we'll have to bring both of them back, won't we?"

Throughout the long, fast journey, Jocelyn mercilessly examined her past relationships in an attempt to comprehend her shattering grief at David's declaration of love. She thought of the many men who had claimed to love her, and the handful that she herself had cared seriously about, and how the two categories had been entirely separate until David had insinuated himself into her life with his kindness and laughter.

By the time she reached London, Jocelyn was exhausted by the thoughts that had jolted around her head in rhythm with the pounding hooves of the horses. While she had not yet achieved full understanding, the facts were forming a pattern too clear to deny. One bitter conclusion was unavoidable: the pain of the present was rooted in the unbearable past that she had always refused to acknowledge, and the time had come to face that past, no matter what it cost her. Tonight she would sleep in London, and tomorrow she would continue to Kent to find Lady Laura, the only person who could give her the answers.

When Jocelyn entered the majestic foyer of her home, she examined its familiar grandeur. Familiar, yes, but so incredibly empty. What was one lone woman doing with so much space? Marie walked past with her mistress's jewel case, but Jocelyn felt unequal to the two flights of stairs and walked into the salon, wearily stripping off her gloves before she rang for coffee.

She was sipping the coffee and waiting for it to invigorate her when the door opened and Lady Laura stepped in, fashionably dressed in a teal-blue evening gown. "Jocelyn, I just heard that you had returned. Is David with you?"

Jocelyn shook her head tiredly, then stood and went to her aunt for a long, silent hug, ignoring the fact that she was crumpling her aunt's finery. Stepping back, she said, "I am so glad you are here. I was going to travel down to Kennington tomorrow to talk to you. Is Uncle Andrew in London also?"

"Yes, he had business at the Horse Guards. We are to meet later at a dinner party." Lady Laura eyed her niece narrowly. The girl looked at the end of her emotional tether, with no trace of the frivolous Lady Jocelyn who had floated and charmed her way through half a dozen London Seasons.

"Do you have time to talk before you go out?" Jocelyn tried to sound casual, but her aunt didn't miss the bleak note in her voice. Choosing a seat, Lady Laura said, "Of course. It won't matter if I am late at the Matsons'; they always sit down to dinner late. What do you wish to discuss?"

Laura expected her niece to pour out a tale of confused feelings for Major Lancaster; it was a shock when the girl looked her straight in the eye and said, "Tell me about my mother."

Her aunt was silent for a long moment before saying, "I have often wondered why you never showed any curiosity about her before. Why do you ask now?"

"I don't know why. I just know I need to understand. What kind of person was she? Why did my father divorce her?"

When Laura still hesitated, Jocelyn asked bluntly, "Was she really a whore, like they say?"

"My dear girl, who ever told you that?" her aunt said in an appalled voice.

"Any number of people," Jocelyn said harshly. "Servants called her that when she left. So did girls at that exclusive seminary in Bath Father sent me to, the one I ran away from. And the noble lord who tried seducing me at his own daughter's come-out ball because he assumed I was no better than I should be."

"Oh, Jocelyn, why did you never tell me?" Laura's eyes were huge and sorrowing, and she felt deeply guilty. "You always seemed so carefree. You were only four when your mother left, and you had spent most of your time with nurses. We thought you didn't miss her, didn't even know that anything was wrong." She should have guessed what her niece would be exposed to, but Laura had been newly married herself, involved with her own concerns.

"Your mother was no harlot. Clea was a beautiful, headstrong woman. She and your father had a whirlwind courtship and married within weeks of their meeting. When the first flames of passion burned out, they found they really had very little in common. In fact, they were both so strong-willed they made each other miserable." She shook her head sorrowfully. "They could have gone their separate ways, like so many members of the *ton*, but each wanted the other to be the perfect lover and they could not accept each other as they were. The fights were extraordinary. They fought in public, they fought in private. There was some kind of love at the bottom of it, but it came out as anger and hatred. You don't remember any of this?"

Jocelyn shook her head. "I'm not sure. A little, perhaps." A memory ripped through her mind, her father's voice shouting, *You're a whore, and if you ever come back here I will kill you with my own hands.* She gasped, then said in a choked voice, "Yes, I do remember some. What happened?"

Laura's own voice tightened. "They began to do their utmost to hurt each other. Your father started keeping one of the most beautiful Cyprians in London and brought her to one of Clea's balls in this very house. I was there, and it was a wonder she didn't kill him on the spot with one of his own pistols. Instead, she openly left the ball with Baron Rothenburg, a Prussian diplomat who had been pursuing her.

"Clea and Rothenburg began an affair that gave your father an abundance of evidence for a divorce. She never returned to this house after that night—your father refused her admittance. He and Rothenburg fought a duel. Neither was killed outright, but Rothenburg took a bullet in the lungs that contributed to his death just five years later."

Laura looked at her niece earnestly and said, "You mustn't blame your mother for the divorce. It was just as much your father's fault. I always loved them both. Clea was so lovely and gay. You are like her in many ways. It was just something between Clea and Edward that made it impossible for them to either love each other in a way that would make them happy, or to let each other go.

"Clea really did come to love Rothenburg, you know. He would have married her, but he was a Catholic and his family would not countenance a divorced woman. Did anyone ever tell you how your mother died?" When Jocelyn shook her head mutely, Laura said, "It was the day after Rothenburg's funeral. She took his stallion out riding and tried to jump a gully that was too wide. Both she and the horse were killed." She closed her eyes with remembered pain, then opened them to say quietly, "Please don't think too ill of her, Jocelyn. She might not have loved wisely, but she loved with all her heart."

"If she was so wonderful, then what was wrong with me?" Jocelyn's voice was a raw cry of agony. "What was so horribly wrong with me, that my own mother could leave me without a single word, without any remorse or regret?" She was shaking with anguish as her aunt came to her side and embraced her, rocking her as if she were an infant.

"Oh, Jocelyn, my dear girl, is that what you have believed all these years? Why didn't you ever ask me? I could have told you the truth." Laura held her niece closely, feeling some of the girl's own pain as she relived her own memories of that ghastly time.

When Jocelyn's sobs had diminished, Laura continued, "Your mother loved you and tried everything she could to take you with her. She even went to Charlton once to see you when she thought Edward was away, and he threatened her with a horsewhip. He said he'd kill her if she ever tried to come near you again.

"She tried to convince Edward that since you could not inherit the title, you should be with your mother, but he refused to let you go or to let Clea contact you in any way. In a divorce, a woman has no rights at all and there was nothing she could do. Your father had you guarded until Clea's death."

Jocelyn's breath was still ragged, but Laura could sense her listening. "I stayed in correspondence with

Clea until she died, sending her drawings you made, telling her how you grew, what you were doing." She stopped a moment, then said, "She wanted to know if you ever talked about her, but you never said a word. I could not bear to add to her unhappiness, so I lied and said that you remembered her and asked after her."

"I thought of her all the time, but I was afraid to ask," Jocelyn whispered.

Laura stroked the girl's head gently. "Why were you afraid?"

"I think . . . I was afraid that if I ever asked about her, Father would send me away, too."

"Oh, my dear, if only you had talked to me or to your father." Laura felt tears in her own eyes as she continued, "He loved you more than anyone else in his life. One reason he never remarried was to have more time and attention for you. He and I discussed you often, wondering how you felt about the divorce. There was such a terrible scandal. I avoided fashionable parties for years because I hated the gossip and whispering. It was a relief to follow the drum with Andrew. Eventually new scandals came along, and by the time you had grown up it was ancient history. Neither your father nor I ever dreamed how you felt, or that you were the victim of such taunts and insults."

She hesitated, then asked cautiously, "Do you know about Mrs. Michaels?" Jocelyn nodded; there had been no shortage of people anxious to tell her about her father's long-time mistress. Elvira had said once, "She isn't even pretty, my dear. One has to wonder about your dear father's taste."

"After your father met Anne Michaels, much of his bitterness toward Clea subsided. Since you never asked about your mother and seemed perfectly happy, he decided it would be better for you if he never raised the subject of the divorce. He was grateful because he thought you had escaped unscathed." Laura sighed. Perhaps it was as well her brother never knew what scars had been left on his beloved daughter; he would have been unable to forgive himself.

"Edward and Anne Michaels found genuine happiness with each other, but he had no wish to remarry and she had an estranged husband living in the colonies. Your father left her well provided for. I believe she is living in Italy now."

"And you think my mother really loved me?"

Jocelyn's voice was that of a despairing child, and it hurt Laura to the heart. She lifted her niece away from her and looked into the swollen hazel eyes as she replied, "I know that she did. I received a letter Clea wrote just before her death, and she said her greatest regret was that she had lost you and would never see you grown up. She sent you a gift, but I never gave it to you because the time didn't seem right."

She stood and helped Jocelyn up. "The time has come."

Laura led her niece upstairs to her own bedchamber. Opening her jewelry box, she took out a flat, oval-shaped cloisonné box about three inches long and handed it to Jocelyn. It was a portrait case, and an exquisitely lovely one.

Jocelyn held it in her hands for a few moments, then pressed the catch on the side. It opened easily to reveal the miniature of a golden-haired woman of striking beauty but with a suggestion of sadness in her eyes. On the opposite side was a piece of parchment with delicate script saying, "To my daughter Jocelyn, with all my love."

Jocelyn stared at her mother's face as memories flooded back to her. Her mother playing with her in the garden, lifting her onto her own horse, dressing her in her own satins and laces, casually unconcerned when Jocelyn accidentally ruined a new bonnet. Jocelyn had suppressed all the good memories along with the unbearable pain, but now she could remember, and the tears she shed were healing.

Laura put her arms around her and let her cry. When her tears had finally stilled, she asked, "Do you understand now?" When Jocelyn nodded, she continued, "Do you want me to stay with you this evening? I can easily forgo the Matsons' party."

"No, thank you, Aunt Laura." Jocelyn's voice was low but calm. "I'd rather be alone this evening. I have a great deal of thinking to do. Thank you for explaining. Perhaps now I can sort out the muddle I've made of my affairs."

"Are you in love with David Lancaster?"

"I don't know. I don't think I understand love at all."

Laura gave her a hug and sighed, "Oh, my dear. Love is not for understanding—it just *is*."

"I shall try to remember that." She glanced at her aunt and smiled faintly. "I'm afraid you will have to change your gown. The one you are wearing has not been improved by my weeping all over it."

"No matter," Laura said as she rang for her maid. "A small price to pay for having cleared the air after too many years. You are sure you will be all right tonight?"

"Quite sure." She kissed her aunt's cheek shyly. "I always thought of you as my real mother. Now, I have two."

"Thank you, my dear. That means a great deal to me. I always wanted a daughter, but I could not have loved one of my own more than you."

Tears threatened them both for a moment, but Lady Laura's abigail entered before emotion gained the upper hand. As Jocelyn left the room, she was beginning to understand how the past was influencing her present.

# 15

Jocelyn was up very late that night, sitting in her window seat with Isis purring sympathetically in her lap. As she had told Laura, she didn't understand love at all. She had thought she loved the Duke of Candover, and just the memory of his face caused a tingle of excitement. Was that love, or the kind of hollow passion that had drawn her parents into their doomed marriage?

David Lancaster called up more complex feelings. She had married him at random, laughed with him, come to think of him as a trustworthy friend, and in a tangle of emotions she had taken him as her lover. She didn't know if that was love, but the thought of not having him in her life produced a wrenching sense of loss. Would he follow her to London, or had she already destroyed what was between them? Questions . . . By the time she retired to restless slumber, her mind was numb with wondering.

She awoke the next morning to an unnatural calm and joined her aunt and uncle for breakfast. General Kirkpatrick looked at her sharply before leaving for the day, but he asked no tactless questions about his former staff officer. Jocelyn was grateful; she would have been quite incapable of carefree chat about David.

Lady Laura invited her niece to join her for a morning at the *modiste*, but Jocelyn refused, unready to deal with the normal trivia of existence. Instead, she went to her room and started writing an account of how she felt about her aunt's revelations in the obscure hope she would achieve a better understanding.

Late in the morning she stopped to sip a cup of tea. If David came to London after her, he could be here by evening. And if he did come, how could she see him? What could she possibly say? That perhaps she loved him but she really didn't know for sure? He deserved better than that.

As Jocelyn sighed and flexed her cramped fingers, a footman entered with a card on a silver tray. She picked it up and felt a shiver as she read the name: "Rafael Whitbourne, Duke of Candover." The man who had filled her fantasies for three long years, a man she might be in love with. At the very least, a piece of unfinished business. Today was only August 29, so he had returned to London early. "Until September . . ."

Well, she had wanted answers, and here was an opportunity to get some. She stood and glanced at herself dispassionately in the mirror. Marie had done her job well, Lady Jocelyn Kendal was her usual elegant self. She tried smiling. Not entirely convincing, but reasonable. Then she sallied forth to greet her visitor.

The duke was leaning casually against the mantel in the salon, disdaining the comfort of a chair. He was darkly handsome as always, and his cool gray eyes openly admired Jocelyn as she entered.

"Good morning, your grace. This is an unexpected pleasure."

He bowed, then said, "I was called back to London by business and saw that your knocker was up as I drove by. To find you like this was more than I had hoped for."

He strolled across the room with lazy grace to stand within an arm's length of Jocelyn, saying softly, "A marriage of convenience sounds confoundedly dull. Though it is not yet September, dare I hope you are ready"—he lifted her hand and kissed it lingeringly— "for diversion?"

Jocelyn felt a confused thrill at his touch and realized that part of his attraction was the faint aura of danger that surrounded him. Life would never be dull around such a man, but was that what she wanted of love? She smiled with all the charm she could muster. "The subject is open for discussion, your grace."

"I think you should call me Rafe. I much prefer that to Rafael. Naming me after an archangel was singularly inappropriate, don't you agree?"

There was a sparkle of amusement in his gray eyes, and Jocelyn smiled back in response. *This would all be much easier if he wasn't so attractive!* Rafe Whitbourne had been fascinating women since he was in leading strings, and Jocelyn doubted there was a female alive who would be impervious to his charm.

The duke lifted her chin to study her face, saying softly, "You are the most exquisite creature, Jocelyn. I have been admiring you since your first Season, hoping you would marry and then, perhaps, seek a wider field of activity."

She gave him a searching glance, trying to penetrate that lazy, well-bred charm. "Do you think that is all marriage can be, Rafe, a posting stop on the way to other pleasures?"

His eyes were thoughtful as he answered. "That has been my observation. What else could it possibly be?"

He brought his lips down to hers and began to kiss her with all of his considerable skill. Jocelyn found herself experiencing his embrace with a curious duality: as her body responded to his touch and his closeness, it was quite clear how he came by his reputation as a magnificent lover.

But that was a superficial reaction that paled next to an explosion of understanding that resolved all her questions. Her feelings for the duke were a frail, rootless thing next to the tempest David had aroused in her.

She knew now why David's declaration of love had terrified her. More important, she knew why Aunt Laura said that love was not for understanding, it simply was. The wonder was that it had taken her so long to recognize an emotion that was now revealed with such overpowering strength. She was about to step back from Rafe's embrace when the door to the salon swung open.

David Lancaster and Hugh Morgan had traveled hard through most of the moonlit night, reaching London hours faster than normal post-chaise speed. They went directly to Cromarty House, David bounding up the steps two at a time. Mossley himself let them in, his face mirroring his surprise. As Hugh went upstairs to find Marie, David asked the butler, "Where is Lady Jocelyn?"

"She's in the salon. But she has company . . ."

David brushed past Mossley, the last words still in his ears when he opened the door to the salon and found his lady wife passionately entwined in the arms of a man who could only be the Duke of Candover.

He stopped frozen just inside the door, gripped by a murderous rage that surpassed anything he had ever known in battle. So the instinct that had guided him with Jocelyn was no more than a treacherous illusion, compounded of his hopes and dreams. The summer over and her unwanted virginity gone, Jocelyn had flown back to London, back to her lover. His fists clenching, David scanned the duke's imperturbable face. No doubt Candover had much experience of angry husbands.

David had thought the situation could not be worse, but he was wrong. Jocelyn cried out, "David!" as she turned toward him, her face shining with happiness, as if she had been longing for his arrival, not halfway into bed with another man. Or had she moved from virgin to *ménage à trois* in two short days?

She moved toward him quickly, her beautiful face glowing, hands lifting with welcome. "How did you get here so soon? I would not have thought you could be in London before tonight." Then she stopped abruptly, alerted by his expression.

As always, she looked honest and innocent, and David's stomach twisted with the sick knowledge that he had never known her at all. She was indeed the fashionable lady, the perfect hostess even under these circumstances. He couldn't speak at first. The only words he could find were furious denunciations. After an endless moment, he managed to say tightly, "It's obvious my arrival is both unexpected and unwelcome." His eyes raked her, then went to the duke.

"I presume this is Candover? Or are you spreading your favors more widely?"

As Jocelyn gasped in shock, the duke nodded at the intruder, saying coolly, "Servant, sir. You have the advantage of me."

Lawyerly detachment came to David's aid. Jocelyn had never pretended to want him for a real husband, and he had no just claim on her behavior. He had promised she would have her freedom, and their mockery of a marriage carried no license to be rude to her under her own roof. She had done a great deal for him, and if she was incapable of giving love, that was his loss, not her crime.

David's furious green eyes met Candover's cool gray ones and he nearly succumbed to the temptation to take the man apart, preferably with his bare hands. For all the duke's athletic build, there wasn't a Corinthian in London David couldn't best in his present mood; a fashionable sportsman was no match for a trained man of war. He damned himself for his unwanted sense of fairness; violence would relieve some of his angry pain. But appealing though the idea was, he had no right to murder Candover—the duke was there by Jocelyn's choice.

When he spoke next, David's voice was perfectly polite and of a hardness that would cut glass. "I am Presteyne, passingly the husband of this lady here." He glanced at Jocelyn. "My apologies for injecting my presence where it is so clearly unwanted. It will take only a few moments to remove those of my belongings that are still here. Then I will disturb you no more."

He turned and was gone, the door slamming behind him with a force that rattled the windows. Jocelyn's knees weakened under her and she sank onto a chair, her hands pressed against her breast. She had been so happy in her new understanding that she had not even considered how compromising her circumstances were . . . not until she had seen the look of furious revulsion on David's face. If she lived to be a hundred, she would never forget his expression, that combination of anger and raw, betrayed pain.

From that first meeting in the hospital, David had opened himself up to her with complete generosity, always giving her kindness and understanding, teasing and comforting her about his imminent death. He had even committed near perjury about a humiliatingly intimate matter to give her an annulment. And how had she repaid him? When he had declared himself and was most vulnerable, she had spurned him, running away without any real explanation; and when he put aside pride to follow her, he had found her passionately embracing someone of greater rank and fortune.

Jocelyn stared at the door where he had disappeared, knowing that the paralyzed numbness she felt was a tissue-thin shield against a sea of pain. He would never believe she loved him now, and it was the ultimate irony that in the moment she discovered the love she had always dreamed of, she had destroyed her chance of ever sharing it with her husband.

The duke's presence was forgotten until he drawled, "Do you know, Lady Jocelyn, from the look on your husband's face, he does not share your belief that your marriage is one of convenience."

She raised her eyes to him mutely. After a probing glance, he continued, "If you will forgive a personal observation, you don't look precisely casual yourself. Just what kind of deep game are you playing? I can tell you right now he's the wrong man to manipulate with jealousy. He may leave you or he may wring your neck, but he won't play that kind of lover's game."

His voice hardening, the duke added, "Nor do I enjoy being a pawn. I might have to kill your husband in a duel, which I would not like. Having seen him, I must admit there is a strong possibility that he might kill me, which I should like even less." As he looked at Jocelyn's blanched face, he said more gently, "Nor does playing games seem your style. Just what exactly is afoot?"

With an effort, Jocelyn pulled her disordered senses together to speak. "A great deal of stupidity and confusion is afoot, all of it mine. I have been trying to understand my heart, and I have done so too late."

The duke said firmly, "If you are the romantic I take you for, go after him. You won't get what you want from me, I promise you. I gave my heart away many years ago to someone who dropped and broke it, so I have none left to give.

"On the other hand, if you throw your charming self at your husband's feet with abject apologies, I have every faith in your ability to bring him around your finger, at least this once."

As Jocelyn stared in astonishment, he said dryly, "A man will forgive the woman he loves a great deal. I would not, however, recommend that you ever let him find you in anyone else's arms. I doubt he would forgive you a second time."

Jocelyn felt a bubble of near-hysterical laughter in her throat. "Your sangfroid is legendary, but even so, the reports did you less than justice. If the devil himself walked in, you'd ask him if he played whist."

"Never play whist with the devil, my dear. He cheats." The duke picked up his hat from a chair, then paused to lift Jocelyn's hand and lightly kiss it. "Should your husband resist your blandishments, feel free to contact me if you wish to resume our . . . discussion. However, I shall not expect it." He held her hand for a moment, then said softly, "You remind me of a woman I once knew, but not enough. Never enough."

Then he was gone. Jocelyn spared one regret that a man so worthy of love had cut himself off from it. Then she raced out into the hall, running up the stairs at a speed she hadn't achieved since she was twelve years old.

She burst into the Blue Room without knocking to find her husband packing his few remaining possessions into a portmanteau. She gasped, breathless from two long flights of stairs, "Please, David, give me a chance to explain. That was not what it looked like."

He raised a sardonic eyebrow. "Oh? Are you trying to say you weren't wrapped passionately in Candover's arms? I hadn't realized my eyesight was so poor."

Before today, Jocelyn had never seen him angry.

There had been kindness, intelligence, humor, and heart-melting tenderness, but never this icy, terrifying rage. She drew her breath in, then said calmly, "Yes, I let him kiss me. I wanted to understand my feelings for him, and it seemed the quickest way to find out." She moved a step closer to him, her voice pleading. "Please, David, don't go. I don't want an annulment, I want to be your wife."

"Oh? Have you decided that a nominal husband will give you the freedom to cast your net wider than just the duke?" He slammed down the lid of the portmanteau. "I regret to inform you that my values are shockingly bourgeois. I have no desire for a wife with fashionable morals. If you want a husband for propriety's sake, you can buy yourself a more complaisant one after you regain your freedom."

He lifted the case and looked down at her, his face expressionless but the lean body taut with tension. "I will not oppose the annulment. If you try to withdraw from it so you can maintain the fiction of being married, I shall divorce you. Would your duke find you a suitable partner then?"

"David, stop it!" Jocelyn cried. "I kissed the man once, I didn't join the muslin company. I don't want him and a fashionable life, I want *you*! I'd be happy to live with you at Westholme forever!"

His lips tightened and she realized with sick despair that she had said the wrong thing. "Hungry for my acres, Lady Jocelyn? You could buy my dying body, but not my living one. Now stand aside."

Instead of moving out of the way, she planted herself in front of the door, blocking his escape. With aching empathy Jocelyn knew that the depth of his anger was a measure of his hurt. She who had spent a lifetime nursing her own feelings of rejection had inflicted the same kind of wounds on the man she loved. Feeling his pain as sharply as her own, she reached for a possibility that might break through his anger. "What if I am carrying your child?"

There was a spark deep in his eyes and for a moment

she thought she had reached him. Then the shutters came back down and he said bitterly, "If you work quickly, perhaps you can use it as a lever to convince Candover to marry you. I believe he needs an heir."

It was too much. "Stop it!" Jocelyn cried out in agony, twisting sideways to hide her face. She was shuddering with reaction and would have fallen if the door hadn't supported her, but she forced back the tears, drawing her breath in ragged gulps. David's hard hands were on her shoulders and he was moving her out of his way when a faint idea occurred to her. Turning to face him, she said with what calm she could muster, "You trained as a lawyer and pride yourself on having a fair mind. Will you judge me without hearing all the evidence?"

That gave him pause, but he said, still with that icy detachment, "I found the letter from your aunt. The contents made it seem probable that you decided virginity was no longer an asset and set out to seduce me for that reason. I arrived here and found you in the arms of a man you yourself claimed to have loved for years. How much more evidence is there?"

Jocelyn looked up into his green eyes and ached for what she saw there. "Oh, my love, is that what you believed, that I invited you to my bed from cold-blooded calculation?" Shaking her head in denial, she said, "I have been many kinds of fool, but never a calculating one."

Her gaze locked to David's, she tried to project every ounce of sincerity she possessed as she said slowly, "I don't know when I first loved you, but my heart and my body knew the truth before my mind. My own fears prevented me from understanding that you were the man I have been searching for all my life."

David was utterly still and she sensed that he wanted to believe her. He asked flatly, "Why did you run away and say we should not see each other again?"

Her answer came with great difficulty as she struggled to express the enlightenment she had found when she kissed Candover. "Because . . . when I came to you, I thought you were in love with your Jeannette. For complicated reasons I am only beginning to understand, I have only cared for men who had no room in their hearts for me. When you left the note saying you loved me, I ran away because of fear and confusion."

David's face mirrored his perplexity as he attempted to make sense of her words. She couldn't blame him; she only dimly understood herself.

But at least he was listening now. Jocelyn knew that she must explain more fully, giving him the reasons to believe her. Swallowing hard, she elaborated. "When I returned to London, I talked to Aunt Laura to learn more about what I had been hiding from all my life."

Even now, it was almost impossible to say the words. "My parents were divorced. It was a great scandal many years ago." Ignoring his sharp intake of breath, she continued doggedly, "I was scarcely four when my mother left, and I believed there was something horribly wrong with me. My mother had abandoned me, and I feared my father would also if I wasn't the perfect daughter, always bright and happy. It was a role I learned to play very well."

Her eyes slid away from his, her words wrenched from the tortured depths of memory. "When I grew up . . . on some level I believed that men who claimed to love me must be liars who were after my fortune, or worse yet, sincere fools who would come to despise me if they knew me better. Since a man who came too close would find my fatal flaw, I fixed my attentions on those who would not care enough to look closely. Only after Sally said you wanted to marry someone else could I begin to acknowledge my feelings for you."

David felt his anger dissolve in the face of her gallant, painful honesty. He remembered Richard Dalton saying that Jocelyn had liked him better than her eager suitors; David himself had wondered at her unrequited love for Candover, had sensed that under her bright confidence lay fear. The pieces came together into the whole Jocelyn, the wounded child as well as the bewitching woman, and he cursed himself for having forced her to lay bare her soul. Overwhelmed with love and compassion, he raised one hand, trying to stop the flow of agonized words.

Jocelyn's eyes were closed and she didn't see his gesture as she forced herself to her faltering conclusion. "Candover is an attractive man, easy to dream about. But when I kissed him, I realized what I liked most . . . was that he didn't love me, which was perfect since I didn't feel I deserved to be loved.

"When you left me that note, I thought my heart would die of the pain. If you truly loved me, eventually you would discern what was wrong with me." Her voice breaking, she finished, "I could survive losing the regard of someone I do not really care for, but losing the man I do love would destroy me. So I left . . . before you could send me away."

Her voice was a barely audible whisper, but she struggled on, trying to find the right words, until David's arms enfolded her, pulling her tight against the full length of his body as if his touch could heal the wounds she had borne all her life. His voice as husky as her own he said, "Jocelyn, love, you don't have to say anything more. I'm sorry for the beastly things I said. You did nothing to deserve such cruelty on my part."

She clung to him fiercely, as if his love depended on her never letting him go. David's shoulder was reassuringly solid against her cheek, and his warm hand cradled her head, then stroked down her neck and back soothingly. There was apology in the beautiful deep voice as he continued, "You see why I try to be a cool English gentleman: when the wild, emotional Welshman escapes, I am immune to logic and good sense. I hadn't known I was capable of that kind of jealousy. But then, I've never loved anyone as I love you."

With a trace of humor, he added, "It didn't help that Candover is a wealthy, handsome duke. If you need to sort out your feelings in the future, do you think you could restrict yourself to short, elderly fishmongers?"

Between laughter and tears, she finally raised her face to him and he kissed her. With all the defenses down between them, they were joined in an emotional closeness that came from their souls, leaving them both shaken.

Reconciliation flared into passion, the need to be as close as humanly possible. Once more David lifted Jocelyn and carried her to a bed, but this time there was none of the tentativeness of new lovers. Jocelyn pulled him to her, wanting to know every inch of him, to forge a bond that would bind them for a lifetime, and beyond.

They made love with the desperate hunger of two people who had nearly lost what they valued most, staying tangled together even in the hazy aftermath of loving. As their bodies cooled, David released Jocelyn only long enough to pull a blanket over them before once more cradling her in his arms.

They talked as lovers do, of how each had begun to love the other, of the small landmarks and discoveries that laid the foundations of their personal miracle. There was no reason to rush, and every reason in the world to savor that sweet sharing.

Much, much later, David chuckled and said, "I'm grateful your servants have the sense not to walk in on us without knocking. I would hate to embarrass one of the maids."

Jocelyn felt so full of joy that anything would have made her laugh. "If I know anything about my household, they have deduced exactly why we have been closeted in here for hours, and they're celebrating with a champagne toast in the servants' hall. From what Marie has said, they've been worried about my impending spinsterdom and had decided you were the perfect solution."

Her head was lying on his chest and she could feel as well as hear his laughter. Lifting her head to look at him, she said, "Is it safe to assume that Jeannette is no longer relevant?"

His green eyes crinkled mischievously. "It is. To be honest, I'd forgotten that I wrote Sally about her. It was a lightning-bolt affair that ended when she sorrowfully informed me that a man of greater fortune had offered for her and she really could not support life on an officer's salary. After the initial shock wore off, I discovered I didn't miss her in the least. Jeannette is entirely ancient history, as is our annulment." He leaned over to kiss Jocelyn. "It is too late to change your mind, lady mine. I'm not letting you go again."

Jocelyn heard once more the echo, "Till death us do part," this time with a resonance of infinite warmth and protection. Even so, she rested her chin on his chest, her hazel eyes searching his green ones as she said hesitantly, "Now I am aware of why I've believed myself unworthy of love, but it will be a long time before my fears are gone. I hope you will be patient if I cling too closely."

David rolled over so that he was above her, putting his hands on both sides of her face. In a husky whisper he said, "If you have trouble believing that I love you, then I will just have to repeat the words every day for as long as we both shall live. Will that help?"

She pulled his face down to hers, tasting the salty sweetness of his lips. "I rather think it will."

David and Jocelyn let the world continue to think they had met in Spain. Since their wedding had been so hasty and private, they gave a large reception to officially announce the marriage to friends and family. Richard Dalton was still bedridden and unable to attend, but before the reception they called and presented him with a gold-headed cane engraved with the words, "To Richard, with love and gratitude." The captain made no objection when the bride kissed him.

Elvira, Countess of Cromarty, went into a hysterical rage when she learned that her wretched niece had withdrawn the application for an annulment. It was bad enough knowing that Jocelyn's fortune was forever out of Elvira's reach; it was worse discovering that the girl and her husband were besotted with each other. As she told the long-suffering Willoughby, the very least one could have hoped for was that they would be as miserable as most married couples.

Jocelyn wrote a brief note to the Duke of Candover, thanking him for his forbearance and good advice and urging him to matrimony as the happiest of all states. He smiled a little sadly when he read the note, drank a solitary toast to the lady and her lucky husband, then smashed the glass in the fireplace.

Hugh and Marie were delighted that they would not have to decide which well-loved employer to leave when they themselves married.

When Sally told Ian Kinlock that her brother and Lady Jocelyn had discovered they were in love, he looked up from his anatomy text with a twinkle in his eyes, agreeing that being in love was a very good thing and that marriage to a woman as beautiful as Lady Jocelyn was bound to make the major happy. Sally cuffed him on the shoulder, leading to an applied anatomy lesson that both of them found a good deal more enjoyable than the one Ian had been studying.

General Andrew Kirkpatrick reminded his wife that he had said the Kendal women were irresistible to army men. She laughed in agreement and put out the candle.

Though she took a dim view of sharing her mistress, Isis continued to sleep on Jocelyn's bed. After all, she had been there first.